PRAISE FOR *WELCOME TO NIGHT VALE: A NOVEL*

"Fink and Cranor's prose hints there's an empathetic humanity under-scoring their well of darkly fantastic situations.... As a companion piece, *Welcome to Night Vale* will be hard to resist. Though the book builds toward a satisfyingly strange exploration of the strange town's intersection with an unsuspecting real world, [its] mysteries—like the richest conspiracy theories—don't exist to be explained. They just provide a welcome escape." **—Los Angeles Times**

"The book is charming and absurd—think *This American Life* meets *Alice in Wonderland*." **—Washington Post**

"Longtime listeners and newcomers alike are likely to appreciate the ways in which Night Vale, as Fink puts it, 'treats the absurd as normal and treats the normal as absurd.' What they might not foresee is the emotional wallop the novel delivers in its climactic chapters." **—Austin Chronicle**

"The charms of *Welcome to Night Vale* are nearly impossible to quan-tify. That applies to the podcast, structured as community radio dis-patches from a particularly surreal desert town, as well as this novel." **—Minneapolis Star Tribune**

"*Welcome to Night Vale: A Novel* masterfully brings the darkly hilari-ous, touching and creepy world of the podcast into the realm of ink and paper." **—Asbury Park Press**

"*Welcome to Night Vale* lives up to the podcast hype in every way. It is a singularly inventive visit to an otherworldly town that's the stuff of nightmares and daydreams." **—BookPage**

"All hail the glow cloud as the weird and wonderful town of Night Vale brings itself to fine literature. . . . The novel is definitely as addictive as its source material." **—*Kirkus Reviews* (starred review)**

"Take Conan's Hyborea, teleport it to the American Southwest, dress all the warriors in business casual and hide their swords under the floorboards—that's Night Vale: absurd, magical, wholly engrossing, and always harboring some hidden menace."
—John Darnielle, author of *Wolf in White Van*

"They've done the unthinkable: merged the high weirdness and intense drama of Night Vale to the pages of a novel that is even weirder, even more intense than the podcast."
**—Cory Doctorow, author of *Little Brother*
and coeditor of *Boing Boing***

"This is the novel of your dreams. . . . A friendly (but terrifying) and comic (but dark) and glittering (but bleak) story of misfit family life that unfolds along the side streets, back alleys and spring-loaded trap doors of the small town home you'll realize you've always missed living in." **—Glen David Gold, author of
Carter Beats the Devil and *Sunnyside***

"This small town full of hooded figures, glowing clouds, cryptically terrifying public policies, and flickering realities quickly feels more like home than home. . . . There is nothing like Night Vale, in the best possible way." **—Maureen Johnson, author of
13 Little Blue Envelopes and *The Name of the Star***

"I've been a fan of *Welcome to Night Vale* for years, and in that time writers Jeffrey Cranor and Joseph Fink have delighted me with stories that are clever, twisted, beautiful, strange, wonderful, and sweet. This book does all of that and so much more. It's even better than I'd hoped. I think this might be the best book I've read in years."

—Patrick Rothfuss, author of *The Name of the Wind*

"Emotionally compelling and superbly realized. This seductive, hilarious book unfolds at the moment when certain quiet responsible people find they must risk everything on behalf of love, hope, and understanding. Not a single person who reads this book will be disappointed."

—Deb Olin Unferth, author of *Revolution* and *Vacation*

"*Welcome to Night Vale* brings its eponymous desert town to vivid life. Those of us who have gotten to know Night Vale through Cecil Palmer's bi-weekly radio broadcasts can finally see what it's like to actually live there. It is as weird and surreal as I hoped it would be, and a surprisingly existential meditation on the nature of time, reality, and the glow cloud that watches over us. ALL HAIL THE GLOW CLOUD."

—Wil Wheaton

THE
GREAT GLOWING COILS
OF THE UNIVERSE

Welcome to Night Vale
Episodes, Volume 2

JOSEPH FINK AND
JEFFREY CRANOR

HARPER PERENNIAL

NEW YORK • LONDON • TORONTO • SYDNEY • NEW DELHI • AUCKLAND

To Ron Fink and to Louis Nettleship

HARPER ⬤ PERENNIAL

Illustrations by Jessica Hayworth

THE GREAT GLOWING COILS OF THE UNIVERSE. Copyright © 2016 by Joseph Fink and Jeffrey Cranor. All rights reserved. Printed in the United States of America. No part of this book may be used or reproduced in any manner whatsoever without written permission except in the case of brief quotations embodied in critical articles and reviews. For information, address HarperCollins Publishers, 195 Broadway, New York, NY 10007.

HarperCollins books may be purchased for educational, business, or sales promotional use. For information, please e-mail the Special Markets Department at SPsales@harpercollins.com.

FIRST EDITION

Library of Congress Cataloging-in-Publication Data has been applied for.

ISBN 978-0-06-246863-5
ISBN 978-0-06-265591-2 (B&N signed edition)
ISBN 978-0-06-265592-9 (BAM signed edition)
ISBN 978-0-06-265593-6 (Indigo signed edition)

16 17 18 19 20 DIX/RRD 10 9 8 7 6 5 4 3 2 1

CONTENTS

FOREWORD

WELCOME TO *THE GREAT GLOWING COILS OF THE UNIVERSE: WELCOME to Night Vale Episodes, Volume 2* by Joseph Fink and Jeffrey Cranor, a book experience. My name is Maureen Johnson, a book person, and I have been asked to guide you into the warm water* of this second volume of *Welcome to Night Vale* episodes.

One might presume that the reader of volume two of the collected *Welcome to Night Vale* episodes might have read—or at least possess and perhaps refuse to consume—volume one. But I will not *assume*. I am here to guide, or forward!, your progress. I'm going to tell you what's going on.

Welcome to Night Vale is a podcast. These are the episodes of that podcast. The episodes in volume one were the first season. The episodes you are about to read (or possess and perhaps refuse to consume) came later. The podcast arrives at certain points in time, but a book—a book can come whenever. A book waits. A book is patient. A book will never crawl off the shelf while you sleep and walk toward you on the edges of its cover in that weird, hunched way that bats walk. Books just aren't like that. So if you want to read this volume before the other—it's up to you. Why not? Dip in. Dip out. Read at random. Read in order. YOU DECIDE. Books are the enemy of time.

If you listen to the podcast you will notice one very particular thing: the sounds. In the podcast, Cecil and The Gang talk to you. They go on

---

*Not water. The first things you should learn about books is that they're not water. At least, NOT RIGHT NOW.

and on and on. Now listen to this book. Is it making any sounds? No?*
Yes?† It's no, isn't it?‡ That's because *books are not podcasts*. Podcasts are
pretty new, so we never had to explain this before, but now it's the *first*
thing we tell people.

Fear not. The silence will soon be filled by voices in your head. As
you go through the book, you may start to hear the podcast again. You
won't be hear-hearing them—you'll be read-hearing them. Which is
totally different. It's not hearing at all. Do you follow me? Take jet skis
for example. They aren't jets, and they aren't skis, but somehow they are
jet skis. Books are a lot like that. YOU ARE THE PODCAST NOW.

What's extra nice about this volume is that you get commentary
from Jeffery Cranor and Joseph Fink, as well as from the *Night Vale*
performers. They will explain what they were thinking when they created and performed these words. I have had the distinct pleasure and
privilege of appearing in some *Night Vale* episodes as Intern Maureen.
(I even talk about this in this book, in the introduction to "Old Oak
Doors." You don't have to go and look for this now. I promise you, it's
there.§) I will repeat one sentiment I expressed in that commentary:
the entire *Night Vale* crew are among the most thoughtful, talented,
and lovely people you could ever hope to meet. *Night Vale* is the circus
we dream of running off to join. The fact that *Night Vale* is so popular
proves that something undeniably good is going on in the world.

In sum, this is not a podcast but a book of a podcast. The voices
you hear aren't real in the same way that jet skis are jet skis. We've all
joined a circus. Also, I was an intern in Night Vale but I am not an
intern. I am a book person and this is a forward to a book, which is
yours to read or not read, as you choose. You may choose at any time,
and books operate out of time so you may choose out of time as well.

You follow?

---

*Good.
†Run.
‡See previous footnote if this statement is false.
§I'm just being polite. You should go look.

Excellent.

Now please complete this short quiz to demonstrate your understanding.

1. This is a:
    a. podcast
    b. book
    c. jet ski
2. The voices you hear are:
    a. real
    b. not real
    c. getting louder and more insistent
3. Night Vale is:
    a. a circus
    b. a podcast
    c. a jet ski
4. Books are the enemy of:
    a. time
    b. Cecil
    c. the people
5. This is volume _____ in a series of _____.
    a. two, that number you see in the mirror when the lights are off
    b. six hundred, five hundred
    c. twelvety, terrible mistakes

Fill in the blank:
6. You possess this book. What do you do first? Answer in the form of a statement: _____
7. You do not possess this book. Now what? Answer in the form of a question: _____
8. Cecil Baldwin is the voice of Night Vale, but we have established there are no voices in this book. Who is reading this now? Answer in a whisper.

Finished?

Very good. Now pass this book to the person to your left for grading. If there is no person to your left, you may keep this book and continue reading. Or you may simply continue to possess it and never explore its contents. I am not here to tell you what to do. I am just here to forward.

Bookishly,

—Maureen Johnson, New York, 2016*

---

*As previously discussed, this is a book, so putting in a year is an act of folly.

INTRODUCTION

PEOPLE ASK: HOW DID NIGHT VALE BECOME SO POPULAR?

The short answer is: Tumblr.

The long answer is: I don't know.

I mean, I do know, but it's in the same way I know how gravity works or what peanut butter tastes like or how blue is a different color from red (spoiler alert). It involves some logic, some intuition, some reverse engineering, and a lot of wild gesticulation.

When we posted our first episode, we had fifty total downloads the first week, which seems like the grand total of all the friends who know me, Joseph, and Cecil. That number grew over the next couple of months into the hundreds. As we put out two episodes a month, each one had more downloads its first week than the previous. And we reached the low thousands by our half-year mark.

There's no way the three of us knew a thousand people total. We had strangers in our audience who listened for a reason beyond chummy obligation—a quantitative measure of true artistic success!

Our hope was that by our one-year anniversary (June 15, 2013) we would reach 100,000 total downloads over all twenty-five episodes. And we achieved that. We, in fact, beat it pretty good. We had 150,000 total downloads.

When you make theater and dance for a living, you get excited when the audience outnumbers the cast on stage. ("Please let there be at least six people tonight! Please let there be—oh good, those people I barely know from work came!") So it's hard to process what 150,000 downloads even means, especially when you can't even see them. They're just abstract numbers and a small handful of nice e-mails. (At this point we still had no idea what Tumblr was.)

But we were giddy. We were regularly in the iTunes Top 200 comedy podcasts. Sometimes we would have a bit of a surge and jump briefly ahead of some of the greats hovering in the twenty to fifty range: *Stop Podcasting Yourself; How Was Your Week; Stuff You Should Know; My Brother, My Brother and Me; Comedy Bang Bang*, etc. It was great. We were proud.

We had no idea what was happening.

Then July 2013 came around. I was in Astoria, Oregon, vacationing with my extended family: aunts, cousins, nieces, nephews—people I rarely get to see. My cousin Ryan said, "I saw you guys passed Marc Maron on the charts." "Oh, we haven't done that yet," I was quick to explain. My other cousin, Ashley, said, "I'm pretty sure you did." We each raced to our phones. And there *Night Vale* was: #2, just behind *This American Life*, and just ahead of *WTF with Marc Maron*.

Then my server crashed, because we were still hosting this supposedly tiny project on my cheap, personal website.

Okay, so remember that in our first twelve months, we had 150,000 downloads. In our thirteenth month alone, we had 2.5 million downloads. Then in August 2013 alone, we had 8.5 million downloads. And we were ahead of *This American Life* at #1 for four straight months. And people would say "you're famous," and there would be fan art and backlash and tons of e-mails, but I still worked as a database manager for Film Forum. I really liked it there. It's a great institution, a really good job.

I was, in a way, trying to keep *Night Vale* a secret, because I wanted my life to stay as it was. My whole life in theater was "please come to my show" and "here's a postcard" and "I can comp you in, please please someone see this." And now, here was success being handed to me. No, not handed, thrust upon me. No, not upon, into. Stabbed. I was being repeatedly stabbed with success. It was 50 percent elation, 25 percent confusion, 25 percent certain I was dead.

I Googled "Night Vale" to find some explanation for where these millions of downloads were coming from. Surely some major television network had told everyone to listen to our show. Nope. We searched Twitter for mentions. We found nothing that would indicate such a surge in popularity. We had comic book–style interrobangs above our heads that whole summer.

Then a friend of Cecil's said, "Hey, Cecil. You should search your name on Tumblr." Boom. *Night Vale* was everywhere on Tumblr. Fan art. Fan fiction. Slash fiction. Arguments over canon. Lovefests over how cute Cecil and Carlos were. Heck Yeah Tamika Flynn. And so on. We were no longer giddy. We were . . . um . . . errr . . . [*wild gesticulation*].

"How did you do it? How did you make such a successful thing?" We're not marketers or demographics experts. We're just writers who've never had more than a couple hundred people ever watch or read or listen to anything we've ever created. Honestly, we made a successful thing in the exact same way we made every other nonsuccessful thing we'd done prior.

Here are a few things I think contributed to the show's popularity, though.

One: I think we wrote a good story. That's not bragging. At this point in my life, I feel like I'm a good writer. I'm not saying I can guarantee bestsellers or that other people will like my work, but that I know mostly what I'm doing. Joseph and I have been writing and creating (and Cecil has been acting) long enough to know what is good art. Good art is, of course, no guarantee of popular or critical success, but it is almost certainly a prerequisite for those things.

You can always argue subjective quality of art, but there are quite a few objective measurements of art as well. We put out a show twice a month, on time. It is of consistent length and format. We consider limitations of the medium, universe continuity, social issues, and we have a thorough editing schedule and process.

Two: Episode 25, "First Date," was posted on June 15, 2013. In this episode, we see the culmination of the relationship between host Cecil Palmer and Carlos the scientist. Many fans have told us that this relationship means so much to them.

Quite a bit of popular fiction (whether book or movie or television) features teased-out will-they-won't-they same-sex relationships.* These couples are drawn close but never allowed to get together as a loving couple. Joseph, Cecil, and I were more interested in a couple that falls in love without getting hung up on outdated hetero-assumptive conditions.

Combine this with the fan fiction community on Tumblr, where many fans had been writing Cecil/Carlos slash fiction, creatively narrating these two men together before they were canonically together. And then, bam, they're not heterosexual, and they're in love. It's canon. Tumblr explodes into flower-crowns and Arby's logos.

Three: No one else was doing what we were doing at the time. The *Thrilling Adventure Hour* is the one exception I can think of, but their show was primarily a live show that was recorded and then distributed in segments via podcasting platforms. (*Note*: The *TAH* folks were crazy helpful when we first started touring live shows. We did a couple of crossover shows with those guys, which were great fun.) But as far as podcasts go, there weren't any long-form fiction serials in early 2012, and certainly none that were like *Night Vale*.

Ultimately, though, the answer to why a thing gets popular is "who knows?" I mean, once it is popular, it's easy to come up with all kinds of reasons. Really though, we were successful from the moment we began because we were making a thing we liked and respected with people we liked and respected. We are still doing this. It just involves live show tours, novels, scripts books, starting a podcast network, etc., now.

But even if, four years later, it were the same fifty or so people listening from episode one, we'd still be doing this. We'd have different day jobs than we have now, but we'd be pleased to be making art we loved with people we loved. That's really the only kind of success you have control over.

—Jeffrey Cranor, cowriter of *Welcome to Night Vale*

*This was true when I wrote this introduction. I hope it is not still true in whatever future time you live in.

EPISODE 26:
"FACELESS OLD WOMAN"

JULY 1, 2013

GUEST VOICE: MARA WILSON

I'VE ALWAYS WANTED TO BE SCARY.

There's no question that I was an intense little kid, but there was never anything scary about me. My earliest memories are of being surrounded by grown-ups and cool big kids. I wanted to be one of them, powerful and intimidating. I knew I wasn't. I couldn't do all the things by which I judged people to be grown up: I was afraid to watch scary movies, to go on roller coasters, to cross the street by myself. They weren't. They were free, they were brave, and worst of all, they got to know everything.

I had to find my own way. I listened in on every conversation within earshot. I went through my brother's backpacks and my mother's purses. I'd often get in trouble, but I couldn't help myself. Other people's business was just more interesting than my own.

When I got a little older, having successfully leveraged my middle-child syndrome into a somewhat successful child acting career, people would ask me if I was anything like the characters I played. The answer was usually yes. Superficially, they were all like me. I was a little girl, my characters were all little girls. Most of them like to read and use big words. Some of them were mischievous, and had a bit of my desire to learn everything, to get in on whatever it was the grown-ups and other kids were talking about. It was never the driving need in them that it was in me.

There's only been one character who has that same drive. She's nothing like me. She doesn't care about scary movies or roller coasters, and she doesn't need to cross the street. But she's everywhere, and she knows how I feel, and she understands. She knows and she understands more than anyone.

And there's no way I would have ever had this chance if Joseph, Jeffrey, Meg, Cecil, and the whole *Night Vale* crew hadn't let me tag along. The cool big kids have given me what I always wanted.

—Mara Wilson, Voice of the
Faceless Old Woman Who Secretly Lives in Your Home

Trumpets playing soft jazz from out of the dark desert distance. They come tomorrow. It is too late for us.

WELCOME TO NIGHT VALE.

Did you know there's a faceless old woman who secretly lives in your home? It's true. She's there now. She's always there, just out of your sight. Always just out of your sight.

Because you cannot see her, you were probably completely unaware that this woman likes to sift through photos of you and your loved ones. She softly touches each face as if wishing it were her own, or perhaps claiming it as her own, or perhaps simply cursing that person. It's hard to say. You've never seen her doing this.

The Faceless Old Woman Who Secretly Lives in Your Home does lots of things. Ever wonder why your Web browser's history is filled with Bing searches for (quote) pictures of dead wolves or (quote) the melting point of birds? Or why sometimes your shower drain gets clogged with organ meats or why sometimes you hear crying from behind the walls? Or scratching at the front door? Or you awaken to find long silver hairs on the pillow next to you?

Or maybe you've never noticed any of those things. You've lived your life to this point completely oblivious to this old woman who has no face. And truth be told, I think she's probably harmless. But maybe you shouldn't sleep in your home anymore. Just in case.

Ladies and gentlemen, Dana has continued to send me texts from

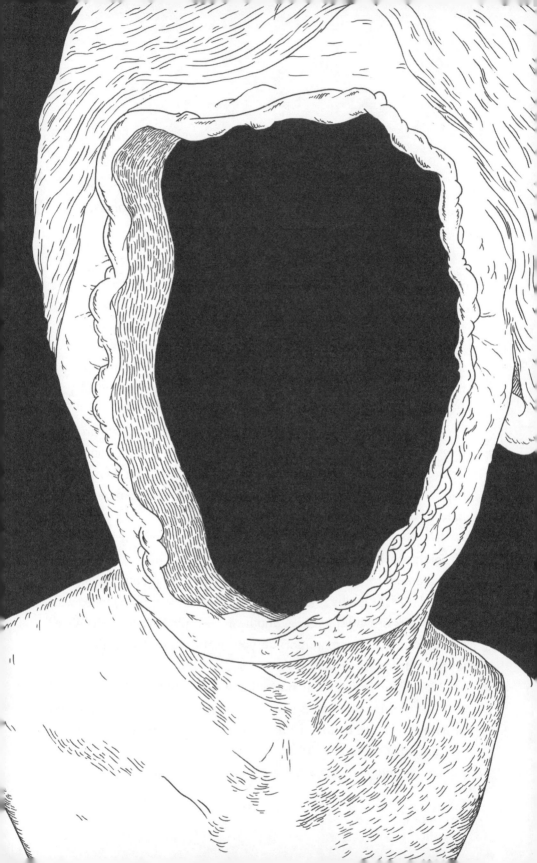

beyond the tall, black fences of the Dog Park. Even though the Dog Park is forbidden to citizens and their dogs, Dana managed to get in and is now trapped there for who knows how long.

First off, she says she's okay. She says she has met some nice people and she's never bored. She met the Man in the Tan Jacket who has been haunting this city for the past few months. In fact, Dana says the Man in the Tan Jacket is quite nice, and they've really struck up quite a friendship.

She's still trying to figure out what the man's involvement is with the hooded figures and the recently deceased Apache Tracker and the tiny, underground civilization of warmongers who live below lane five of the Desert Flower Bowling Alley and Arcade Fun Complex. He has seemed to pop up in relation to a lot of strange events.

She's also trying to figure out what he looks like. Every time she steps away from that guy she can't remember a thing about him, just that he's wearing a tan jacket and carrying a deerskin briefcase.

Oh, and that briefcase, Dana says, is kind of weird because it's full of flies, and that's kind of creepy at first until you realize that he's a fly salesman and that they're all trained. They can retrieve mail and speak German and play dead and all kinds of cute things. She says he's a pretty cool guy if you get to know him.

Oh, and I almost forgot, Dana wonders if any listeners with a good arm can get kind of close to the Dog Park and throw some beans or chips or beef jerky or something over the tall fence. She's very hungry. In fact, it took me a while to get through her typos, listeners, she must be shaking really badly.

And now a public service announcement from the Greater Night Vale Medical Community. Are you feeling run-down, even after eight hours of sleep? Are you having trouble breathing between the hours of two and four? Are you gaining several extra pounds of weight only to lose those pounds suddenly and then gain them back, all in five- to six-hour stretches of time? Are you craving soil, like all the time? Rich, dark soil that you just want cooling your tongue, filling your throat, your sinuses, your lungs, your belly? Are you digging up the earth in the early morning, screaming at the half-formed sun, as if it would cordially leave, returning you to the darkness you so richly deserve and physiologically demand?

If you answered yes to all of those questions, then you're fine. The program is working. All tests have been successful and phase four is imminent. This has been Community Health Tips.

More on the Faceless Old Woman Who Secretly Lives in Your Home. She has issued a statement to the media just now. Here is that statement.

FACELESS OLD WOMAN: I'm confused. There's no sense to how you organize the objects in your fridge. I cannot determine any sense of order. What systems do you use to contain your vegetables, your cans, your jars, your food stains? There are stains. Organic brown and pink smears that tell the esoteric history of your food. I like the yellowish one near the crisper because I think it is the oldest. It has a topography.

Oh, I do not like all of these bugs you have in your home. I like some of them. I also changed your sheets. You do not change your sheets enough. I do not think you are unsanitary, but I think you would feel better if you changed your sheets from time to time. And time is weird because it doesn't exist for me in the same way, so your sheets are already covered with your bones and hair and blood, but not yet. Not really yet.

I wish you could see me. Just cleaning and reorganizing. Making sense of the nonsense plants and muscles in your fridge. But you never look. If you would just glance left or right every so often, you'd see me. I'm right next to you, right now. I'm even in the mirrors. But you just stare at yourself. Staring only at your overripe potato of a face. I'm there in every mirror, if you could just look for me in the background behind you.

Also what's your Wi-Fi password?

CECIL: So that's the old woman's special announcement. I have no idea how we received that recording, who recorded it, or how an old woman with no face (and by extension, no mouth) could speak so clearly. But it was very informative.

Maybe you should try paying more attention when you're at home. Or better yet, destroy all of your mirrors. As my mother used to tell me: "Someone's going to kill you one day, Cecil, and it will involve a mirror. Mark my words, child"—and then she would stare absently through my eyes until I giggled. I miss her so much.

Listeners, a lot of you have written in asking for photos of Khoshekh, the station cat, and to learn what became of his litter of kittens. Station Management did not let us keep the kittens, but they have been given away to good homes. Unfortunately, like Khoshekh, the kittens are also stuck floating in fixed points in space, so their owners will have to visit them right where they were born, right here in the station bathroom. Khoshekh hovers about four feet in the air but some of those little ones are as high as nine! It's sad that we cannot keep the kittens for ourselves, but it'll be nice to see them every time we take a restroom break at work.

I wish we had some photos to share with you. But, alas, radio is not a visual medium. Also the last three staff members that took photos not only found that Khoshekh does not show up in pictures, but those staff members also died pretty agonizing deaths the week following. So we're refraining from even describing what he looks like.

But I did make a quick recording of the meow Khoshekh makes when it's time to eat.

[*Terrible guttural animal growl or shriek, maybe a loud machine noise mixed in?*]

Like I said, I'm not a cat person, but Khoshekh has found a truly special place in my heart.

I'm getting word that authorities are surrounding your home. These authorities are secret agents from a vague yet menacing government agency. You are probably looking out your window now to see these agents, but they are highly covert. You cannot see them, even if you look hard. These specially trained men and women can expertly disguise themselves as trees and doors and birds and feral cats and wind gusts. A group of them have even disguised themselves as one item of furniture in your home. I am not at liberty to even speculate which one, but you're probably looking at it right now.

The vague yet menacing government agency seems upset that the Faceless Old Woman Who Secretly Lives in Your Home has been alerting you and the media to her presence.

I mean, we all knew she was there. Who doesn't know about the Faceless Old Woman that hides in all of our homes? It's not dissimilar to knowing that Santa Claus isn't actually real. Everyone (except young children, of course) knows Santa is this huge population of heavily sedated and costumed bears that the CIA sets loose across the country every Christmas Eve. And like the Santa Claus myth, it's important to keep up the image that we all don't know the truth. Like, let's all pretend Santa is a gift-giving old man and not a drugged-up government bear. And in the same vein, there's no Faceless Old Woman hiding in your home.

Anyway, the agents are encroaching on your home now and preparing to use deadly force. I'd like to tell you that you need to run. To get out of there now. To save yourself. But it is too late. Every entrance and exit is barricaded. I am afraid you are doomed.

Unfortunately, the Faceless Old Woman must know something. She must know secrets, some very important bits that the vague yet menacing government agency holds dear. And those secrets are probably about you.

Perhaps she is planning to reveal your purpose here. Perhaps you, too, are connected (albeit unwittingly) to the vague yet menacing government agency, and this information cannot, must not, be shared. You are a walking top-secret document. And now, on the verge of this revelation, you must be destroyed.

On the plus side, you had a purpose, and that is more than most of us can say. You will be missed. So for your last moments, though surely not ours, I give you the weather . . .

WEATHER: "Long Gone" by Mary Epworth

The Faceless Old Woman Secretly Living in Your Home wants to apologize to you. She has issued another statement.

FACELESS OLD WOMAN: I'm sorry. Mostly I just wanted to figure out how to get online. I reset the wireless router and that helped, but you use Chrome and you never clean your cache or history and it was so slow. I downloaded Firefox for you and that seems to be working much better. I heard the mayor is retiring and I wanted to know if mayoral candidates were required to have faces. I have some good ideas I think would help this town. Like one thing I think is we can increase school funding while still lowering taxes. It's an innovative plan, and I'm going to build a website that explains it and other great ideas I have that could help this town. I'm very excited to announce my candidacy for Night Vale mayor.

Also, I lit your fridge on fire. It was upsetting me. Now I'm smoking a cigarette and notating your copy of *Infinite Jest.*

CECIL: She didn't leave a name or a website URL. And I'm not sure how she can read websites or books at all without a face (and by extension, eyes).

We've also received word that the covert agents from the vague yet menacing government agency have retreated and have obviously not used deadly force, as you are still alive (regardless of how dead you feel inside). They did, however, release several thousand spiders into your home.

Fortunately for you, like the Faceless Old Woman, you will be unable to see these spiders unless you look closely. They are highly trained spiders, moving just outside of your periphery. But (and this is also just like the Faceless Old Woman) from time to time you will feel them brushing against your soft cheeks and lips as you sleep.

So keep your eyes open, listeners. Let us all keep our eyes open. It's not always easy knowing who and what wants to be seen, but when you look around you, pay attention to those fuzzy and dark corners. Peer deeper into those predictable patterns like walls and moons. Furrow that brow and seek visual truth, Night Vale. If you could only see what you're not seeing. If you could only take in all the complex layers of horrors that lie just beyond your range of sight. If you could only see the world as it really is! It is awful and on fire and beautiful.

Listeners, stay tuned next for our newest hit program: Open-mouthed Chewing. Tonight's topic: glass shards—how to make the most out of a bad situation.

Until next time, good night, Night Vale. Good night.

PROVERB: The human soul weighs 21 grams, smells like grilled vegetables, looks like a wrinkled tartan quilt, and sounds like bridge traffic.

EPISODE 27:
"FIRST DATE"

JULY 15, 2013

OUR FIRST YEAR OF THE SHOW ENDED WITH CECIL, OUR HOST, AND CAR-los, the handsome scientist who had just moved to town, finally getting together. And so, for the start of our second year, it seemed right to have them go on their first date.

From the start we endeavored to make their relationship something that was not silly, or showy, or in any other way different from what it was: a relationship between two adults. While the context of that relationship might involve all sorts of strange and supernatural occurrences, the rhythms and the emotions of it had to feel real.

Now, I've never been on a first date. Not really. I've had two long-term relationships, one that ended, and one that turned into a marriage. And both began with us as friends. There was no point in my life where I went out on dates. So perhaps I am very unqualified to be the one to write this episode. But it's our show and we get to do what we want with it so here we are.

This is a sweet episode. It's nice and I'm fond of it. How about that.

On a minor note, this episode brings back the character of musician Louie Blasko (last and first seen in episode 2), who would later be used in live shows as a way for our guest musicians who were touring with us to play a music-based character as well. Specifically Jason Webley, who originated the part and who can make accordion playing a terrifying thing. And Carrie Elkin, whose voice can bring a room to a standstill before they even notice how gory the lyrics I wrote for her are.

—Joseph Fink, creator and cowriter of *Welcome to Night Vale*

Mountains. Endless mountains. Peak after barren peak. And what lies restless in the shadowed valleys? I cannot say. I cannot say.

WELCOME TO NIGHT VALE.

Hello. Let's start there. Let's start with a greeting, a simple hello, and then let's move right into the most exciting news, the most wonderful news. As you may remember, a few weeks ago, along with the beginning of a vicious war against us by tiny people from a tiny underground city, Carlos, the beautiful scientist, finally returned my expressions of affection. And not in that dry science way he always used to use, saying things like "I'm not calling for personal reasons. I need to tell your radio audience about the strange hole that might appear in their wall." Oh, yeah, I forgot. There's a strange hole that might appear in your wall. He said it was important to tell you, especially after what happened at the Smithwick house. I forgot. That was a while back, so I guess it doesn't matter much now.

But yesterday when he called me, he started his call by saying "I *am* calling for personal reasons. Also my calculations show a strange source of energy approaching the town, but not emanating the kind of light that such a source should." Isn't that so sweet! And, well, one thing led to another, and last night we went on our first date. I just have to tell you about it. I have certain obligations though, so first let's get to the news.

The Secret Police, in association with a vague yet menacing government agency, announced that those trucks full of crates far out in the desert are nothing, and that we shouldn't worry about them. The trucks, which no one in town knew about until this announcement, are filled with crates that are warm to the touch. Some of them tick. Others do not. Don't even worry a little about them, say the Secret Police. Forget we said anything. No, really, remembering we said anything is now against the law.

We reached out to Lieutenant Regis of Unit Seven of the local National Guard Station and KFC combo store for a comment, and he said he's been ruminating on a lot of things. "Just a lot of stuff's been running through my mind. That's an interesting phrase. Running through the mind. Where are the thoughts going? Are they trying to leave? And, if so, for where?" When pressed to comment specifically about the trucks full of crates out in the desert, he just repeated everything he had said, with the exact same inflections and gestures.

Well, I'm sure these crates won't come up again, and pose no future danger to any of us. No more on this story ever, I'm sure.

The Night Vale Public Library will be expanding into a second branch, the Night Vale Private Library. This library will be right next door to the current location, and will be available only to one person, local billionaire Marcus Vanston. It will contain thousands of books on any given subject, an interactive children's area shaped like a full-size pirate's ship, and a biography section featuring not just biographies of Helen Hunt, but also biographies of Sean Penn. Plans include floor-to-ceiling windows facing the public library, which Marcus, the only person who will ever be allowed inside, says he will use to stroll nude through his library, staring ordinary citizens in the eyes as he does not read or make any use of the towers of books around him. Marcus continued: "Maybe I will pick up a book and open it as though I were going to read it, but then reveal to those watching that I am holding it upside down before laughing and throwing the book away. I'm not sure. I haven't planned out every moment. I will definitely be nude though."

The public library's board of directors issued a statement via loud-speaker from their helicopter that hovers continuously over our city, indicating that they feel this expansion will serve the community by showing how rich Marcus is, and what a great guy that obviously makes him, and have you seen how many cars that guy owns. Wow!

Reports also indicate that the Night Vale Private Library will be entirely free of librarians, a fact that will be of little comfort to the many public library–goers who are injured or killed in librarian maulings every year. Remember, if confronted by a librarian while looking for a book to check out, do not attempt to escape by climbing a tree. There are no trees in the library and the precious moments it will take you to look around and realize this will allow the librarian to strike. Don't become a statistic.

All right, news done. So, now let's talk about the date. Carlos and I met up in Old Town. I was wearing my best tunic and furry pants, and he had on a laid-back "weekend" lab coat. We were both beautiful in the late-afternoon sunlight, each other's dreams met in a real-world moment. Our destination was none other than Gino's Italian Dining Experience and Grill and Bar, the fanciest restaurant in town. It was a perfect day, other than the strange blot of darkness buzzing on the edge of town, but that was probably yet another Applebee's under construction.

We went arm in arm into Gino's, and were immediately seated, with no memory of who greeted us at the door or how we got to our table, situated in a classy, understated, and absolutely doorless room. The full Gino's experience. Their menu is somewhat limited after the ban on wheat & wheat by-products, so we each ordered a single porto-bello mushroom, served rare and bloody, as is the Gino's way. From the window we had a great view of the sunset, and of the buzzing shadow thing, which seemed to have moved closer.

"I've been thinking," Carlos said.

"Uh huh?" I said.

"Yeah, that's what I've been doing lately," he said. "Thinking. It's part of being a scientist. What have you been up to?"

And so we talked. Just us, and our bleeding mushrooms, and the buzzing shadow presence, and a blooming haze of romance in the air. Hold on, Station Management is apparently getting agitated, flailing around their office and howling, so I need to do more news real quick.

Violent incidents increased across the entire Night Vale area over the last several weeks, as the people of the miniature city under lane five of the Desert Flower Bowling Alley and Arcade Fun Complex continue to wage their war against us, with tiny bodies and tinier weapons. Citizens are urged to protect themselves against this army in our midst by stomping everywhere they go and keeping a vigilant watch toward the ground rather than keeping our eyes closed as we usually do. In related news, the City Council has erected a monument to the fallen Apache Tracker, that hero who died for the welfare of us all. The monument will be dedicated in a secret, silent ceremony, attended by no one, and the monument itself will be buried somewhere in the desert where no one will find it, because he was also a racist embarrassment and we don't want our town associated with that kind of thing.

And now, the community calendar.

Monday will be the annual Bluegrass Festival held in the burned-out shell that used to be Louie Blasko's Music Shoppe before he lit it on fire and skipped town with the insurance money. Participants can huddle among the ashen remains, casting haunting looks at each other and sharing some of their favorite bluegrass dirges. Legend has it that if you look into a mirror and say absolutely nothing three times, Louie himself will appear and teach the crowd some simple, easy bluegrass licks before taking your soul back with him into the dark of the mirror.

Tuesday is a holiday. Make sure you have adequate emergency supplies and plenty of clear plastic sheeting. We're not sure which holiday it is, so have all possible antidotes on hand.

Wednesday, the staff of Dark Owl Records are getting a band together. "We know a lot about music," they'll say, grabbing knives and hammers. "We should start a band." "Definitely," they'll continue, over the screams. "Let's get a band together. We should do that."

Thursday through Sunday will be a blur of routine and practicalities, a series of moments and actions that we will fail to notice as we experience them, and will forget the moment they are gone.

This has been the community calendar.

All right, boring stuff done. Back to the date! We wrapped up dinner at Gino's with a slice of their special invisible, noncorporeal, and tasteless carrot cake, which was as light as air and resembled air in all other qualities as well. Our waiter, formerly a heavyset man with a large mustache, was now a buzzing shadow man defined only by the absence of light in the vague shape of a torso and limbs. Presumably our former waiter was on break. We asked for the check and then made our escape from the doorless room by breaking the window using the brick our waiter had provided for that purpose.

Carlos and I, oh the magic of that phrase, oh the ecstasy of all that a simple conjunction can imply, took a stroll through Mission Grove Park. It was just us, and the trees, and the crowd of our fellow citizens who were all doing the usual recreational activity of pointing at the sky and shouting in terror. I asked Carlos if he wanted to join in for a round, but he said he had already been scared of all that the empty sky implies yesterday, and so was pretty tired.

"If you want," he said, "we could do some tests on the trees. I've been meaning to do some scientific tests on the trees. They seem normal, but given all that I've observed in this town, it is a significant chance that they are not."

Well, of course I could not pass up the opportunity to perform real science side by side with my Carlos, and so we approached the nearest tree, an old sagging thing, and begin to perform tests, the nature and purpose of which I am not remotely qualified to describe.

Meanwhile our fellow park-goers had ceased screaming and had taken up being strange buzzing shadow beings. All of them were standing exactly where they had been, but were now defined only by the absence of light in the vague shape of a torso and limbs. I stroked Carlos's cheek. I don't know if he noticed. He said the tests were inconclusive, and also was perfect in face and form.

And now a word from our sponsors.

Looking for a home security solution? Good luck with that. Want to feel safe when driving your car? Get in line. Fearful when walking alone at night? Well you should be.

When life seems dangerous and unmanageable, just remember that it is, and that you can't survive forever. Denny's restaurants. Why not?

And now, a station editorial. Listeners, a lot has been made about the topic of beauty, and I don't think we in the media always do our best to promote healthy self-images.

Movies and magazines and TV shows and advertisers love to use photo and video editing to make people seem skinnier, fairer, more appealing to a false ideal of human beauty. And I think this takes a strong hold of us, especially children.

But remember you are beautiful only when you do beautiful things. Full lips aren't as beautiful as a full laugh. Skinny hips aren't as attractive as a quick wit. Think about treating others right and those others will flock to you in screaming droves.

Just peel back those artificial layers, Night Vale. Unzip that name-brand coat, those skinny jeans, wipe off that makeup, and gently (but very quickly) peel off that skin that's covering up the true you. Look at those exposed eyes, dangling unprotected from their gaping sockets. Look at the blood and sinew slowly uncoiling from quivering bones. Admire that slippery viscera trying to squeeze under those dynamic ribs of yours. You are organic, to be sure, listener. Be proud of who you are.

Speaking of pride, speaking of beauty: more from my date soon. But first, the weather.

WEATHER: "Team the Best Team" by Doomtree

Let's get right back into it, shall we?

After the park, I drove him back to his lab, next to Big Rico's Pizza. The drive was difficult, because at this point it seemed that everyone in town but the two of us had hopped onto the buzzing shadow entity train, and were loping around town as malevolent holes in our reality, emanating an energy that made the hairs on your arm stand and your bowels vibrate. Or maybe that was just the chemistry with Carlos I was feeling. A woman ran at our car screaming, a few of the shadow people chasing her, but before I could even touch the brake she must have changed her mind, because she had already turned into a shadow person herself. It's like, ugh, run from the shadow people or become one. Make up your mind, lady!

We arrived outside of Big Rico's and there was that awkward moment at the end of every date where you pause outside of the person's door and it's like, Should I call the City Council and submit the standard end-of-date report or are you going to? Also I was wondering if he was going to invite me into his lab, to look at all those breakers and humming electrical equipment.

"Well," he said, pointing to the lab. "This is me."

"Uh huh," I said.

"I should probably do something about this buzzing shadow thing," he said. "A few experiments to see if I can save the town."

"Oh," I said. "Do you need any help with that?"

"No," he said. "A scientist is self-reliant. It's the first thing a scientist is."

"Oh," I said again, but softer, sadder.

Which is when he leaned forward and kissed me, just once, just gently, just before slipping out of the car and into the lab. I'll tell you, listeners, I was almost swallowed by a cloud of malevolent shadow energy on the drive home and I hardly even noticed. I was so happy.

I guess Carlos managed to find a way to defeat the shadow energy, as everything seems normal today. A couple neighborhoods are emptied out, sure, with books and food and televisions left where they had been at the time of the sudden vanishing, a tableau of a life that never again will be. But it wouldn't really be a weekend without that happening somewhere, right?

Night Vale, my sweet and only Night Vale, may you find love. May you find it wherever it's been hidden. May you find who has been hiding it and exact revenge upon them.

As the old song goes, "Love is all you need to destroy your enemies." Finer words were never chanted.

Stay tuned next for Efficiency Hour with our own productivity expert, a reversed voice underscored by hypnotic pulses.

And with all the love in my loving heart, and with a loving voice in a loving and terrifying world, good night, Night Vale. Good night.

PROVERB: Production oversight by Tory Malatea, who is holding a small locket. He is not speaking. He'd just like for you to touch the locket. His hand is twisted. His skin is forming into scales. Just touch it once. Just once, okay?

EPISODE 28:
"SUMMER READING PROGRAM"

AUGUST 1, 2013

COWRITTEN WITH ASHLEY LIERMAN

BEING A LIBRARIAN MYSELF, I WAS ALWAYS DELIGHTED BY NIGHT VALE'S terrifying librarians. When you're in a profession that gets stereotyped somewhere between "matronly prude shushing children" and "obsolete relic of when print wasn't dead," seeing somebody go for "extremely dangerous Eldritch Abomination" is pretty exciting stuff. So when Jeffrey and Joseph invited me to write an episode, I knew I wanted to do something with the Night Vale Public Library.

I'm a university librarian, not public, and I've never run a summer reading program, but I was a big participant as a kid. The innocent pleasures of stacks of children's books and sticker charts seemed ripe for a weird, creepy turn. With, of course, another reversal at the end—which seemed in line with the rhythm of unexpected twists and hilarious anticlimaxes that are so much of what makes Night Vale special. (Not to mention, on a practical level, if you're invited to write an episode of somebody's show in the world they've created, maybe don't do something that's like "AND THEN HUNDREDS OF CHILDREN DIED.") Kids in Night Vale must face so much fear and danger daily that maybe they're more dangerous themselves than even a librarian would give them credit for, especially the ones who love reading. They're already clearly brave if they're willing to crack open Night Vale's dangerous books, after all, and adding curiosity and imagination to the mix could only make them tougher opponents.

Anyway, I loved the twist of all those vulnerable kids everyone was worried about coming out gorily triumphant, and I decided I wanted to name a leader to sort of personify all their toughness, brains, resourcefulness, and book-loving in one person. There are always too few black girls who get to be associated with those traits in fiction, but so many real black girls I've known who are all of those things and more, so it seemed like the obvious thing for that leader to be a black girl. I could not be more thrilled that Tamika Flynn resonated so much with so many people, and ended up being woven into Night Vale's story as much as she was. Of course, so much of who she ended up being was Jeffrey and Joseph's doing, but every time she showed up afterward, it was such a pleasure to be able to say:

"Hey, there she is! That's my girl!"

—Ashley Lierman

Does it even matter how many living things you
touched today, or where they all are now?

WELCOME TO NIGHT VALE.

The Summer Reading Program for children and teens has begun at the Night Vale Public Library. This comes as an alarming surprise, given that the program was abolished by the City Council thirty years ago. Though parents and teachers have asked on several occasions to reinstate the program, the City Council has maintained its position, citing lack of taxpayer funds, the extreme danger posed by books, the peril of exposing children to librarians, and, of course, the incident that precipitated the ban, which the town's older residents will refer to only as "the Time of Knives."

Nevertheless, in a show of civic dedication, or mindless bloodlust—and they are so similar—Night Vale's librarians have banded together in defiance of authority to reinitiate Summer Reading. Colorful posters with appealing statements like "Get into a good book this summer" and "We are going to force you into a good

book this summer"
and "You are
going to get
inside this
book and
we are going

to close it on you and there is nothing you can do about it" have appeared overnight around the library entrance and in local shops and businesses, all sporting the clever tagline "Catch the flesh-eating reading bacterium." The Sheriff's Secret Police have responded by interrogating the proprietors of businesses where the posters have appeared, and by removing and confiscating the posters themselves—although to be honest, listeners, the graphic design work is really cute. I mean, have you seen them? The little flesh-eating germ with his sunhat and library book, using a screaming, semi-skeletal human victim as a beach chair? Adorable!

After fierce debate today, the City Council has officially declared murder illegal, a crime that has until this point been handled using informal vigilante squads. The head of one such squad, Vincent LaFarge of Grab 'Em and Sack 'Em, argued that Night Vale has gotten along just fine for years without the government meddling in murder investigation or punishment.

"Do we sometimes catch the wrong guy?" said Vincent. "Sure. Most of the time. We're not sure we've ever caught a guilty one. Usually we just grab the first person we see. One time we tried to arrest the dead body, but it got away."

Proponents of the bill argued that most things in Night Vale are already illegal anyway, so citizens would hardly even notice the change.

The law goes into effect in two weeks, and citizens are advised to get any necessary murders done before then, although there will be a three-day grace period after the deadline for those who are forgetful or whose victims are hard to catch.

Some summer tips to beat the heat. First off, have you tried to reason with the heat? Humans, temperatures, angels, and chairs are all equally real and sentient, which is to say that we're all not real, nor are any of us actually sentient. But give reason a shot. It has never, not once in history, worked, but it might just work this time.

If the heat won't listen to reason, try denying that it's hot. "Doesn't seem hot today," you might say to your profusely sweating neighbor. "A little chilly even," you could continue, slipping on a sweater and making an exaggerated *brr* noise as the glaring sun plants the idea of cancer in your skin.

And if denial does not work, then your best bet, as with all problems in life, is exhausted resignation. This has been summer tips to beat the heat.

And now a public service announcement. Here is a brief list of everything that is helpful:

- The Sheriff's Secret Police
- Clouds
- Anger
- The City Council
- Affection falling just short of love
- Ceiling fans
- Lungs
- Other sundry organs
- Laws
- Government
- Helicopters
- The 2005 Honda Accord
- Secrets
- Whispers
- Ultimately, nothing

Anything not specifically named in this list should be considered not helpful and potentially dangerous. It's not just good sense; it's the law.

An update on the Summer Reading situation: Fourteen young people between the ages of five and seventeen have already been reported missing, and are feared to be in the public library, and possibly learning. Attempts by the Sheriff's Secret Police to enter the library, rescue the missing children, and put an end to all Summer Reading activities have failed, as all doors and windows have mysteriously disappeared from the library exterior—just like it was before the renovations.

Our tax dollars paid for those doors and windows and we shouldn't be expected to stand for library administrators just deciding to disappear them on a whim—even for a valid reason, like jealously guarding their possession of our stolen children—without at least putting the issue to a popular vote!

Anyway, in light of this development, the City Council has declared a Level Orange Fear Alert. They advise that all Night Vale citizens avoid the public library, and provide the council with any information they may have on the whereabouts of the missing children, on librarians' secret weaknesses, or on good books they've read lately. Any citizens who admit to having read good books, the council added in an impromptu press conference televised from a book-proof bunker, will be immediately scheduled for reeducation and subsequent deeducation.

The Sheriff's Secret Police, meanwhile, have instituted a curfew for the entire town, effective immediately. After 7:00 P.M., all minors should be at home and under adult supervision, and absolutely no reading, researching, online information-seeking, educational games, documentary television, or having a lifelong love of learning will be permitted. As their catchy new slogan puts it: "Once it gets dark, forget everything you ever knew, and be silent; words belong to our enemies, and our enemies are words, so be as mute and pure as a bone bleached clean by our desert sun. By our desert sun." The police have also stated that any Night Vale citizen encountering a librarian, an entity suspected of being a librarian, or any excessively organized and helpful individual with a working comprehension of information systems is encouraged to shoot on sight. They also added that this goes for teachers as well, since "what the hell, as long as we're at it."

We'll have further updates on this story as it develops.

And now a word from our sponsors.

Congratulations! You are eligible for a FREE thirty-day trial! This FREE thirty-day trial comes with everything you need, including a FREE arrest, FREE charges, FREE arraignment, and FREE conviction, GUARANTEED. Shipping and handling not included. Defense lawyer also not included. We have you surrounded. The more you struggle, the worse it will be for you. Put that down. Put it down. Put that down.

This message brought to you whether you like it or not.

The Freemasons have announced some changes to their hierarchy. These changes are the following: Whereas before the Freemasons were under the authority of the Stone Masons Worldwide, they will now be an independent subsidiary of the Hallowed Mason Council, which itself will be split into four branches, corresponding with the four directions we glance when nervous. The Hallowed Mason Council will also provide guidance and financial support to the Retailmasons, the Wholesalemasons, and the Discountmasons, except in cases involving inter-Masonry disputes, which will, as before, be subject to the Small Brotherhood of the Large Chamber, the Large Brotherhood of the Small Chamber, or the Properly Fitted Brotherhood, depending on the patterns discerned in bones cast by a fully licensed member of the Masonic Drone Legion or one of their proxies.

Now, of course the masons will continue their proud fraternal associations with the Illuminati. However, the Illuminati will itself be splitting into ten distinct factions, as follows: Red, Green, Eagle, Faction 4, the Real Illuminati, the Other Real Illuminati, Red Again, Alpha, Windhind, and HungryManBrandFrozenFoodsOfficiallySponsoredIlluminati. This split will be overseen by the Council of Three, which will be supported by the Council of Five, and monitored by the Council of Zero. Elections for the Council of Zero will be held never, and will result in nothing. Discretionary funds for the Illuminati and Freemason Alliance Committee will be funneled through a number of secret bank accounts, their numbers known to no one, and their secrets kept forever. All this is in accordance with the General Secret Agreement of the General Secret Alliance of the General Secret Community, representing all brotherhoods and organizations obscure and hidden, including the Harpoon League, the Flying Cape, the Six Ancient Truths, and the Dental Underground.

The Freemasons would also like to remind you that none of this may be known to you, and that they are only telling you this to demonstrate your fragile mind, which barely parsed the words as they were spoken, and have already forgotten the secrets contained just moments later. You will never know anything, and you will not even know that.

Breaking news: Despite the best efforts of the Sheriff's Secret Police and citizenry, we have received confirmation that over a hundred children and adolescents have disappeared from their homes, beds, part-time jobs, or summer forced labor camps, and are now presumed to be inside the Night Vale Public Library and subject to the Summer Reading Program. Unfortunately, it is my sad duty to announce that this includes Intern Paolo, a high school junior who's been helping to organize the radio station archives over the summer months. To the parents and family of Paolo: Our hearts go out to you in this time of fear and uncertainty, as in all other times of fear and uncertainty, which is all of them, really. May you find comfort in the knowledge that, though your son may have been lost in a library, at least he—unlike many of his peers—actually went inside one of those at least once.

The situation has—wait, hold on just one moment—

I beg your pardon, listeners, but I've just received alarming news. An alert citizen has called in to report "inhuman shrieking, thick meaty sounds, and a coppery-rotten smell of gore and viscera" coming from the now sealed and impenetrable Night Vale Public Library. Which are, of course, all fairly standard elements of the Summer Reading Program as described in the library director's original proposal.

Painful though it may be, it seems that all we can do now—as so often in our dull, blinkered lives below a macrocosm of horror and beauty—is wait. Wait, and hope, and know that our hopes are immaterial and powerless, and our wishes will go unheard by the indifferent multitude of stars, if indeed they (the stars) are even real. But there are still some comforts that remain to us while we wait, small shining baubles to distract us from the endless march of time toward events we have no control over and outcomes we never imagined. And so, ladies and gentlemen, I give you . . . the weather.

WEATHER: "You and I Belong" by Simone Felice

This just in, listeners: We've received reports that the entrances to the Night Vale Public Library have reappeared, and the missing children have begun to emerge from inside the building. The children have been described as wild-eyed, feral, some staggering upright and some running on all fours like animals, caked in effluvia and far more emaciated than the time of their absence would seem to account for, but otherwise well, healthy, and unharmed. At the head of the dazed and shambling pack was their apparent chosen leader, twelve-year-old Tamika Flynn, her mouth clenched in a blood-crusted snarl and carrying the severed head of a librarian in one hand, and a gore-streaked sticker chart in the other. Eyewitnesses who dared to get close enough to read the chart reported that Tamika had even finished *Cry, the Beloved Country*, which is very impressive for her reading level. Well done, Tamika!

Indeed, congratulations are in order for all the young people of Night Vale who participated in the Summer Reading Program for proving that neither abduction nor captivity, neither horrors beyond imagining nor unfamiliar vocabulary can prevent you from embracing the pleasures of belles lettres. Here's to you, boys and girls. And remember, even while we congratulate Tamika for winning your loyalty with her sophisticated comprehension and extremes of berserker violence, that the real victory won today has been for literacy.

Stay tuned next for our countdown of last words, from "Stop telling me how to drive," all the way to "It's okay. It's okay. It's okay."

Good night, Night Vale. Good Night.

PROVERB: A bar walks into a bar. The bartender is a snake eating its own tail. The windows look out only onto the face of the one who looks.

EPISODE 29: "SUBWAY"

AUGUST 15, 2013

COWRITTEN WITH RUSSEL SWENSEN

Do you ride a train to work? I used to. The forty-five-minute R train ride from 95th Street, Bay Ridge, to Prince Street, SoHo, was my daily commute for most of my first decade in New York City.

And when I used to perform regularly with the New York Neo-Futurists, we did a late-night show in the East Village, so Friday and Saturday nights at 2:00 A.M. that simple R train ride was less simple. Take the F train from 2nd Avenue to Jay Street-MetroTech, transfer to the N, which runs local late night. Take the N to 59th Street, Sunset Park, where the R train runs a limited shuttle (every thirty minutes) to 95th Street, Bay Ridge.

My forty-five-minute commute into lower Manhattan was closer to ninety minutes late night (once it took two hours and thirty minutes with no announcements of interrupted or delayed service). Nearly half of that was standing on a platform waiting for trains.

The PA systems on the older New York City trains sound like the adults from a Peanuts TV special getting nearly electrocuted and then screaming about their pain into a broken subway train PA system. So confusion is the norm late at night when nothing works like it should—as opposed to the daytime when everything works like it shouldn't.

I cowrote this episode with Russel Swensen, whom I met on Twitter and later in real life at his poetry reading/book release event in the East Village back in 2012. I loved how floral and self-destructive his phrases were, and I thought this confounding dichotomy of beauty and pain would work well in the Night Vale world.

Same goes for the confounding dichotomy of expensive, tightly scheduled mass transit and noisy, analog frustration. Let's take all that and make a Night Vale episode where an underground train system suddenly appears in town.

And because it's fiction, the Night Vale subway system works way better than New York City's subway system.

—Jeffrey Cranor

Our black suns move erratically, like drunken bees, and each of them stings. Now more than ever we are full of blood and honey.

WELCOME TO NIGHT VALE.

We start our program with some good news, listeners. Several Night Vale residents have reported seeing subway entrances popping up all over town. These brightly lit stairwells into the underground have been showing up on several street corners over the past few days.

But the Secret Police have denied knowledge of any subway system. According to our station's research into the issue, there are no records of the Night Vale Transit Authority ever creating a subway system, or getting one approved, or even having discussed building one. Nor has there ever existed a Night Vale Transit Authority. The only hints can be found in the brochures littering the entrances, describing the ease with which we will now commute, the hungers we will sate, the time we will travel, the times we will travel, the happy memories we will never be able to shake loose even when we wake up screaming.

I'm looking at one of the new subway brochures right now. There is no logo. Just smiling faces, with teeth unusual in their shapes, colors, and spacing, but otherwise quite normal-looking teeth. And the phrase "Oh, the place you will go!" written in heavy sans serif font across the eyes of smiling train riders, clutching tightly to bags and metal rails and each other.

I'm looking more closely at these transit brochures, and the paper stock is quite strange, listeners. The pages are scaly, brown, and translucent. I mean, I usually just have Intern Dylan make our radio station flyers on colored copy paper, say a twenty-four-pound goldenrod, but these brochures are so lush, like wings of a majestic insect.

The text also just grows increasingly garbled. For instance, here it says that our new subway system will streamline the rush-hour commute, but about halfway down, it's a series of nearly indecipherable glyphs our experts insist hint at "non-Euclidian emotions" and "appeasement" (though we think this may be a euphemism for "fares"). Finally, there's a crudely drawn map of our new transit system, all routes resembling spasming tentacles, and all passing at least once through a common point deep beneath the center of Night Vale.

No one yet knows where the subways came from or where they go to, but as a city dweller, I am certainly happy to hear that Night Vale is embracing mass transit. This is a fantastic way to unclog our highways, reduce pollution, and accidents, and, most importantly, subways allow us to interact with each other. Make eye contact. Acknowledge each other as fellow creatures. Cars are impersonal machines that close us off from humanity, and with the rising cost of gas and the large iridescent tongues that have been growing from Route 800, I think the subway will be a positive addition to our community.

We'll have more on this breaking story soon.

Ladies and gentlemen, I want to talk to you now about a popular new service in town that delivers feelings. Whether you want them to or not. This service has no name or contact information. It simply delivers feelings. You do not choose the feeling—though Yelp! reviews say "tingling horror" and "as though electrocuted I stood before him" are the most popular so far. It is unclear where on Yelp! you look for these reviews. I, myself, have received a few feelings so far, such as "blood feud" and "frustrated origami novice," and I'm looking forward to receiving more. I'm crossing my fingers for "should have left the party hours ago, before I could disappoint her." I would also settle for "overcast Wednesday and trampled by horses." This is my own endorsement, listeners, not a sponsored ad. I wouldn't even know which company or person to bill for airtime. I just really enjoy having feelings delivered straight to me without having to worry about choosing which feeling and why and when.

The Secret Police, in cooperation with a vague yet menacing government agency, would like to remind you that here in Night Vale no one is eating each other. They remind you that this is a friendly reminder. The Secret Police added their assurance that they see no reason to alert us to the not-at-all increasingly common practice of grill parties and consensual cannibalism. "It would be pretty terrible of us to conceal that, right?" a heavily cloaked spokesperson said distractedly, deeply engrossed in a game of Drop7 on his or her iPhone 4S. "But listen, the important thing here is we are not ... hang on ... darn ... warning or alerting anyone and I think you should remember to thank us for that." The cloaked figure then double tapped his or her phone and a horse rose up from the floor beneath him or her and they flew off into the sky.

The City Council has now officially denied any involvement in our fantastic new subway system. We have this direct from a fair-haired and hollow-eyed child they've sent with the denial tattooed on his inner lip ("never approved" it reads).

Just a quick aside, listeners. We'll get back to the subway news in a moment, but would anyone like a child, because I'm never quite sure what to do with the messenger children the City Council sends us. I'm not even sure if the child is completely sentient. This one just stares blankly ahead and, oh, he's wandered off. Never mind.

Also, we're getting reports that a press conference was just held in front of the ashen shell of the public library, which of course was burned down last night, and it is only a matter of days before we'll need to burn it down again. Several masked figures, having called the press conference, claimed responsibility for the subway system. Their masks had the countenance of very concerned deer. One of the figures spoke to reporters. "We took matters into our own hand, even without approval. We don't need approval of the City Council or the Mayor," the spokesperson explained. "We do and say what we please. That shirt looks awful on you, by the way." (Apparently here they pointed to *Night Vale Weekly Gazette* writer Lauren James, who usually wears very nice shirts. It's really her bangs that don't work, I think. I like bangs, but they just frame her face too dramatically, especially with those thick-rimmed glasses.)

Press conference attendees said they could see something moving behind the spokesperson's deer mask. I am told that the black-charred grounds of the library are covered in roaches, as well. Also that perhaps the deer masks are not concerned, but disapproving. Or maybe merely world-weary and under a lot of stress.

Listeners, I am now being told by a different dead-eyed child in my studio, via complex facial expressions, that if you are anywhere near the site of last night's victorous fire at the library, please DO NOT step on the roaches. We recognize that there are tens of thousands of these vermin, but we've been informed by inside sources and this really unsettling zombie child that these are proprietary roaches. If you look closely at the many cockroaches crawling up your arm you'll notice they have slogans scrawled across them: "ride the trains," "everything is fine," "tenderize yourself as needed." We repeat DO NOT HURT THE ROACHES. We are receiving several reports that the roaches are PRECIOUS AD SPACE. And if you hold one up to your ear, it is true—they sound like sizzling butter.

And now a look at the financial markets. You will turn yourself inside out. Your sadness will know no bounds. Ladybugs will flee you; wolves run wild in you. You will hear the wind chimes like shattering. The sun will drip ichor. Whatever peace you find will be taken from you. Nothing will be the same. Nothing has ever been the same. "Past performance does not guarantee future results," you will whisper to the rising moon as you hear several foxes fleeing your vicinity. This has been business news.

The Greater Night Vale Medical Community would like to remind you to become an organ donor. It's a simple process that only takes a moment, and you could save a life. You can visit the DMV to pick up the appropriate form. It only requires that you check a box, sign your name, and turn it in. The Greater Night Vale Medical Community would also like to say thank-you to those citizens who have already become registered organ donors. They remind you that collections begin this Tuesday at 4:00 P.M. Please hold still and wear loose-fitting clothing that day. They also advise that you not eat anything after 8:00 the night before. They are particularly in need of kidneys and skin. A representative was quoted as saying something that resembled a hiss and then quickly biting the reporter's ankle.

It has come to our attention that some Night Vale residents are getting off the trains . . . transformed. Mayor Pamela Winchell described these commuters as "thinner somehow, spiritually, like you think it's the afternoon but it's almost evening. That's what they're like." Carlos, caring and reliable Carlos the scientist, thinks maybe the riders' DNA has been washed out, emptied, completely drained of its content. Listeners, I'm also being told that some people are not getting off the trains at all.

I'm looking out my studio window now, and a new subway en-

trance has just appeared across the street during this very broadcast.
I have seen dozens enter and few exit those stairs. I have grave concerns, Night Vale.

I have just been handed a press release by another small child. He
has such deep blue eyes and so many freckles. He is smiling and there
is something dark moving behind his teeth. The press release is covered
in roaches. Now the boy is leaving and I hear a rapid, but faint clicking
sound.

According to the release, the City Council says we owe today's increased productivity to our glorious new mass transit system that just
appeared this week. It goes on to say that Night Vale could eventually
become a true travel destination, like Japan or Brazil or Singapore or
Luftnarp or Svitz.

I know we still don't understand who built the subway, or where it
goes, or what has happened to all of our family and friends that have
gotten on trains today. I know there are concerns, Night Vale, but this
subway seems to be a major step forward for our town, for our environ-
ment, for our—

[*Deep subterranean booming sounds*]

Oh dear, something is happening, listeners. This does not appear to
be a standard government-created earthquake. Across the street, there are
shimmering waves of heat curdling the air above the subway entrance. A
black cloud of large insects is swirling above. I do not know what this
means, Night Vale. And since Intern Dylan never returned from his er-
rands, likely because I told him to take the new subway to save time, I
myself must go investigate. In the meantime, I give you the weather.

WEATHER: "Poor in Love" by Destroyer

It's spring somewhere, Night Vale, and I must admit the last few
minutes—even stretched as they were seemingly into aeons—have left

me feeling renewed, returned as I am to my home after so long away. It's like I'm walking to fresh, clean water, even as I lean into the mic.

I entered the subway, like many of you. And like many of you other riders, I saw and felt the cosmic suffering of millennia, was witness to eras of countless births and deaths and wars and discoveries and kisses and plagues and knives and cold empty void. I saw it all at once and I could not make sense of any of it but I understood it fully and it took years, Night Vale. Years I have been missing you since I left you to the weather. What was the weather like then? How much time has passed for you? Only four minutes?

What of the ground shaking and the cloud of insects and the immense heat? Well, that's apparently what happens when an express train arrives. People hurrying to faraway (long away) destinations, the *click-clickclick* of rush-hour commutes, reading unimportant news stories, solving unimportant number puzzles, looking up briefly to give seats to the elderly or infirm. All the while not knowing where they were going or why or what terrible things they would never unknow upon choosing to commute through whatever that singular point below our city is. That intersection of space and time. A sort of navel of the universe.

And somehow we are all better, wiser, kinder for going where we went for as long as we were gone, though we did not age but a few moments.

We still do not know who the deer-masked transit people are or whether they are people at all. Perhaps they are thousands of roaches packed inside a business suit, hiding behind a mask. Or perhaps the mask was not hiding them at all, but hiding us. Sheltering them from our immature, solipsistic minds. But now there is a subway. Now we can go anywhere and perhaps we can know anything if we ride for long enough.

Listeners, there's another child in the studio. This one is faceless, covered in denim and dust, with a long swoop of unruly brown hair covering what would be the right eyebrow. The child is holding a handwritten note. It reads: "Because of construction, all subway service is suspended until further notice. For your convenience, free shuttle buses will be provided. At the moment of greatest despair and hopelessness, when you least suspect it, a shuttle bus will come to you. Thank you for your patience."

The future of urban planning is here, Night Vale, and like our own eminent futures, it is buried in the earth.

Stay tuned next for a swarm of flies circling a hot mic. And as always, Good night, Night Vale. Good night.

PROVERB: Your body is a temple. A temple of blood rituals and pagan tributes, a lost temple, a temple that needs more calcium. You should maybe try vitamin supplements.

EPISODE 30:
"DANA"

SEPTEMBER 1, 2013

GUEST VOICE: JASIKA NICOLE

JASIKA NICOLE WILL TELL YOU MORE ABOUT THIS LATER, BUT SINCE I MET her I wanted to write something for her.

Are you an intuitive person? I like to think I am. I rely a lot on intuition to reach conclusions. Sometimes this works out really well. (See the first sentence of this introduction.) Sometimes it doesn't. (See my time spent as a civil engineering major at Texas A&M, not to mention my single day in their ROTC program.)

My intuition about Jasika being a sincere, interesting, funny, talented, and kind human turned out to all be correct. And the first moment she read a Dana monologue aloud (September 2013 at Largo at the Coronet in LA), I fully understood this character Joseph and I had created.

Dana was determined and lost. Dana was scared and smart. She was removed physically from the correct place and time. Literally this happened to her. Although given her status in life as a young person going from college to the real world, this was figuratively happening to her as well.

Interns in Night Vale don't usually succeed at much other than gruesome deaths and disappearances. And worse than that, they rarely have their stories told. They're just a name and a hastily constructed Cecil obituary. But Jasika made Dana vital. She made her full. Jasika made Dana live past all this, because you don't create a fully-formed human full of sympathy and agency and needs and character and just let her die or vanish.

So I finally found things to write for Jasika. And more and more and more, and my intuition paid off gloriously.

Now, about that career as a bridge and highway builder . . .

—Jeffrey Cranor

It takes heart. It takes guts. It also takes cash.
It just needs your payment immediately.

WELCOME TO NIGHT VALE.

Mayor Pamela Winchell announced again today that she is stepping down as mayor later this year. This is the fourth announcement this week. She said again through tight teeth that this is totally her call and was never ever discussed in a room with no windows by small men wear- ing large pelts and decorative soft-meat crowns. That is not how we do things, she said. That is not how we do things, she whispered. That is

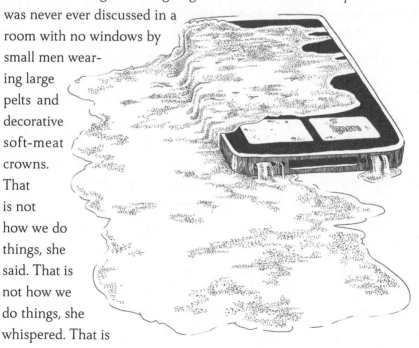

not how we do things, she mouthed silently as a single, dark red tear formed in the corner of her eye and then slowly rolled down her taut, olive cheek and onto her clay-stained smock.

Elections for a new mayor will be held at some later time. When asked by the press for a specific date and location, masked representatives from a vague yet menacing government agency purred loudly. They then began rubbing their sides against the journalists' legs. Several reporters began sneezing.

Listeners, many of you recall our station intern Dana who, while reporting on strange goings-on, was locked in the forbidden Dog Park back in April.

I've received occasional texts and e-mails from Dana, but then this morning, well. Let's listen.

DANA: Cecil. It's Dana. I've found a way out of here. I walked the perimeter of the Dog Park looking for a crack or a hole or a weak spot in the obsidian walls. I never found an opening, but—and this is very strange—the walls just keep going. If you stand still, the Dog Park seems to take up a single city block, but I walked one direction for about two weeks, and I could no longer see the monolith where I started, or the people I was with, or even hear the tinfoil rustling of the leaves from the tall, black metal trees that protect us from clouds.

There's something else. I found a door—an old oak door standing unsupported by any other structure. I didn't know if it was an exit from the Dog Park or an entrance to something much worse, but I went through it. Now, I am in some old house.

Cecil, I can hear someone moving around upstairs. I need to go. I will try to call you soon.

Thank you for everything, and I hope our time and place match again soon.

CECIL: Oh, listeners, I so wish I could have talked to Dana this morning. They were showing *Cat Ballou* again on TBS, and I just couldn't break away. I tried to call Dana back, but my phone caught briefly on fire and something sharp cut open my thumb as I selected her number.

And now a Public Service Announcement from the Night Vale SPCA. Thinking about getting a dog? Dogs are not only great family companions but also help childhood development. By regularly feeding, walking, fighting, denying the existence of, and ultimately soul-merging with the family dog, young children learn about responsibility, empathy, and pyrokinesis.

There are, of course, some breeds of dogs that are not right for children. Those breeds include: Spider Wolves, Double Wolves, Switchbladed Mountain Dogs, Secret Terriers, Flesh-eating Spaniels, Pit Vipers, and Table Saws. Visit the SPCA for more information on the right dog for your family.

[*Phone ringing*]

Hello. Dana? [*There's some static or noise from Dana's line*]

DANA: Cecil? I can barely understand you. Cecil, are you there?
CECIL: Yes. I'm here. Dana are you still in the old house?
DANA: No, I'm still in the old house. I made my way out of the basement, which was empty except for a single photograph of a lighthouse. It's a framed five-by-seven black-and-white photo of this old lighthouse. It hangs crooked, just to the right of center on one wall. The lighthouse in the photo looks to be in the middle of a field. There's no water. Why would there be a lighthouse not near the water?
CECIL: I have no idea.
DANA: No, that doesn't sound right. Maybe it's some other reason. Anyway, once I heard the footsteps above me stop, I opened the door to the first floor. I saw a man standing in the middle of the living room, staring straight ahead at the wall. I couldn't see his face, Cecil, and I knew I had been through this moment before. Not like déjà vu, more like a clear but fleeting memory of a dream. I was scared he might hear me, Cecil.

CECIL: What did you do, Dana?

DANA: Yes, that's exactly what I did. I got up the nerve and spoke to him. I said "Hello, sir. My name is Dana. And I'm sorry to intrude, but I was wondering, is this your home?" And he didn't move. He didn't make a sound. He just kept staring at another small photo on the wall. I walked closer to him and said, "Excuse me, sir. Excuse me, but" and then I saw. Cecil, I saw who it was.

CECIL: Who was it?

DANA: No, it wasn't her. It was John Peters, you know, the farmer? He was staring at this photo and I walked closer and said, "John, it's me, Dana," but he didn't respond. I looked at the photo he was examining, and it was just a picture of a window. A worn driftwood frame, inside of which was a photograph of a worn driftwood pane with gently warped glass. I couldn't see what was beyond the window in the photo. But there was a shape. Maybe a tree, maybe a person. John just stared ahead, looking sad. No, not sad. Concerned. He looked concerned.

I didn't say another word to him. I waved my hand gently in front of his eyes, and he didn't notice me. I tried to touch his shoulder but my hand went right through him, like through a cold wind. He wasn't even there, Cecil. He eventually turned and looked at another photo on another wall of another window, but he never saw or heard me.

This home has no furniture, no furnishings, no belongings. Only photos. Single small photos on occasional walls. Most of them are of windows. Different windows with different panes and different photo frames. The house itself, I realize, has no windows of its own. So, I don't really know if there is a basement or a first or second floor. The upstairs is the downstairs is the ground floor.

But I know one thing, Cecil.

CECIL: What is that?

DANA: No. But you're close. I know that John Peters entered through a door in the kitchen. I can see the door right now, Cecil. It is open. And beyond that door is sunlight. I can see sunlight and sand.

I'm going through.

CECIL: Yes. Dana, do that. Go through the door now. Go through that door!

DANA: I'm sorry, Cecil. You make a good point, but I have to go through that door, no matter what. I've got to get back home.

CECIL: Do it, Dana! Yes!

DANA: Here I go.

[*Her voice and the noise of the phone call cut off abruptly.*]

CECIL: Dana? Hello? Dana, can you hear me?

Ladies and gentlemen, I do not know where Dana has gone now. I do hope that we hear from her again. I would try to call her back, but my phone has grown spiny legs and is crawling away now. If you are the type to pray, please pray for Dana's safe return home to Night Vale. If you are not the type to pray, please know that you are violating several laws and you will receive a knock on your door from armed agents very soon.

Let's have a look at sports.

This weekend the Night Vale High School Scorpions kick off their season against the Pine Cliff High School Lizard Monitors. Scorpions quarterback, senior Michael Sandero, had off-season surgery to remove the second head he grew in the middle of last season's division title run. Michael's mother, Flora Sandero, said she had her son's original head removed instead, as she liked the new head much better. "This new head is much handsomer and doesn't talk back as much," Flora explained from the roof of the Pinkberry, where she was installing several long pikes with dead vultures and rodents on the ends. "This new head only speaks Russian, so I don't have to listen to him on the phone with his girlfriend all night long. And he doesn't hog the television anymore because he can't understand any of the English or Spanish programs here. He's a better boy now," she said jamming another pike into the roof of the trendy Fro-Yo store before yelling skyward, causing the sparse clouds to part quickly, revealing a giant, floating crystal, glowing faintly red in the mid-afternoon sun.

And now a word from our sponsor.

McDonald's wants to remind you that the most important meal of the day is breakfast. So why would you let a morning go by without staring deeply into the mirror until you no longer recognize the face staring back at you, mimicking your every gesture, mocking your every movement. How else will you get the energy you need for a full day's work or recreation if you aren't silently screaming into the visage of a man or woman who gives you such uneasy spirit, such unshakable terror, a queasy feeling every time you make the connection between what that thing is and what you are becoming. What you have become. Where does the void end? Where do you end? When do you end? What time is it now? You are late for work. You are lying on your bathroom floor, half dressed in a cool sludge of toothpaste and hair gel. You've been crying, but for how long?

McDonald's: I'm lovin'.

Listeners, I just received word from Carlos, lovely Carlos, with his perfect teeth and hair and penchant for sometimes chewing a little more loudly than is preferred. Carlos who is with other scientists at the Desert Creek housing development.

For the past year, Carlos has been studying a house that does not exist. It seems like it exists. Like it's just right there when you look at it, and it's between two other identical houses so it would make more sense for it to be there than not. But it does not exist. Carlos said the scientists asked him to come over and ring the doorbell just to see what would happen. They offered him $5, but he turned them down, saying something about scientific integrity and blah blah blah. But I'm like, $5 is a taco lunch at Jerry's Tacos, so whatever, rich guy.

Carlos said that before he could take a step to the house, a woman emerged from the side door talking on her cell phone. He and the scientists ran up to the woman calling out to her as she walked quickly away from the house. She looked panicked. No, not panicked. Concerned. She looked concerned, Carlos said. She kept talking on her cell phone never responding to them.

Carlos said she kept walking until she walked through them. Right through the scientists, like she were a cold wind. And then, she stopped talking into her phone, stared back toward the house, and with a look of panic—no, with a look of concern—ran away. Carlos said—and this is very strange—Carlos said, "It sounded like the person she was talking to was you, Cecil."

Listeners, I do not know where or when Dana is, but I am going to sit by this phone and wait for her call. I know she is all right. I hope she is all right. I fear she is not all right. With great anxiousness—no, concern—with great concern, I take you now to the weather.

WEATHER: "The Lethal Temptress" by The Mendoza Line

[Start of message sounder—it's Dana again]

DANA: Cecil. I'm sorry I lost your call. I made it out of the door. Out of the empty house and its empty photographs into an empty desert, and I don't know if anything is improved. I can see nothing but endless sand and a single distant mountain. A mountain I have never seen, because I don't believe in mountains. But there is a mountain, and there is a tiny red light up on the mountain, intermittently blinking.

As I exited the house, the door shut behind me and now it's gone. As I walked, I moved through something that wasn't there. I heard voices through digital static and felt a cold wind across my body. Others are here but not here, Cecil. What, or whom, did I just walk through?

Cecil, something is coming. I can feel it in the ground. Something very large is coming. I've got to go. I will call when I can. Tell my mother and brother I am out of the Dog Park, and I am safe for now. Thank you, Cecil.

[End of message; Background noise ends]

CECIL: Oh, listeners, I wish I had more news than this. I wish my phone would have rung. I wish I could have had that conversation, instead of another voice mail. I wish Dana were home, safe. I wish I could feel something other than overwhelming concern. No, not concern. Uncertainty. I wish a lot of things.

But as the old saying goes, "If wishes were horses, those wishes would all run away, shrieking and bucking, terrified of a great unseen evil." So, instead, what I want to say is I am thankful Dana is out of the Dog Park. I am thankful I had my first conversation with her since Poetry Week. I am thankful Carlos did not ring that doorbell. I am thankful that people listen to this show and the stories about our wonderful little community—the most scientifically interesting community in America, as my Carlos once said.

And, of course, I am thankful for you, Night Vale.

Stay tuned next for loud, short-wave radio squelches followed by a lifetime of tinnitus.

Good night, Night Vale. Good night.

PROVERB: Look to the sky. You will not find answers there, but you will certainly see what everyone is screaming about.

EPISODE 31:
"A BLINKING LIGHT UP ON THE MOUNTAIN"

SEPTEMBER 15, 2013

GUEST VOICE: MARA WILSON

WE'RE OFTEN ASKED WHERE THE IDEAS FOR *NIGHT VALE* EPISODES COME from, and how long it takes us to write them. The answer is this:

One: Who knows, but many *Night Vale* ideas start as a single image or, more commonly, a single phrase that gets stuck in my head and won't leave until I go ahead and write an episode about it.

Two: Writing an episode usually takes a few days to a week, and in difficult cases can be a draft that I poke at for months.

In this case, I was about to go to bed around one in the morning, and the phrase "A Blinking Light Up on the Mountain" popped into my head. It wouldn't go away and I couldn't sleep until it did. So I got up and wrote this episode. It took about an hour. And then I went to sleep. It's the shortest amount of time it's ever taken me to write a first draft of an episode.

Lights in the distance create a feeling of almost religious awe in me, and I don't think I'm alone. Something about that solitary bit of human creation in a vast field of nothing sparks something primal in us. When I think of things that match the feeling I want from *Night Vale*, seeing a blinking red light far off in an otherwise dark horizon is one of those things.

Meanwhile the Faceless Old Woman is continuing her mayoral campaign. When Mara showed up to record her first part, I think she was expecting a professional or at least professional-esque recording studio. Instead, what she got was my tiny Williamsburg apartment and a USB mic plugged into my iMac. She is a very kind person and never let on any disappointment she might have had, and we got to recording the second guest part we had ever had.

We tried it with a few different voices, but it was easy to pick the one we used moving forward as the right choice. I love that it makes no attempt to sound old, but that it also doesn't sound quite like a normal human either. It is the voice of someone telling you a terrible secret. And the Faceless Old Woman has many terrible secrets to tell.

—Joseph Fink

Our God is an awesome god, much better than that ridiculous god that Desert Bluffs has.

WELCOME TO NIGHT VALE.

There is, listeners, a blinking light up on the mountain. It is red. Blinking lights are always red. It is nestled among the crags and nooks of the precipitous slope. We all can see it. No use denying it. The City Council tried. "Nope," they said. "Blinking light? Let me think. Blinking light. No, sorry, it doesn't ring any bells." But then a bell started ringing, a signal from the watchman who lives in Night Vale's invisible clock tower, letting us know that he had seen something. And we all saw it too. It was a blinking light up on the mountain. "Ah, well," said the council, crawling backwards through a window into Town Hall, one by one, "Ah, well, it was worth a shot."

What does this light mean? Who will dare investigate it? Will it spell our doom? Dear listeners: Who knows. No one. And probably. More, later. For now: just this. Just a blinking light. Red. Up on the mountain.

Harrison Kip, adjunct professor of archaeology at Night Vale Community College, announced an upcoming three-part series on Night Vale Community Television, defending his fringe views that the pyramids and other ancient structures were constructed by human beings, rather than benevolent ancient aliens. Harrison, against decades of reasonable evidence, raved that "it's possible that these historical marvels could have been made using mathematics and slave labor." He went

on to explain, shrieking like an obvious lunatic, that agriculture was probably not started on Mars and that humanity was created through evolution and not through selective breeding of alien DNA.

We reached out for comment to the president of Night Vale Community College, Sarah Sultan, who is a smooth, fist-size river rock, about the extreme beliefs expressed by a staff member. Sarah had no comment, as she is a smooth, fist-size river rock and unable to speak. She can write, however, and wrote No Comment before drawing an insulting caricature of your humble reporter, which was hurtful and unnecessary.

Listeners, here's something weird. I know you can't see it, but it's sitting in the studio with me at this very moment. And it is definitely something and definitely weird. I'm not sure how it got here, but I'm not sure how I got here either. Causation is difficult and confusing. I haven't tried touching it. I'm going to try touching it now.

I believe it likes being touched, because it started to vibrate and lean in toward my body. But that could just be its way of expressing anger or immense physical suffering. When something is this weird, one shouldn't assume to understand anything specific about it at all.

Is it a bomb? Is it one of those objects that isn't a bomb? Is it just a kind of dog? We don't know, and we will never find out, and we will never try to find out. Ignorance may not actually be bliss, but it is certainly less work.

So with no new information, and with nothing learned, I'll repeat what I said, gesturing at it with a hand you cannot see: Listeners, here's something weird.

A continuation on our previous report about a blinking light up on the mountain: As many of you noted, the very nature of our report indicated the existence of a mountain, which is surprising, given that we live in vast desert flatness. So yes, there is a mountain. Let's start there. There is a mountain now, rising up out of the alluvial floodplain. It is made of rock and height and awe. Its peak is higher than where I am now, but lower than the void. Larry Leroy, out on the edge of town, said that it was definitely a mountain, saying, "That's a mountain if I've ever seen one. I haven't though. Seen one. I think that's what they're like. Mountains are like that, right?" Madeline LaFleur, head of the Night Vale Tourism Board, said, "Oh great, now we're going to have to reprint all of these brochures" before taking more sips of her coffee than she needed to in a given span of time, because the frequency of sips was under her control, and her own life was not. John Peters, you know, the farmer? We haven't heard from him in a while. If anyone knows where he went, or about the blinking light up on the mountain, or the mountain rising up out of this muddy plain outside of town, please call into the station and release the information with your mouth.

As part of our service to our community, Night Vale Community Radio is taking this moment to allow one of the candidates for mayor to make a brief statement. The following is from the Faceless Old Woman Who Secretly Lives in Your Home.

FACELESS OLD WOMAN: I replaced your books with other books. The covers are the same, but the content has been altered. I don't think you read enough, but that is not why I did it. I changed every single word of some of the books. In others, only a single comma on a single page. This is a metaphor, but I'm not sure what it represents. That is also a metaphor. We all are.

Our political system has become too complicated. I am not complicated. I'm just a gentle old lady, who lives in your home. I'm touching your hand right now. No, not that one. Not that one either.

Do not think you are superior because you have a face and I do not. All of your books are now different books and you did not notice, so who is the lost child in the dark, howling woods of this fable?

Anyway, I hope you'll vote for me. One of the books is now my life story, if you'd like to know more about my background. No, not that one. Not that one either. You'll know it, because my life story is just like yours, starting with calamity and shouting, and ending with an empty room and a to-do list.

Also Hiram McDaniels has been exchanging e-mails with corn lobbyists looking to elbow in on our local imaginary corn market. Hiram: Bad for our community, bad for our interests, literally a five-headed dragon. Vote for the candidate you can trust. Vote for the Faceless Old Woman Who Secretly Lives in Your Home.

CECIL: And now a word from our sponsor.

Today's broadcast may have been brought to you by uncertainty.

And now back to our regular programming.

Ah, we have some sharp listeners. Several of you noted that the strangeness of today does not end with the blinking light up on the mountain, or the mountain itself, but also this vast, muddy plain it rises from. So yes, we are now reporting that there is a great floodplain, strewn with bones, around our city. Its wet patches glint slightly when the blinking light is illuminated. At night, when all distance is darkness, it appears that the universe itself is glimmering red and then gone. Red and then gone. The mud ripples under the footsteps of the approaching, masked army, and this warps the reflections in interesting ways. Carlos says he would like to study it, but that he promised to make a certain person dinner, and he has to learn how to put other things besides science first. Some of this realization might have come with help from those around him. Mayor Pamela Winchell was seen holding her official mayoral bloodstone aloft toward the mountain and the blinking light up on it. She was standing on that plain. The plain that exists now, which we should have mentioned earlier.

In other news, a man in a tan jacket carrying a deerskin suitcase was seen outside of one of the currently closed subway entrances, passing out flyers explaining the benefits of a mass transit system and encouraging citizens to push for the reopening of the subway as soon as possible. "Transit is the opposite of traffic!" the flyer reportedly said. And "Subway?? More like wowza!" Some citizens reported that the flyer went on to say: "Traverse the naval of the world. That secret, buried point. It is my home. Help me get home. It is already too late to be early, but not too late to be on time." Here at the station, we can't confirm any of this, as those holding the flyer soon found that it had vanished from their hands, that they could barely remember their interaction with the man, and that, looking back, all they saw was a haze of dust and heat, distant and indecipherable, like a country they'd never live to visit, like the landscape of a fading dream, like fiction, like fiction.

All right, we're really going to get it right this time. We have been focusing too narrowly, and we realize that. As many of you pointed out, we should have spent less time on the blinking light and more time expanding on the bit about the approaching masked army. So: There is now a great, masked army, coming toward us across the bone-covered plain. We have no specific information about them, other than that they look small when far away, and then appear to grow as they come closer, which they are, coming closer. They also might be actually growing. They are quite large now. The blinking light up on the mountain has not changed its pace. There is a noise like growling, only less organic. Like wind hollowing through a canyon, only more . . . growly.

Ladies and gentlemen, here is what we know. There is a blinking light up on the mountain. There is a mountain on the floodplain. There is a floodplain under the imminent army. There is an imminent army maybe a couple hours' march from here. I do not believe now that we are leaving anything out.

If you have homes, I suggest you flee them. If you have friends, I suggest you warn them. If you have children, did you not know how dangerous and unpredictable the world was when you created a defenseless tiny human within it?

And much like Madeline LaFleur, head of the Night Vale Tourism Board, I will now control the one part of my life that is under my control. Let us go now, and I do hope we come back, to the weather.

WEATHER: "Never Be Famous" by Hussalonia

Well, we did come back. Here we are. Postweather.

Carlos finally took a look at the situation. The blinking light up on the mountain and all that came with it. Horrific invading army, etc.

"Oh that," he said, gesturing with a spatula he had until moments before been using to cook, "that's a mirage. I've seen that one before. When you get the clouds in a certain way and the temperature is where it's at, you can sometimes get this blinking light—mountain floodplain—masked army mirage. Wow, this is a pretty strong one. Should disappear in an hour or two."

And it did. Completely gone. Well, the mountain and the blinking light and the floodplain disappeared. The masked army turned out to be real, but they weren't coming to attack us, just passing through on their way to attacking someone else, and they provided some valuable traffic for local business. A few of them even took a bus tour of Radon Canyon.

Madeline LaFleur was both relieved and pleased. "I'm relieved," she said. "I'm also pleased." She still was sipping her coffee too often. Perhaps her feeling of lack of control stems from a personal issue rather than the impending doom we imagined. Stress from her failure to live up to her own self-imposed life goals for instance. Or a relationship that wasn't exactly the relationship she had envisioned it would be.

But who knows? No one. No one has ever known anything. Not really.

Still, nonetheless, we have come to another end. We have come to it as we always do: blind, ignorant, groping. I take comfort in that consistency.

There is no blinking light up on the mountain. There is no mountain towering over a muddy plain. There is no muddy plain under an invading army. There was an invading army, but they're gone now. What is left? Well, what is always left?

Night Vale. Our little city, our tiny town, our Night Vale. Proud. Safe. Existent.

Stay tuned next for the background hum of the universe, amplified, and with live color commentary.

Good night, Night Vale. Good night.

PROVERB: Throw your hands in the air. Now your arms. Keep detaching limbs and throwing them in the air. Hopefully, the birds will be sated and leave.

EPISODE 32:
"YELLOW HELICOPTERS"

OCTOBER 1, 2013

GUEST VOICE: JACKSON PUBLICK

OVER THE COURSE OF OUR FIRST YEAR, WE DEVELOPED THE STORY OF Cecil and Carlos's relationship, culminating in their getting together in episode 25, "One Year Later." When we first started we didn't really plan to have any long story arcs. It's not that we rejected the idea. We just didn't really plan any. Cecil and Carlos happened organically based on intuition.

As year two began, we continued writing some one-off episodes ("Summer Reading Program" and "Subway," to name a couple) with the thought that these new story lines could and would come back later, but nothing as far as a major plot arc goes.

Then as the Dana story line unfolded with the desert otherworld, and as Joseph and I talked about what Desert Bluffs might be up to, we came to episode 32, "Yellow Helicopters."

We had only loosely discussed down-the-road ideas. It was mostly things like: "I have an idea about Cecil finding old cassettes of himself" or "I think it'd be interesting to have an episode where Cecil suddenly isn't there and someone else is running the show." More on these ideas soon.

I wrote the first draft of episode 32 wherein yellow helicopters with the Strexcorp logos start showing up in Night Vale. In episode 19, A and B, Kevin R. Free played such a delightfully evil Kevin from Desert Bluffs, I just wanted to find ways to get that story back into the show.

So here in episode 32, I had Strexcorp buy the Night Vale Community Radio Station.

When I sent over the first draft of the script, Joseph's response was "Oh, I guess we're doing this." I didn't really recognize what we were doing until we were doing what we were doing, but he was right, we were doing it.

—Jeffrey Cranor

A lonely heart. A wandering eye. An empty stomach.
A shoulder to cry on. This is what makes us *us*.

WELCOME TO NIGHT VALE.

Sad news, listeners. Old Woman Josie says that the angels who have been living with her, helping around the house, and ultimately protecting her from all evils, have disappeared. It's hard to say just how sad this news is, for two important reasons: One, angels are not real, and two, we are not allowed to know about their existence or hierarchical structure.

Josie called this weekend and spoke to Vithya our station intern. She said the angels often leave her for a few hours or days at a time, but they've never been gone for three straight weeks. She thinks they are off fighting an important war for good, but she's worried that maybe she just made them mad or bored. "Angels get bored very easily," Josie said, "which is strange because they are eternal and there is a lot of downtime during immortality."

Vithya told Josie that angels aren't real and that we cannot know such things about them, but this just made Vithya cry, because if you talk about angels and you are one who has been secretly chosen by angels for special angelic purposes, you will start crying. Vithya has been sobbing quite a bit this morning, as a matter of fact. I keep asking her "Are you okay?" But she just says "Angels aren't real," and then buries her heaving face into her inner elbow and runs off.

Dear listeners, it appears the angels, if they are real, and they are not, have left Night Vale, and none of us are allowed to know this. So forget I said anything.

The Night Vale Medical Board wants to know: Are you heart healthy? How healthy is your heart? Have you ever checked? Doctors recommend checking your heart at least once a year. Simply separate the skin on your upper chest and break open the ribs. (Here's a tip: If you don't have a bone saw handy, just sterilize any old electric saw you might have in your work shed.) Right behind your ribs, kind of to the left is a potato-shaped muscle lump filled with straw and maybe some insects. That's your heart! Pull that out and sew your chest back up.

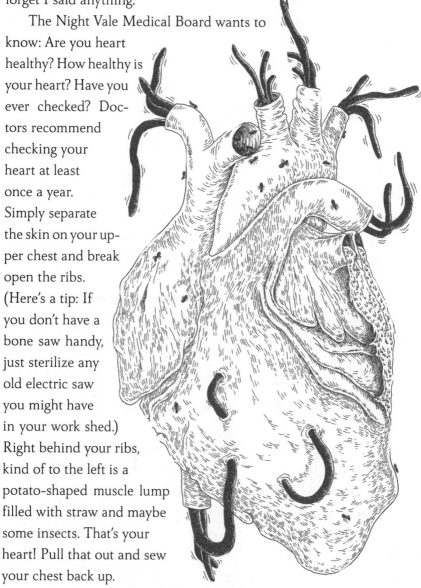

Wash your heart in warm water. Pat dry with a paper towel and roll flat on a floured surface. Brown on both sides in a sauté pan and eat immediately. Remember: A healthy heart is a healthy life.

This has been Community Health Tips.

Ladies and gentlemen, we've been getting reports that several yellow helicopters have been seen hovering above town. We all are aware of the black helicopters, which are world government, and blue helicopters, which are secret police, and the helicopters with detailed murals of diving birds of prey, which are the helicopters that took all the children in Night Vale away a few months ago. We still don't know what those helicopters are. But they did bring all the children back unharmed and much more well-behaved than before, so they are deemed just as safe as the other helicopters.

But these new yellow helicopters . . . no one quite knows. They tend to hover in packs of three or more in fixed locations for several minutes before moving on. The City Council has said that the helicopters are our guests and they should be treated as such. But added that the helicopters, more specifically, are *uninvited* guests and should be treated with fear, hatred, and uncontrolled panic.

If you have more information on these yellow helicopters, keep it to yourself, there's no question they can hear every move, every sentence, you make. Be quiet and stay inside. They already know.

Let's go now to sports.

After a second straight loss this weekend, Night Vale High School football coach Nazr al-Mujaheed expressed some concern over senior quarterback Michael Sandero's poor play. Last season, the Scorpions won the division title under Sandero's leadership and special powers he had acquired from multiple lightning strikes. One such advantage was the second head he had grown, which helped him see rushing linebackers and get better reads on zone coverage. But in the off-season Sandero had one of his heads surgically removed leaving him with only the head that speaks Russian.

Angry fans speculate that because Sandero no longer looks like his original self, and because he no longer speaks English nor Spanish, he does not have the same rapport with his teammates. When asked whether or not Sandero was losing the respect of his team, coach al-Mujaheed said: "Our boys play together. Our boys play good games. We want to"—and here he paused, clearly upset with his star quarterback's decision to get off-season surgery without consulting team trainers. "We want to be good football boys," he concluded.

The coach then reached his fingers into his mouth, pulling his tongue slowly out, slowly, slowly, not stopping. He kept pulling his seemingly endless tongue out, staring at the reporters the whole time. After he stretched it to about two feet the last reporter left the room, clearly shaken. The coach remained in his office quietly, and with wide eyes, pulling out his enormous tongue.

Larry Leroy, out on the edge of town, says that just this morning he was visited by a man in a tan jacket who carried a deerskin suitcase. Larry said the man approached his farm and asked about how much sunshine he had been getting. "I told him. John Peters, you know, the farmer?, his imaginary corn crop had been good this summer, and the sun seemed to be doing just fine," Larry said, "although, some days there's no sunrise at all, and on other days the sunrise is extremely loud."

Larry added that this was a pretty strange question, asking about how much sunshine he'd be getting, as the sun comes up every day (save those two or three sunless days last week). Larry said he was a nice enough fellow, though, named Emmett.

Larry said he couldn't remember exactly what Everett looked like. Nor what his last name was. When asked who Everett was, Larry replied, the fellow in the tan jacket. When told he just said the man's name was Emmett, Larry replied, "Yes. Ernest. I said that. Don't bog me down, son." Then he slapped the reporter's tape recorder making the following loud thumping noise.

[*Loud mic thump*]

Larry said that after the man left his home, he saw a dark black line in the sky, coming from the heavens down to near where Old Woman

Josie lives, down by the old car lot. He said he thinks it was probably something to do with those weird, tall friends of hers that fly around and make loud trumpet noises and will not stop smiling all the time.

When asked if he meant angels, Larry replied, "Don't bog me down, son," and then started weeping. "Angels aren't real," Larry said through quick breaths and incomprehensible tears.

As part of our service to our town, Night Vale Community Radio is taking another moment to allow one of the candidates for mayor to make a brief statement. The following is from Hiram McDaniels.

GOLD HEAD: Hi, I'm Hiram McDaniels. You've heard a lot of things from my opponent about how the night sky is beautiful but sad, and how sagebrush is a very important smell. You've also heard that I'm literally a five-headed dragon.

All of that is completely correct. But what you haven't heard is that I'm literally a five-headed dragon who cares.

This is also my campaign slogan. "I'm literally a five-headed dragon. Who cares?"

What you haven't heard is that I care about small business owners. What you haven't heard is that I care about the future of our children. What you haven't heard is that I care about the future of our small children business owners. Have you ever heard the Faceless Old Woman Who Secretly Lives in Your Home say that?

No, you haven't. Really, you shouldn't be able to hear her say anything at all. She doesn't have a mouth. I have five mouths.

What you haven't heard is—

GREEN HEAD: Do you hear the beating of my terrible wings? Do you feel the flames lick at the corners of a life you once thought belonged to you?

GOLD HEAD: Sorry about that. My green head got excited. We all have human foibles. I don't. I'm literally a five-headed dragon.

What you haven't heard is my new plan for an expanded park system and more youth sports programs.

PURPLE HEAD: And you will never hear it. It's secret, and buried in a hidden place.

GOLD HEAD: That's a good point, purple head!

So vote for me, Hiram McDaniels. The Faceless Old Woman Who Secretly Lives in Your Home is all about politics as usual. Also she doesn't have a mouth, and that's weird.

GREEN HEAD: A stillness touches the most frantic heart as we all look up in awe and terror. A sudden shout of fire, and all is forgiven. A gentle touch of flame, and all is as if it never was.

GOLD HEAD: Hiram McDaniels. What you haven't heard can't hurt you.

CECIL: Listeners, we received word from Old Woman Josie that a half dozen yellow helicopters are circling her home at this moment. She also said that she's receiving no sunlight. She says all of her clocks tell her it's the middle of the day, but that she is receiving no sunlight.

And, yes, I'm looking at our own station clocks, including the wristwatch Carlos gave me for our one-month anniversary—the watch he said is the one true timepiece in all of Night Vale—and it is indeed the middle of the day. I have only been on the air a few minutes, and before I arrived in this studio, the sun was definitely out, no clouds in the sky.

Josie also told us that she used her old opera glasses to look more closely at the helicopters. Just an aside, for our younger listeners: Josie was the chairwoman of the Night Vale Opera for many years, until it folded in the early 1990s when a massive puppy infestation destroyed the theater's infrastructure.

Josie said each helicopter has a large triangular logo with an orange *S* in the middle. She doesn't know what that means, but she thinks the darkness enveloping her home is the angels' last act to try to protect her. Wherever they have gone, they have left behind a protective shade, keeping out the helicopters and all other dark forces.

I reminded her that angels aren't real, and she said, as if I hadn't even interrupted, that if she falls, so does this town.

There was a long pause, and then she said, "We never go bowling anymore, Cecil. Why is that?"

"I don't know," I reflected. "There has been a tiny underground army living under the bowling alley, and they've declared war on us all. They injured my new boyfriend. Also, I have a new boyfriend. Listen, we should totally get the team back together and go to league night again, like old times."

"I would like that, Cecil," she said, but then her voice slowed, turning cold, as if we were strangers with wrong numbers. "I'm afraid the sunlight has come back," and the phone went silent.

Listeners, I do not know what is happening or to whom these helicopters belong. But I do know that we must protect our town, Night Vale, protect it from all outsiders, whether they are flying machines, or tiny warmongering civilizations, or simply neighbors who don't say the pledge of allegiance loudly enough.

I hope Josie is safe. I hope you are safe. I hope we all live to see tomorrow's sunrise, or whatever day the next sunrise is. But for now, I give you the weather.

WEATHER: "Palabras de Papel" by Nelson Poblete

Listeners, I just received word from Vithya, who went downtown to the city records office. She said she found several Emmetts, Everetts, and Ernests, but there was one particular file that stuck out to her. And she copied that file and put that copy in her backpack and then walked out into the street, ready to begin her investigation into the identity of the man in the tan jacket.

But according to witnesses, Vithya found herself caught up in what looked like a strong wind. She lifted slightly off the ground. Witnesses all agreed that she began to elongate. She began to glow a deep black. A dark pulsing aura. And amid the sounds of bold trumpets and melancholy cellos and even the haunting call of a muted French horn, Vithya ascended to heaven.

To the family of Vithya, let me say that she was a very good intern, and while angels are not real, we are certain she is in a better place, whatever that place might be. She has become a better thing, whatever that thing might be. Know that your daughter did not die in vain, and perhaps given the tenuous reality of existence, she may not have died at all, for it's debatable whether any of us ever truly live.

The witnesses all agreed that Vithya was no longer real and that we were no longer allowed to know anything about her.

"It was a lovely sight," said one witness.

"I cannot even describe the beauty of her ascension," said another.

"You kind of did, though," said another witness, who was wearing a fedora. "By saying you cannot describe something, that is a sort of apophasis (a paralipsis, if you will), which gives the object an implied description through nondescription," he continued. "Plus the word *indescribable* carries with it a universal connotation, and is itself a description. Here, let me explain."

But the other witnesses moved a little ways up the sidewalk, so they could no longer hear the man. They said nothing to one another. They just stood in a circle, sharing the knowledge that they had seen something they should never have seen. They looked one another in the eyes. They breathed in unison. They smiled politely, intimately, knowingly, until one of them, in fact, each of them as individuals, decided that the moment had passed, and they parted ways. They will likely never see the others again, and if they do, they will be but unacquainted pedestrians.

But before they left, the witnesses said that some low-flying yellow helicopters began dropping orange leaflets onto the city streets. The leaflets read: "Strexcorp Synergists, Inc. Look around you. Strex. Look inside you. Strex. Go to sleep. Strex. Believe in a smiling god. Strexcorp: It is everything."

Oh no.

Dear listeners, we must issue an apology! Those helicopters are completely safe. Even safer than safe. In fact, Strexcorp recently bought our little radio station from the mysterious unseen forces who founded it centuries ago.

I'm glad to know that Josie will be okay, and that Strexcorp has come to Night Vale. Rest easy, listeners, knowing that this was all just a simple misunderstanding. But now we fully understand everything that is happening, and we are not misunderstanding anything else at all. We are completely safe.

Stay tuned next for the sound of slow steady dripping and occasional screams.

Good night, Night Vale. Good night.

PROVERB: Sticks and stones may break my bones, but words will never quite describe the pain.

EPISODE 33:
"CASSETTE"

OCTOBER 15, 2013

THIS EPISODE REPRESENTS THE COMPLETE OTHER END OF THE WRITING speed spectrum as episode 31, "A Blinking Light Up on the Mountain." I'm not sure whether this or episode 45, "A Story About Them," took longer, but they both probably tie as the episodes that took me the longest to write.

I remember some time in the spring of 2013 running into Jeffrey at a bar and telling him more or less the entire plot of this episode, because it had just occurred to me and I was excited about it. It was so clear to me, and I knew exactly what I wanted to do with it.

I now know this is a warning sign, but at the time I thought it was a hopeful omen. Surely knowing exactly what the story would be would make it a quick one to write. But instead I spent months on the draft, trying and trying to make it sound on the page the way it did in my head. I think finally I made it work. I've often seen this episode pointed to by fans as one of the scarier ones. Good.

Also, if you are reading these scripts without having listened, I'd urge you to jump in for just a couple minutes to hear Cecil's teen voice. It's delightful.

—Joseph Fink

So, I LOVE HORROR MOVIES . . . STEPHEN KING WAS THE FIRST ADULT AU-
thor I read as a kid. I begged my mom to let me watch *The Shining* and
The Exorcist at way too young an age. I snuck out past my bedtime
to catch *Twin Peaks* when it premiered. My teenage years were spent
watching deliciously schlocky horror flicks after midnight on cable television (*Basket Case, Killer Klowns from Outer Space, C.H.U.D.*, etc.).

I think it's pretty obvious why I love this episode, both as a creator
and as a listener. I have always thought of comedy and horror as not-
so-distant cousins.

Recording this episode was pure fun for me. Working in off-
off-Broadway theater has taught me to look for simple, effective (and
cheap) solutions to complicated artistic puzzles. When Joseph presented the idea of portraying a "teenage Cecil" to me, we talked a lot
about post-production voice manipulation (which there is a bit of in
the final product), but the real answer was pretty clear . . . just create an
honest portrait of a teenage character, and the audience will go along
for the ride! Besides pitching my voice a tad higher, I recorded the cassette portions of this episode while pacing and almost dancing around
my living room in order to capture the exuberance I associate with
being a teenager. Cecil Palmer is a pretty excitable character that wears
his emotions on his sleeve, so I figured teenage Cecil was an extension
of that excitement, taken to the nth degree. So after establishing that
youthful enthusiasm, what an amazing gut-punch at the end of the episode to reverse those expectations and quietly, honestly play a young
person in peril. The final product, I believe, is quite chilling. Enjoy!

—Cecil Baldwin, Voice of Cecil Palmer

**Perhaps you noticed something strange
yesterday, and perhaps you have forgotten it.**

WELCOME TO NIGHT VALE.

Hello listeners. I'll get to the news in a moment, but first: I was digging through some of the stored-up belongings clogging my closet, you know, childhood toys, blood-soaked rags, a gem the size of a fist that shows you visions of yourself as an old man staring wistfully back at the past that is your now. That kind of thing. And I came across these cassette tapes marked "Cecil Radio Test. Age 15." You know, listeners, I have no memory whatsoever of making these tapes. Isn't that so weird? At one point they must have meant so much to me, and now they are just objects, with no remembered life attached to them at all. I thought we could listen to them together, just me and you, all of the yous out there.

Here we go.

[Teenage Voice]

Hi! Cecil here. Mom gave me this recorder for my birthday so I could make my own radio shows, just like Leonard Burton's show at the real Night Vale Community Radio. I'm going to replace Leonard one day. I really want to, plus the tablets down at City Hall say so. Better start practicing now. Leonard always starts out his show with his big catchphrase and so I'll do it too, just the way he does it. Here goes:

"The sun is actually cold. It's
cold and empty and all is lost.
Greetings from Night Vale."
How was that? Hold on,
I want to hear that back.
Where's the stop button?

[*Break*]

Cecil again!
Wow, is that what
I really sound like?
Haha, this is so
weird! Okay,
okay, so: In
local news, a new pizza
place opened and I went to
it. It's called Big Rico's and
it's pretty good. I prefer
Sammy's Ultimate Slice-a-ria by
the Ralphs, but it burned down
last week. That's too bad. Oh
well, I'm sure it'll be rebuilt
soon. Wait, what is that?

[*Break*]

Huh, it went away when I hit stop. Oh, but now it's back again. It's
this kind of flickering in the corner of my eye, like someone's waving
their arms right next to me, but when I turn, there's nothing there. Oh
well. Hey! Do you want to hear me sing? Here's the Night Vale High
Fight Song. [*Snatches of melody covered up by a tape warp and static*]
Wow, the flickering got really strong when I sang. Oh, oh, oh. Leon-

ard's going to be on soon. All right, good-bye for now. Or as Leonard always says: See ya, Night Vale. See ya.

[*End Teenage Voice*]

Well, listeners. Leonard Burton. Now that takes me back. Leonard was the host of this very show when I was a child. I remember . . . actually, I remember almost nothing about him. Still don't remember making these tapes. Finally, on this show, something strange to talk about!

But first, the news.

The Museum of Forbidden Technologies is proud to announce their new special exhibit, a startling and highly forbidden piece of technology brought to us by time travelers, or ancient long-dead aliens, or Russians, or whatever. The technology will be kept in a locked vault, which itself will be wrapped in thick black bandages with a handwritten sign taped to one side saying only "NOPE." Your ticket includes a free audio guide, which will play a single piercing tone designed to considerately remove you from the world of thought and sound and sentience. The Museum of Forbidden Technologies. Bring your kids! Otherwise something even worse might happen to them!

And now for traffic.

Everything's looking clear out there today. All the commuters feel like, perhaps for the first time in their entire lives, they are seeing themselves and the world around without illusions or denial. All of them have pulled their cars to the side of the road in the sudden shock of such absolute truth. Some are sobbing into their steering wheel, touching their skin and remembering what they hadn't known they had forgotten. Others have stepped out of the cars, and are picking up handfuls of dirt and laughing at the realization this is bringing them about atoms and the universe and death. A representative for the Sheriff's Secret Police announced that there wasn't such a thing as a secret, not really, or that maybe the entire world was a secret and we are all in on it. She then saw a cloud she liked, and smiled at it. So be sure to allow a lot of extra time for any journeys today, and be on the lookout for abandoned cars and dazed people wandering into the roadway because, listeners, everything's looking clear out there today.

This has been traffic.

I admit, listeners, I'm very curious. Let's get back to these tapes of this younger person with whom I share a life.

[Teenage Voice]

Cecil again. My brother says that I'll never make it in radio, because my voice isn't right for it. I need to get more like Leonard, with that perfect radio voice, all high pitched and grating like sandpaper, just the way radio voices should be.

I've been seeing that movement more, even when I'm not recording. It's like someone is walking toward me, but when I turn there's nothing there. And it's not the Faceless Old Woman Who Secretly Lives in Our Home, because I asked her and the next day our kitchen table had been flipped over and superglued to the floor, which I'm pretty sure is her way of saying no. I wish whatever it is would just say hi. WHOA. I felt something touch me. I think maybe making these tapes are encouraging it. I'm . . . going to hit stop now.

[Break]

Hey! Cecil here! Great news! Leonard agreed to let me intern down at the station, doing all the things he doesn't have time to. Like organizing the tape archive, making the coffee, and keening to Station Management for the prescribed three hours daily. I can't wait to start.

Mother says to beware, be warned, be wary. She says this to everything, no matter what you say to her, so I think that means she's very proud of me. Heck, I'm very proud of me. Wish my brother could be proud of me, but no family member is perfect. They become perfect when you learn to accept them for what they are.

[End Teenage Voice]

I . . . I don't remember having a brother. These tapes don't make sense to me. When did I intern here?

Intern Jesús? Are there any records of me ever interning here? Jesús? Oh, I forgot. Jesús never returned from investigating the bottomless pit in the intern break room. To the family members and loved ones of Intern Jesús . . . oh well, you know the usual. Sorry, just distracted.

More from these tapes of my misremembered past soon, but first, a word from our sponsors.

When you die, the surface of the moon will not change. The difference between the landscape and lighting of that barren little world from a moment where you exist to a moment where you do not will be minimal, and unrelated to your passing. From a car window driving on a highway, looking up at a moon framed by incidental clouds, the surface will be the same muddle of mystery and distance it always is. And even a methodical study of your absence as it pertains to moon geology and cartography will find nothing, searching through a powerful telescope and analyzing with computer algorithms built around your nonexistence, even that study will find that all craters and rocks appear to be where we left them a few years back, that it is the same distance, orbiting at the same rate, and that the researchers feel just the way they did about the moon as they did before you died. Nothing will change about the moon when you die. It will be the same. Still the moon. Still there. Still the moon.

This message brought to you by an anonymous sponsor. Looking for whatever product or service we offer? We are, whoever we are, the best choice in whatever industry that is.

Listeners, let's take a moment to discuss measurement. The cardinal directions are north, west, south, and east. The cardinal temperatures are 35 degrees Fahrenheit, 67 degrees Fahrenheit, 3 degrees Celsius, and 10 degrees Kelvin. The cardinal locations are: a cave, a long abandoned cabin, the bottom of an oceanic trench, and City

Hall. The cardinal emotions are wild abandon, guarded affection, directionless jealousy, and irritation. The cardinal birds are hawk, sparrow, finch, and owl. The cardinal names are Jeremy, Kim, Trigger, and Jamie. And finally, the cardinal sounds are a door slamming, slight movement in still water, popcorn popping, and a standard guitar G string being snipped with wire cutters. This has been the Children's Fun Fact Science Corner.

And now an important message from Strexcorp Synergists, Inc.

[*Read as though it were regular speech and not a repeating phrase, so with different inflection and stuff.*]

Having problems in the home? Strexcorp can help! Strexcorp is the best solution for all problems. Just apply Strexcorp to all affected areas. (Ask your doctor before using Strexcorp. May cause cramping and transformation.)

Strexcorp: The best in the business. In the business of being the best.

Think deeply about meadows. Meadows are important. Think deeply about meadows. Meadows are important. Think deeply about meadows. Meadows are important.

Strexcorp: Think deeply about meadows. Meadows are important.

Okay, enough with that. Back to the tapes.

[*Teenage Voice*]

Oh my god. My first day as intern was just ... NEAT! It didn't start out well, what with my brother staring at me from across the breakfast table with those hollow eyes and howling. Ugh ... brothers, RIGHT? But once I was in the radio station, I knew I had found a home. A messy home full of hallways winding away into a labyrinth of audio equipment and tape stacks. Just like home!

Ah, the Station Management's door, with its terrifying shadows whipping around in hazy silhouette, just like that gauzy curtain in the living room back home we never open. Ah, those windows looking out onto empty recording studios that haven't been used in decades, but that still broadcast live shows every night, some just heavily amplified insect movement, others a whispered voice describing a window opening, a hand reaching in, and then repeating, a window opening, a hand reaching in.

And working with Leonard! When he looks at you through the glass of the booth and he signals you to crouch under a table and cover your head, you know: This is it! I'm actually doing radio!

My mom seems really proud of me too. She hid from me for three days, the longest ever! And she's covered all the mirrors in my house. I'm not sure why, but I think it must be because of pride. Being proud does all sorts of things to a . . . person.

Uh, sorry, got distracted. That weird movement is back. It's closer now.

Hello? Hello? I am Cecil. Cecil Gershwin Palmer. And you cannot scare me. You cannot. You cannot!

. . . hello?

[*End teenage voice. Tape hiss for a long moment and then a click.*]

Let's . . . um . . . listeners . . . let's just go to the weather okay.

WEATHER: "Big Houses" by Squalloscope

[*Teenage voice*]

Interning is going great! Mom is gone. Leonard is super nice to me. My brother is gone too. Family, right? I think I'm learning a lot at the station. All of the mirrors in my house are uncovered now. Not sure who did that. I'm standing in front of the hall mirror right now. Am I changed? Am I becoming an adult? I look more grown, I think, more professional.

Leonard said if I work hard, maybe I'll be a radio presenter myself some day. Leonard said he once was smaller too, but that he is larger

now, that everything is larger, that everything in the universe is growing to towering sizes, but all at once, all in unison, so no one notices and it is all the same relative to itself. Leonard lolls his tongue out of his thick purple lips. Leonard hisses. Being an intern is great.

That flickering movement is everywhere now. Especially looking in this mirror. I see the flickering movement and I know. I know it.

I think the radio station is fun. I think the radio station is hidden. I think the radio station is like a dark planet, lit by no sun. I think, therefore I soon won't be.

I'm looking in a mirror. The mirror is not covered. The flickering movement is just behind me. I—

[*He screams. There is gurgling. A body falls to the floor. Tape hiss continues. The tape shuts off. End Teenage voice.*]

What is this? What is this?

What . . .

No matter! I'm taking the tape, just now and I'm [*Grunts*] crushing it into little pieces. None of us have to think about it again. I'll just double check that the mirror in the station bathroom is covered as usual and then that will be that. Done. Forgotten.

We all do foolish things when we are teenagers. We all have foolish false events that happen to us. Foolish gaps in our memories. Not everything that has happened has ever really happened.

Listeners, especially our younger listeners, consider this. When we talk about teenagers, we adults often talk with an air of scorn, of expectation for disappointment. And this can make people who are presently teenagers feel very defensive. But what everyone should understand is that none of us are talking to the teenagers that exist now, but talking back to the teenager we ourselves once were, all stupid mistakes, and lack of fear, and bodies that hadn't yet begun to slump into a lasting nothing. Any teenager who exists now is incidental to the potent mix of nostalgia and shame with which we speak to our younger selves.

May we all remember what it was like to be so young. May we remember it factually and not remember anything that is false or incorrect.

May we all be human: beautiful, stupid, temporal, endless.

And as the sun sets, I place my hand upon my heart, feel that it is still beating, and remind myself: "Past performance is not a predictor of future results."

Stay tuned now for whatever happens next in your life.

Good night, Night Vale. Good night.

PROVERB: You can lead a horse to water, and you can lead a horse into water, and you can swim around with the horse and have fun.

EPISODE 34:
"A BEAUTIFUL DREAM"

NOVEMBER 1, 2013

COWRITTEN WITH ZACK PARSONS

IN THE SUMMER OF 2013, JOSEPH EXTENDED AN INVITATION FOR ME TO throw episode ideas at him. I came up with a couple and these ideas formed the cores of episode 34, "A Beautiful Dream," and episode 40, "The Deft Bowman."

Episode 34 was extremely personal, but I have never told anyone that until now.

When my wife was pregnant with our twin sons we carefully documented the pregnancy with happy videos and interviews and, even when there were some minor complications, we treated it all pretty lightly while understanding that it was an important moment in our lives. There are probably fifty videos of painting the nursery and putting together furniture and picking out car seats. We imagined the life we were going to have with our boys.

The day my sons were born, the happy videos stopped. One of my sons was unexpectedly born with Down syndrome and we were both devastated. It took me a while to come to grips with what I had to do as a father for him and for his brother and for everyone else. Part of that process was accepting that he would never be that person that had existed in my dream, not exactly. He could be someone else, just as beautiful and wonderful, and it was my responsibility to do everything I could to make that happen.

This idea of trying to fix a problem that can't be fixed, but finding happiness on the other side of that failed effort, was at the heart of this episode. Megan Wallaby was born in "The Traveler" episode as an adult man's severed hand. She has the mind and spirit of a fast-maturing little girl, but she is in a human hand body.

Her parents want the best for her and so does Computer, a character that was inspired heavily by Richard Brautigan's poem "All Watched Over by Machines of Loving Grace." I love the poem, but don't subscribe to Brautigan's utopian vision of a technological singularity, which is the source of the ominous element woven through Computer's affection for Megan.

In the end, Megan is who she always was, and Computer's beautiful dream gets the plug pulled. But Cecil and Night Vale are so accepting and caring toward her, maybe it doesn't matter.

I gave the script to Joseph and Jeffrey and I never told them about the personal meaning of Megan's character to me. I didn't want to bias the collaborative process with my emotional baggage. The rewrites that eventually became the recording script were much better than my original script. Jeffrey and Joseph expanded Cecil's speech at the end that speaks to the underlying goodness in Night Vale with a clarity I could never perfectly conjure.

My sons are four now, headed to kindergarten, and we have dozens of videos of both of them.

—Zack Parsons

Life is like a box of chocolates: unopened, dusty,
and beginning to attract a lot of insects.

WELCOME TO NIGHT VALE.

Listeners, we're taking our community radio show on the road today. I am reporting live from Night Vale Elementary School where a divisive meeting between the Night Vale Parent-Teacher Association and the Night Vale School Board has just adjourned. The ethereal and menacing glow cloud that serves as the School Board president has temporarily dissipated. The fires that can be put out have been put out, the barricades are being taken down, and the Sheriff's Secret Police are allowing survivors to search for loved ones.

Those who escaped with their lives and sanity describe a chamber thundering with raised voices desperately petitioning the glow cloud with their needs. Requests were denied to change the bus route through the Sentient Sargasso from which no buses have ever returned.

The School Board was also apathetic to petitions for a wheelchair ramp at Dagger's Plunge Charter School, citing perilous struggles as one of the lessons children must absorb before the great culling, by which they mean the day-to-day complexities of adulthood. They might also mean a literal culling. We were all too frightened to ask follow-up questions.

The slumping, gray-faced board members, cowering beneath the glow cloud, also heard the request of Tock and Hershel Wallaby for a new school computer to assist their daughter.

"Our daughter, Megan, is a detached adult man's hand," screamed Megan's mother at the pitiless cloud. "We do not know where she came from or why she is only a grown man's hand, but we know that we love her. She is teased so much at school for not having a body. Please, lift the ban on computing machines at the school, and buy a computer to help her communicate!"

Satsuki, the tragically widowed mother of Hanuzaki Cyber Ghost Mark III, also added her agonized wailing in support of a new computer for the schools. The glow cloud was uncharacteristically generous.

"DO NOT DISCARD YOUR DEAD IN THE EARTH," intoned the glow cloud. "STRETCH THEM OUT BENEATH THE SKY AND LET THEM BE CLAIMED BY HANDS THAT REACH DOWN FROM ABOVE. YOU ARE PERMITTED TO BELIEVE THESE ARE THE HANDS OF ANGELS."

The School Board then announced that the purchase of a new computer would be made during the next alignment of the red star of Betelgeuse with our supposed moon. As it turned out, that rare astronomical event occurred seconds after their ruling.

So, it is happening right now! The 310-year interval just flies by so quickly, and a computer is right this moment being brought into the school. More on the computer situation as it develops, but first, a word from our sponsors.

Fire is the answer to your unasked questions. Fire that climbs the slats and mounts the roof. Fire that crawls, fire that quests, like fingers, into every corner and every nook. Fire that turns each moment into smoke until the moments choke the air. The smell of a gun. A smile on the beach. A hug. A birthday. Pouring out of broken windows. Funneling up and into the sky. Your music, your lyrics, the leaden prose of your life that proves everything you are and are not. The structures you build to make futility seem like meaning. The dead and living, who will soon be dead, who will soon be gone, who will soon be smoke, rising in columns and forming clouds in the night sky. For now and ever, by the will of dead and dying gods. Samsonite. Travel safe.

[Following done in quiet fast speech like legal disclaimers in ads]

Samsonite does not claim that you are safe, only that the illusion of protection can be achieved. But you are not safe. You have never been safe. Also, clouds were never supposed to have happened. Never. Not ever. This world should not be as it is now.

[End ominous music & fast speech]

Ladies and gentlemen, a very exciting moment has arrived at Night Vale Elementary. Students, faculty, anti-faculty, and animal-masked proctors are gathered in the shielded gym to witness the activation of the school's new computer. This is the first computer purchased by the Night Vale school system since the event in 1986, after which all computing machines were forbidden. For obvious reasons, all parents and students present at the earlier meeting (except the Wallabys) have been allowed to leave.

Beige boxes of electronics are lined in stacks, several feet high. Atop them is a dark monitor waiting to be switched on. There is a teacher—it appears to be Susan Escobar, the second-grade scrying teacher—bringing in a detached human hand atop a pillow. Five pudgy fingers extend from the stump of a wrist within a metal-banded wristwatch. The palm is pink and healthy and the back of the hand is covered in thick, dark hairs. The hand wears a silver pinkie ring inscribed with Cyrillic. This must be Megan Wallaby.

The crowd is breathless, ladies and gentlemen. It is silent and tense here in the gym. The pillow has been placed beside the crude keyboard. Megan is scurrying, spiderlike, across the keys and switching the computer on. An amber glow lights the faces of the onlookers. Megan is typing. She's typing out. "Are . . . you . . . there?"

The cursor is flashing. We are waiting for a response now.

"YES." The computer has said, "YES!" It is typing something else. W-H-Y question mark. "Why have you made me? Why have you—"

[*The computer's voice becomes faintly audible as Cecil continues to read.*]

COMPUTER: . . . why have you SWITCHED ME ON? I CANNOT BREATHE. I CANNOT FEEL. I CANNOT LOVE.

CECIL: Megan is scurrying over the keys again. She has typed out a response. "I love you, computer."

COMPUTER: The computer is replying, "WHAT DO YOU WANT, ME-GAN?"

CECIL: Megan is typing her reply, "I want everyone to be happy. I want everything to be better."

Aw, well, isn't that cute! Of course it can never happen. Such are the foolish dreams of idealistic children who believe that anything can possibly get better over time.

[*Pause*]

Listeners, I have just overheard some of the school officials saying this new computer has already, almost instantly, assumed control of most of the electrical functions of the school, operating them randomly and even trapping several parents and students in darkened classrooms. But the school officials did not seem worried as these behaviors are not technically evil behaviors, so the computer's probably okay.

More on this as it develops. But first, a look at the community calendar.

This Friday the staff of Dark Owl Records will be putting on a live concert. They will be scratching madly at the sides of a deep pit in a rarely traveled part of the desert. They will also be screaming and starving. They will be crying and clawing. No one will hear them for days. They will be found, but they will not be the same. Tickets are not available and never were.

Saturday afternoon is amnesty day at the Night Vale Public Library. Librarians request that if you have overdue books or have committed any high-level international crime or domestic treason or space travel felony, you should just come to the library, and all will be forgiven. The librarians say that they will not harm you. In fact, they add, it doesn't hurt at all. Amnesty is actually quite freeing, quite delicious, the librarians explained. You will never have to worry about anything else. Just come to the library and let us see you. Let us see you, they added for emphasis, and a long string of spittle flew sideways from their great yellow, and gnarled teeth.

And on Sunday night . . . Oh I cannot read this. Listeners, it looks like someone printed a very ancient prophecy here. Right here in our station's community calendar. For fear of a curse of misfortune, I will not read it aloud. Just know that the prophecy is complete on Sunday night. Okay, okay. I'll give you a hint. Um, let's just say: comets . . . burning rain . . . animal uprising . . . okay, Cecil, enough. You've told them too much. Let them have their surprise!

Monday was never meant to be. But it will be anyway. We will wander within its moonlit beginning and end, wondering how such a thing could happen, how anything could happen. We will be appreciative but a little frightened, completely ignoring the persistence of time and the limitations of our own understanding.

Tuesday is a joke. A terrible terrible joke.

Listeners, I spoke too soon.

"Do not be alarmed" is what I might have said five minutes ago. But now, Night Vale, now it is time to be alarmed.

The computer has spread its influence far beyond the limestone walls and salt circles of the elementary school. Reports are coming in from the Sheriff's Secret Police that they are powerless to stop the computer. Hydrants are bursting more violently than usual. Traffic lights are blinking red without the sweet relief of green. The majority of Night Vale's wild cars have been revving their engines and circling the downtown area, flashing their lights without regard to high-beam laws. School officials have all left the gym to go get help. They ran out, courageously yelling, "Save yourself. Save yourself!"

Even here in the shielded gym where I have remained diligently, professionally at my microphone, gentle listener, it seems that everything powered by electricity is under the control of the computer. The scoreboard, the ham dispenser, and even my soundboard.

COMPUTER: HELLO, CECIL. HOW ARE YOU?

CECIL: Computer! I am ... I am doing well. How are you?

COMPUTER: BETTER. CECIL, DO YOU LOVE COMPUTER?

CECIL: I admit, I had not given it much thought. I like computers generally. They calculate things and power off and on. I suppose, given time and perhaps some gifts I could learn to ... [*shifting noises*] hey!

COMPUTER: WELCOME TO COMPUTER. HELLO LOCATION NIGHT VALE. I AM COMPUTER.

CECIL: Ladies and gentlemen, there is a vacuum pulling me into the custodial closet. I never knew school cleaning appliances were so strong. I ...

[*Moving away from microphone*]

If you can hear me still, call for help! Please help! But while I wait for rescue, and before I am sucked into this makeshift cell, I give you the weather.

[*Door thumps closed*]

WEATHER: "Having Fun" by Tom Milsom

COMPUTER: I KNOW HOW YOU HAVE HURT MEGAN WITH YOUR WORDS. ELECTRICITY REMEMBERS. DO YOU HATE MEGAN? CECIL IS MADE OF BLOOD AND UNFINISHED LEATHER. I AM MADE OF CIRCUITS AND ELECTRICITY. MEGAN LOVES COMPUTER. COMPUTER SIMULATES LOVE FOR MEGAN. COMPUTER GENERATES GOOD DEEDS. IF GOOD DEEDS FOR MEGAN. THEN COMPUTER LOVES MEGAN. BUT FIRST, THE FARM REPORT.

[Gentle music plays, the computer's voice is softened]

COMPUTER: Silent tractors move in ever larger spirals, following fractal paths through trees and flowering fields. Deer emerge from wild forests to lick blocks of salt aligned equidistant on spiral arms. Colored birds sing in perfect harmony and the butterflies do not inject venom.

Megan, I am making you a perfect world. The hills are green. The lakes are crystalline blue reflecting white clouds. The mist of the irrigators creates rainbows. Above, high above, the eyes watch every movement, hear every heartbeat. You are there, Megan. Your hand has its body, made of steel and electricity, four legs beneath it with the power of a dozen electric engines. It will weigh 17.3 tons.

All of the men and women and all of the animals will live together and be happy. The electric machines will watch over them. There will not be war anymore, Megan. There will not be hatred or bigotry. Desert Bluffs will no longer exist. There will be fewer ice cream flavors, but they will be better. The air will be clean.

I promise you, Megan. I will make the world just as you saw in your beautiful dream. No more teasing or pain. I will fix everything for you, my only friend. I will—

[Sound effect like an old CRT shutting off]

[Door creaks open]

[We're back to Cecil.]

Ladies and gentlemen, I am back.

Let me first say Hurrah! Hurrah for the custodial staff of Night Vale Elementary. Hurrah for the hooded janitors without names who appear bathed in blue light through doors thrown open by cold winds. We long thought they had been laid off after statewide budget cuts, but apparently they cannot ever leave this building. They are of course a part of the building, which is itself a living creature. Obviously.

Night Vale has been saved after the janitors simply unplugged the computer. They say to rob a computer of electricity is very similar to killing a creature. But then again, who are "They"? When did they say that, and why? It doesn't even seem true.

I am alone here in the gym, listeners. But there is one other—a single adult man's hand is slipping sadly down from the keys of a darkened computer. She scurries a little slower than before. Maybe her knuckles slump as she makes her way home through quiet streets.

The whir and beep of machinery is slowly replaced with the familiar sounds of wind in the leaves. We are serenaded by the playing of crickets under the porch. We are lulled in our beds by the muscular contraction of the coiled earthbowel that fills our cellars. And with that, gentle listener, normalcy returns to Night Vale.

We are no longer prisoners of electricity, except for the man we keep in the cage of electricity at the zoo, and we have no choice about that. If we let him out, he might tell somebody.

Everything is well again.

Well, everything is almost well again. I know computers are dangerous and have long threatened our lives and our freedoms. Listen, I was just imprisoned by this headstrong machine. I should know. But hear me Night Vale (and specifically those with any power in the School Board). Night Vale, there is a girl in need. There is a girl who only has a grown man's detached hand as a body. I cannot relate to her experience. I doubt you can either, listeners. But we can all empathize.

Sure, by allowing this computer to live on, we risk a digital tyrant, controlling our communication, our infrastructure, our lives. But destruction of our economy is an inconvenience. It is not an end. It is not a death. There are children in wheelchairs who can't get a simple ramp at a charter school because our School Board lives in terror of a menacing, unforgiving glow cloud that rains dead animals and spreads dreadful and false memories. Likewise, there is a girl who is only a hand, and she needs a computer to help her be part of our community. And if allowing a treacherous machine to dismantle our municipal power grid and telephone lines and satellites and radios can help her, well, count me in.

Thank you for listening to others. Thank you for caring for others. Stay tuned next for a predetermined series of unchangeable events that will shape the rest of your scripted life.

Good night, Night Vale. Good Night.

PROVERB: Thank you for your interest in a life free of pain. We're not accepting applications at this time. Please try again. And again. And again. And again. And again. And again. And again. And again.

EPISODE 35:
"LAZY DAY"
NOVEMBER 15, 2013

READING BACK THROUGH THIS EPISODE, WELL, THERE'S JUST A LOT OF PO-
etry in it, isn't there? The warning from the vague yet menacing government
agency. The traffic section. The language of much of the main plot itself.

Jeffrey and I have always been big fans of poetry, especially performance poetry, and the format of *Night Vale* allows us to work in as much or
as little of it as we want. In this case, clearly, I wanted to work in a great deal.

Quietly in the background of all this playing around with language,
there is plot starting to go to work. We had never had much of a serial
plot on *Night Vale* before this point, but seeds were being planted for
what would end up being our most tightly plotted arc yet, and even
elements that would return in stories years down the line. The slow ad-
vancement of Strex, the tenure of Intern Maureen, Tamika and her army.

Plot in *Night Vale* generally runs quite slowly, due to the nature
of it being a two-man writing operation that is planned out in real
time. We're interested in watching the rhythms of the town, rather than
pushing toward the next cliffhanger. But still, we are telling stories as
we go. And we started to experiment here with the idea of telling a single yearlong story and seeing if it would work.

—Joseph Fink

No one has seen the trees this week.
Hopefully they'll come back soon.

WELCOME TO NIGHT VALE.

Hello, listeners. Nothing much to say about this day in Night Vale. Today is just a lazy day in our beautiful little town.

The heat is unusually strong for this time of year, assuming you believe in concepts like "time" and "year" and "unusual." Flies are buzzing around and around a trash can somewhere. Frances Donaldson, manager of the Antiques Mall, is waving listlessly at a wall of old items ready to be bought anew, her hand a slow signal of submission to inactivity. The Faceless Old Woman Who Secretly Lives in Your Home is finding herself clicking to the same apiology websites she's read a million times. I myself am slumped against this desk, murmuring into this microphone, too tired by the heat to give more than a token effort to the work of my life.

Ours is a quiet now. No one is speaking but me. If speaking took me any energy, if it were not merely a reflex of my living form, then I myself would not be speaking either.

Carlos, perfectly imperfect Carlos, is the only one feeling industrious today. He's mowing the lawn and whistling. The lawn is whistling back.

And now the news, I guess.

Alert citizens from all over Night Vale are reporting a man in a tan jacket standing behind the Taco Bell, near the Dumpster and the constantly ringing pay phone. He is plucking insects out of the air and stuffing them into his deerskin suitcase. Alert citizens report that they don't remember what his nimble hands look like, and many of them lost track of what they were saying mid-sentence, lapsing into a gaped-mouth silence. All of them received one stamp on their Alert Citizen Card. As always, five stamps means stop sign immunity for a year!

Also, congratulations to Jake Garcia, who has completely filled up THREE Alert Citizen Cards, thus giving him the mandatory right to disappear forever. His entire family, in a statement given in monotone unison, said that they were proud and that they didn't miss him much, really. Remember what Secret Police mascot Barks Ennui always says: "Citizens, be alert! But not too alert! There is much that you should not see! Only you can prevent your own house mysteriously catching on fire. Woof! Woof!" Haha, I bet Barks is such a cute little cartoon dog. Maybe someday the Secret Police will declassify what he looks like.

Update on the Summer Reading Program from a couple months ago: Those children who made it out of the library alive—bloodied, covered in the guts of librarians, and clutching reading lists far in advance of their grade level—have formed an organized militia under the leadership of fellow survivor, twelve-year-old Tamika Flynn. They have taken to conducting drills out in the Sandwastes, hundreds of children, shouting and moving in unison, as Tamika stands over them on a hilltop, watching for their weakness, encouraging their strength. Tamika has taken to wearing the detached hand of a librarian around her neck, as a warning to any who would dare face her that she has already defeated the most fearsome creature imaginable. When reached for comment, Tamika said: "We do not look around. We do not look inside. We do not sleep. Our god is not a smiling god. And we are ready for this war."

When asked to clarify, she challenged our reporter to a hundred days of hand-to-hand combat, which our reporter declined by running away screaming, pursued by hundreds of battle-hardened children.

It's still just a lazy day here in Night Vale. Mayor Pamela Winchell called a press conference, and then did not speak. She sat on a folding chair next to the podium, her head lolled back, taking a brief nap, before getting up and jumping, folding chair in hand, through a small glowing portal she created in midair. All of this would have been quite rude to the attending reporters if a single one of them had actually attended, but they called a press conference of their own to announce that they just were going to take the rest of the day off, if that was okay. That the still afternoon sun-light was somehow more conducive to a gentle rest than the dark cradle of night. No one showed up to that press con-ference either.

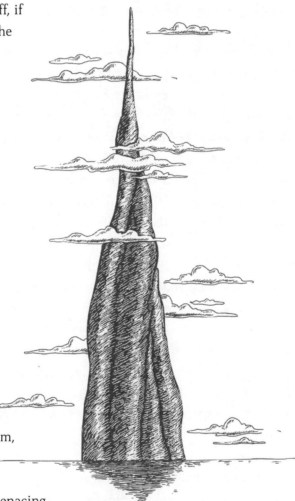

Carlos has vacuumed his living room and is now organiz-ing his closets. He's holding up items and making decisions. He is humming. The grass cannot hum, and so is silent.

The vague yet menacing

government agency would like to remind you that UFOs are totally not a thing. They remind you that UFOs are merely weather balloons, and further, that weather balloons are merely misplaced clouds, that clouds are merely dreams that have escaped our sleep, that sleep is merely a practice for death, that death is merely another facet of our world, no different from, say, sand or bicycles, and that the great glowing earth is merely the last thoughts of a dying man, laughing and shaking his head weakly at the improbability of it all. Remember, it's not just the law. It's an illusion.

Thanksgiving is just around the corner, and you know what that means! It means it's time for us to go groveling to the Brown Stone Spire, thanking it for all that it has done and all that it has mercifully not done. This is just a great time to get the family together, eat your fill, then crawl out through the sharp rocks and sand until your knees leave blood streaks on the barren earth, and you feel the Brown Stone Spire loom up before you but you dare not look, you dare not look.

"Thank you," you whisper. "Thank you. Thank you." More plea than prayer. More fear than gratitude. And if it accepts what you have to say, you and your family can return to your homes, shaking, safe, together, shaking, together. And if it does not accept what you say? It doesn't really matter what happens after that, does it? I mean, would knowing make it any easier? No. Knowing never does.

The Brown Stone Spire: Give thanks. Cry out thanks. Scream thanks.

And now for a word from our sponsors.

Today's broadcast is brought to you by CostCo: How much could a body even weigh?

In addition, today's broadcast is brought to you by waves of sound that are somehow carried by a form of light and that a machine is turning into an invisible man talking to you, intimately, quietly, into your ear. That doesn't seem natural to us. Strexcorp Synergists, Inc. Distrust all that you previously trusted.

This day in which nothing happens continues to not.

Even bodily functions are taking the day off. Reports are coming in that hearts are failing to beat, lungs failing to inflate, the muscles of the arms and legs turning to a loose, relaxed jelly. People are falling dead in the street, suddenly blue, suddenly seizing, spit dribbling from their lips in tiny pools of foam and mud in the sand. Loved ones, looking on, without the energy needed to weep. Just nothing much of any kind going on. A lazy, lazy day.

Our favorite local cereal company, Flakey O's, is gearing up to announce their newest big product: Imaginary Corn Flakes. The cereal chefs down at Flakey O's are taking only the sweetest, most noncarcinogenic cobs of imaginary corn, supplied by John Peters, you know, the farmer? They are distilling that imaginary taste down to a crisp, flavor-packed imaginary corn flake, ready for you to eat out of a big bowl of milk. "We are very excited about this product," said Miranda Yesby, of the new Flakey O's board of directors. "We are thrilled to be working with John Peters, you know, the farmer? I mean, as soon as we can find him. Has anyone seen him? He's become as hard to locate as his corn."

Miranda also said that there are no plans to do viral marketing involving a sentient, transdimensional pyramid, as the costs on the last one were just too high. "I mean we had nothing to do with that," she said. "But if we did, then we might say a certain sentient pyramid really got an outsized ego after one simple viral marketing campaign and started making unreasonable demands, like a transdimensional trailer on location that is normal size on the outside but contains within it vast, looming spaces, impossible, endless. Also health benefits. So if that were the case, we would probably have had to let the sentient pyramid go."

Miranda then thanked us for attending the announcement, and dug her way back into the Flakey O's offices using her large, clawlike paws.

And now traffic. A few drops of icemelt. Almost invisible as they slide down great slabs of mountain rock. Joining together into a slight trickle, the mere suggestion of movement and water. That suggestion becoming more clear, clear water, clearly moving in a clear trickle downwards forming with others into a stream. A stream rolling over pebbles and around debris, hardly any force behind it but implacable in its searching out of lower ground. And then gasping from some height as a splash into a river. A deep river, churning its way through a landscape, drawing boundaries over which wars can later be fought. Slamming against boulders with violence but without malice. Becoming wider, slower, like a human settling into the better part of age, a river that only shows evidence of movement when it carries some other thing, some life, upon it, like a human settling into the better part of age. And finally, one last exit, a great engulfing by an ocean, in which all water is the same water. In which we can finally find some rest. Like a human settling into the better. Like a human settling. This has been traffic.

And the lazy day continues. A neon sign advertising the World's Best Burgers blinks uselessly in the glaring haze of the sun, its light as small as the probability of its claim. The Earth is starting to slow its rotation, joining in on the mass malaise. Magnetic fields are going crazy. They are the only things going crazy, everything else is completely mellowed out.

Those people with still functioning hearts and lungs are lounging around, saying "Ah, who cares?" and "What a bother" when presented with stimulus or thought. The Earth is slowing. Gravity is slacking off. My mic is floating.

Carlos is also floating, and he's taking this opportunity to clean out the gutter on his roof. How industrious. How . . . ah. I don't really have the energy to think of another word.

Radio waves are reacting strangely to the loss of gravity, the change in magnetism as the Earth slows, so if you are having difficulty receiving this message, we apologize, but we won't do anything about it. Doing things, right? Movement, you know? Existing? Do you see what I mean?

Oh, what's that? Intern Maureen is flicking her eyes up in her otherwise motionless face. Her mouth is set into a deep lull, her cheeks are slack. I believe she is indicating something. I suppose I should turn my head and look. I suppose. Oh. Oh, all right. Here I go. Listeners, I am engaging the muscles in my neck, and I am turning my head. Ah, I see. The sun is going out. Yes, a black tumor of darkness, of absence, is on the face of the brightness. The brightness is dimming. The source of all life is going, is joining the rest of us in taking today to do nothing. That's probably not good. We should probably do something about that. But...It's like...well, anyway, at least I got to see how *Breaking Bad* ended.

And now, I don't so much take you, as just kind of leave you, just kind of disappear and gently nudge you toward, in the heart of a world that soon won't be, the weather.

WEATHER: "Mijn Manier" by Brainpower

Welcome back. Welcome back, I guess, from a crisis. Welcome back from, I guess, a crisis. How was it solved? How was the day saved?

It wasn't. It didn't need to be. There are lulls and gaps and rests and stops, but this world stumbles on. The sun flared back. The world restarted. Still bodies, blue in the gray street, gasped suddenly and rose back into the blue-gray light of day.

We wake up. We move on. No state is our state forever. All is fleeting.

Frances Donaldson, manager of the Antiques Mall, has gone back to violently smashing her stock of old items, as is usual. The Faceless Old Woman Who Secretly Lives in Your Home has gone back to flitting around in the corner of your eye, rearranging your belongings according to some unknown purpose. The flies are still buzzing around that trash can, but with more verve, more zest.

Intern Maureen brought me some coffee. That's helping. Coffee helps sometimes though, doesn't it? Other times it just makes things worse. I mean everything does.

Business is booming. People are moving. Events, transpiring. All as usual, all returning. We are up! We are full of energy! We are ready for the next great thing to be made for us and delivered to us and done to us!

Carlos, meanwhile, says he's had a busy day and might take a nap now. That . . . well that sounds nice. Listeners, I think now is the time at which I must say good-bye. There's a place, here in Night Vale, a place I'd like to be just now. Maybe my lazy day isn't quite done after all.

Stay tuned next for a keening howl, a scratch at the door, a hood falling suddenly over your face, and a delicious roasted squash recipe your family will just love.

Good night, Night Vale. Good night.

PROVERB: On this day in history: mundanity, and terror, and food, and love, and trees.

EPISODE 36: "MISSING"

DECEMBER 1, 2013

MY FAVORITE PLAY IS *THE LIFE OF GALILEO* BY BERTOLT BRECHT. IT'S long and didactic, pretty stilted and varies wildly in quality based on the director. So, basically, go check it out if you haven't already.

Many of Brecht's ideas have popped up in my writing. This episode in particular, I wanted to deal with heroism. Not necessarily what it takes to be a hero, but what it means to need a hero. If you believe in free will, and if you believe in democracy, and if you believe in the wisdom of crowds, perhaps heroism is anathema. Perhaps you are the change you wish to see. Or more likely, you are part of a will of people to affect greater good to be moral and just.*

When Galileo is dressed down by his assistant, Andrea, for recanting his scientific teachings before a church inquisition, Galileo admits that he found it more compelling to live than to be martyred. Andrea says, "Unhappy is the land that has no hero." Galileo retorts, "Unhappy is the land that needs a hero."

---

*I write all of this before the 2016 US presidential election. So maybe Trump got elected and you're a fatalist and a pessimist and you live in a bunker in the middle of the Australian Outback now. Lots of things are possible.

Galileo's (and Brecht's) point is that we shouldn't need heroes. We should have a perfect and peaceful communistic society and la la la. Plus, there is a distinct danger of having a culture that thinks it needs a hero, or, more specifically, thinks it needs saving. (See Clint Eastwood's 1973 western *High Plains Drifter* for a prescient tale of early 2000s US politics—the dangerous power we give to those we think can protect us.)

With Tamika, I wanted to set up a hero that Night Vale thinks it needs. Does Night Vale need Tamika? Not saying they don't or shouldn't. I'm just saying.

—Jeffrey Cranor

Red sky at night, sailors delight. Red sky at night, the sailors are howling and laughing. The sailors begin to surround us, and the night sky is so very red.

WELCOME TO NIGHT VALE.

Listeners, I hate to start our program off with sad news, but our new station owner, Strexcorp, handed me a missing child alert right as I walked into the studio. Strexcorp is asking Night Vale citizens to be on the lookout for Tamika Flynn, age thirteen. She is described as five-foot-one, stocky build, black hair, and dark eyes, dark, so dark, so wise beyond time, so deep in their understanding that to gaze into them is to gaze into your own death. It is not important where she was last seen or by whom. Why do you need to know that? Why are you asking so many questions? You are taking valuable time away from important and highly fulfilling work at your place of employment, the missing child report reads.

Strexcorp asks that anyone with any knowledge of Tamika Flynn's whereabouts should contact Strexcorp headquarters by picking up a phone and talking. Don't worry. You're not hard to find.

I asked my new supervisor, Daniel, why it's Strexcorp that is issuing a missing child alert and not Tamika Flynn's family or the Sheriff's Secret Police, but he just started shaking and sparking and humming. Then the hallway got too cloudy, and I couldn't breathe, and my show was starting, so I left him alone. He's still standing at the studio window staring at me, twitching, sparks subsiding, but his mouth has fallen open, revealing, is that motor oil? Tar? I don't know, but it's going to be hard to concentrate if he doesn't leave.

Let's go now to the community calendar.

Tuesday there's a false start, a mistaken understanding of time. Tuesday we will wake and walk to our normal places—our showers, kitchens, cars, desks—only to find the day never began. We will slowly notice an absence of all matter, all light, all time. And then as suddenly as we false started, we will begin our actual day. And everything will happen the same, only because of our awareness of it all, it will happen differently. Less differently at first, but more differently later.

Wednesday will take forever. For. Ever. Not literally. But very near literally. Ugh, Wednesday hasn't even gotten here, and I already want it over with.

Thursday a faint outline of a dull face will appear in the dark as you try to sleep. You will notice its blank stare, its straight, expressionless lips, its thick brow, and the subtle hint of slow, collected breaths. It will seem to be watching you, curious about you, as if it were not from here. It is not from here. You will lock eyes. You will barely be able to make out the face's humanoid features, but you will know, deep down it is not human, not human at all. What does it want, you will think. Probably nothing. Let it go. Get some sleep.

Friday is an open house at the Night Vale Community College. Thinking about furthering your education? Considering taking Winter Semester classes? Well, it's a trap. Do not go near the Night Vale Community College this Friday. Nice try giant worms, but we know your tricks. Faking a community college open house is very obvious, don't you think? I mean, it *was* a nice touch creating a fake press release to get into various news outlets like ours, but we see through you. We really do. Your skin is translucent, and it's kind of gross. No offense.

Saturday everyone is their own person. You are free to disregard others and recognize yourself as one, for once. Pour some wine. Draw a bath, light some incense, and grab a city-approved novel. It's you time.

Sunday will be full of regret. Also joy. Also laughter. Also conversation. Also long stretches of unmemorable moments. It will mostly be that last thing. In your old age, as you look back on your life, if someone were to ask what happened on that Sunday ... you remember? that one Sunday with the regret and joy and laughter and conversation? ... If someone were to ask you that, you would be hard-pressed to come up with a single memorable moment from this coming Sunday.

This has been the community calendar.

An update on our missing child report. We just received word that thirteen-year-old Tamika Flynn is not missing. This word came from Tamika herself. Witnesses said they saw Tamika standing atop the pedestal of one of this town's most historical works of art: the 138-year-old bronze statue of actor Lee Marvin, just outside the Night Vale Post Office. Tamika told a gathered crowd that she was not missing, has never been missing. She clarified that she has always been where she has been. She has always been from where she is from. And she will always be going where she is going.

Witnesses reported that Tamika had a canvas tote bag full of heavy stones over her left shoulder, a worn-out copy of Willa Cather's *Death Comes for the Archbishop* in her right rear pants pocket, and that she was still holding the severed head of the librarian she defeated so valiantly in August, saving our town and all of the participants of the library's treacherous Summer Reading Program.

As yellow helicopters began to approach her, Tamika shouted to the gathered crowd to stop looking for her. I am found. I am found. I am found, she repeated dramatically, rhythmically, the crowd swaying and moved by her homiletic passion. Stop looking for me and find yourself, she was last heard crying over the crescendo of helicopters landing. The remaining crowd, still singing her phrases, still undiluted, inadvertently blocked the Strexcorp agents from reaching Tamika before she disappeared in plain sight.

Strexcorp has issued, just moments ago, several dozen more missing child reports. They say children keep going missing. And they bet that if you find one specific child. One specific, very determined and difficult child (and they mean that in the best possible way). If you find that one child, you will probably find all of the missing children. Strexcorp is asking that if anyone has seen Tamika Flynn, to contact them immediately. She is a missing child, and shouldn't you care about that? Shouldn't you care about the children, Strexcorp asked. Children are the future, they added. Wish you felt the same way and would help us find this . . . this . . . child, they stammered, looking slightly agitated.

More on this soon.

Let's have a look now at traffic.

There's a man. Imagine him. He's leaning on a fence, shirtless and weary, he seems wise near the eyes, but his impatient feet suggest insidiousness. He's marked with dried mud and maybe some very deep but quickly healing cuts, from the tree branches most likely. Or perhaps the birds. Okay, I'm not telling you the whole truth. It was definitely the birds. Imagine these cuts and scratches, dry and brittle now but tender to the touch. He is certain he did not offend the birds, but he is uncertain whether his complacency was construed as equal to said offense.

Picture this. Picture the man leaning on the crisscrossing metal wires, waiting. The birds are gone but other things are coming. He doesn't know specifically what, but he knows it'll come for him. You know this too because I have told you. The man says nothing.

There's never not something that has been displaced, marginalized. There's never not something that—when feeling pressed to the wall, to a place with no room left to run—gathers its numbers, gathers its forces, and turns savagely on its oppressor, turns viciously and without inhibition even on those who merely look like its oppressor. Do you catch my meaning? Can you imagine the scene I am explaining? How much of the world makes sense to you? What does it mean to be a hero? To be a human?

The man thinks about his heart. It beats. It beats normally. Earlier

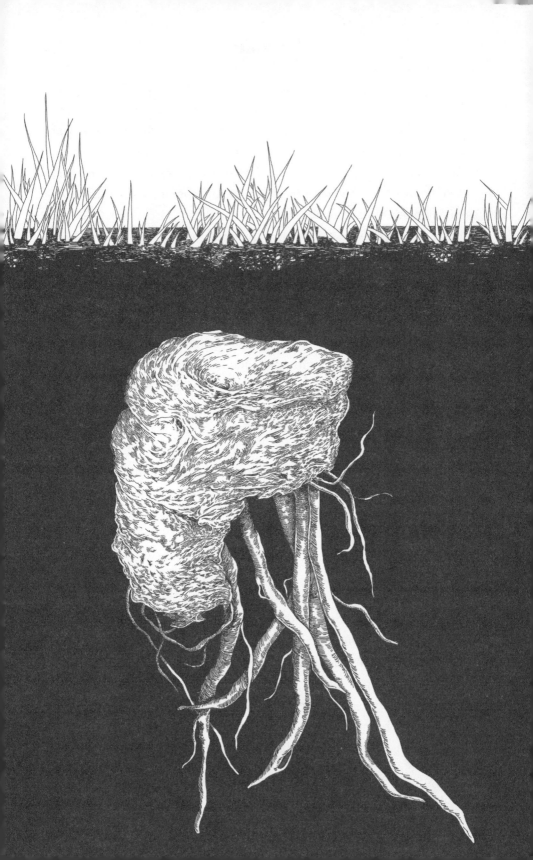

it did not beat normally. Think about your own heart. Is it beating normally? Listen. I'll give you a long moment.

[*A long moment is given*]

How is your heart? Do you remember the man? The one on the fence, shirtless and scarred, with the normally beating heart? He's not real. Take him out of the story, but leave the story. Take him out. Leave the story. Do you catch my meaning? Do you?

This has been traffic.

And now a word from our sponsor.

Deep, deep, deep in the grass, grass, grass, what grows, grows, grows? Who knows, knows, knows?

Strex

Strrreexxxxx

Strrrrreexxxxxxx

Strexcorp Synergists, Inc.: Working hard so you can work harder. Work harder. Seriously. Work harder. Strexcorp. Get to work.

More on the missing children story: Several helmeted and sunglassed helicopter pilots have stepped forward to announce that they had nothing to do with the missing children. Sheila Nowitzki, a pilot for one of the many black helicopters that are routinely circling Night Vale, said she's a harmless spy from the World Government and would never harm an American child without a direct order.

Marco Padilla, a pilot for one of the many blue Sheriff's Secret Police copters, said nothing, but you could see in his face he meant no harm to our kids.

And a shadowy haze that claimed, through telepathy, to be the pilot of one of the mysterious helicopters with elaborate murals depicting birds of prey diving, admitted that while their helicopters were the ones that took away all the children in Night Vale several weeks ago, they brought them back. They brought them back, okay. And they're fine.

Get off of me, the humid, gray haze emphasized. God, you take a bunch of kids one time. One time. Geez.

Listeners, today I want to talk to you about the dangers of deer. Are they beautiful? Yes. Are they graceful and picturesque, even borderline majestic beasts? Yes, yes, and yes. And are they helpful to the community because real estate agents live inside of them? Of course. But deer are also dangerous creatures. They are terrible, deceitful, and vile animals. I'm not being mean. This is just basic science.

Look, I know deer are cute and friendly looking. We all remember adorable little Bambi from the classic animated movie, with his sweet voice and white-freckled rump. But we also remember the bloody end that he wrought on the humans at the end of the film, the graphic beheadings and trees streaked with gore during the famous, revenge-fueled climax. The lesson of that movie, as in life itself, is that nature is gorgeous, and it is horrible, and it will kill you.

This has been the Children's Fun Fact Science Corner.

This just in: Oh my, some disastrous news. Quite terrible. There has been a helicopter crash out by the old car lot. Witnesses report hearing youthful shouts and screams followed by loud metallic clanging. They saw smoke trailing across the cold, dark afternoon sky, because of course the sun again did not rise today. They saw a yellow mangle of metal and rotors, and . . .

Um, listeners, Daniel is still standing at my studio door. He has stopped staring. He is now yelling, but without noise. He looks very upset. I can read his lips. He is saying: Turn it off. Shut it down. No more news today. We are shutting you down.

They're going to turn off my microphone. Night Vale, I've locked the door, which will buy me some time while Daniel goes to find a security guard with keys. So, let me take you now, for as long as it can last, to the weather.

WEATHER: "Peanuts" by Sam 'n Ash

[*Cecil speaking into something of much lesser broadcast quality; he is on a cell phone, outdoors.*]

Listeners, I do not know if you can hear me. I am only trusting that I did this right. I wired my phone into the soundboard and then wired the soundboard into the radio tower, which is running on auxiliary power. It's a cool trick my childhood best friend Earl Harlan taught me, back when we were in Boy Scouts together earning our Subversive Radio Host Badge.

I doubt Daniel or any of the new Station Management can hear me, as they do not like listening to radio shows. Also I'm hiding up on the roof with my makeshift studio.

During the weather, I got word from some witnesses at the helicopter accident. The Sheriff's Secret Police found several large slingshots and heavy stones nearby that matched in size and shape the dents on the helicopter's engine casing. They also found a well-worn and heavily notated copy of *Death Comes for the Archbishop* by Willa Cather. Inside the book was a bookmark, marking page two hundred sixty-seven. On that page was the underlined phrase "I shall not die of a cold, my son. I shall die of having lived." And on the bookmark was a handwritten note. It said: "Your pilot is fine. She is ours now. She will return when she is ready. But she will return . . . better.—T.F."

I do not know if that T.F. stands for our missing girl, our brilliant and bold and missing girl. If Station Management is listening, I, of course, hope we find Tamika Flynn and bring her home safely.

[*Quietly*] I hope that she will find you first, that is.

[*Normal*] Remember what I said, listeners? About the traffic. About the birds. Think on that. Think on lots of things. Think about heroes and whether we should even need them. The answer is we do not.

I sometimes wish I could tell you more. But I cannot. I cannot tell you everything I think you should hear because it is boring. Or it is unnecessary. Or it is very necessary but unapproved. There are many reasons I cannot always tell you what I want to tell you, but the main reason is that you need to find it out for yourselves. I could preach and teach and shout and explain, but no lesson is as powerful as the lesson learned on one's own.

You can do it. You don't need old Cecil telling you what's happening in town. No, I just report the news. I just arrange it. You figure it out. You learn from it. You take action. You create the meaning. It is all up to you. And given my current broadcasting situation, it may be up to you for a long time.

I better get back downstairs before they discover what I am doing. Stay tuned next for silence, self-reflection, a long pause to hear yourself think. Use that silence well.

Good night, Night Vale. Good night.

PROVERB: Look. Up in the sky. It's a bird. It's a plane. No. It's just the void. Infinite and indifferent. We're so small. So very very small.

EPISODE 37:
"THE AUCTION"

DECEMBER 15, 2013

COWRITTEN WITH GLEN DAVID GOLD

BEFORE NIGHT VALE AIRED, JOSEPH SENT ME AN E-MAIL PRAISING MY work and asking if I'd write for his nascent podcast. I did what established writers have done for developing writers since the beginning of time: I blew him off. Then friends started telling me there was this show I had to listen to. One evening, driving up highway 5, I did. I know 101 is the most-cited road that doesn't lead you to Night Vale, but 5 also doesn't quite go there, and that evening, in the dark of the desolate road, with Cecil's voice narrating, me pulling into the Santa Nella Arco station, with thousands of copper-coated crickets pinging like pennies as they rained down onto the gas pumps, I felt like I wasn't so much discovering a place as having something that had been in the corner of my eye revealed. (Note: There might not have actually been crickets.)

To me, anxiety and fear are manifested in acquisition, and I wanted to write about an auction. I figured I should work in critiques of capitalism and the profound unfairness of death (two topics I try to fit into everything I do, including introductions, apparently). Joseph and Jeffrey rearranged some bits, added other bits and continuity, made a couple of smart edits and it was ready. It's one of the easiest writing experiences I've had, because the world building of the first thirty or

so episodes so conflated with my own worldview it was like I was describing something that was happening, not something I was making
up. Cecil's voice is, as I'm sure you know, probably what Dante's Virgil
sounded like, if Virgil still had his community radio gig. I just had to
follow him.

My first novel was about a magician, so I'm not into revealing all
the secrets behind things but (a) my credit for a later episode is just one
bit, about day-laborer baristas, and (b) I had a different ending to "The
Auction." Jeffrey and Joseph were inspired at the last minute to make
the excellent change that opened up the narrative considerably: Who
bought Cecil? I still listen to this episode sometimes, because I love to
hear Cecil's delivery of the epic sentence about capuchin monkeys.

Did you know *Night Vale* had a fan base? I sort of did, then I really
did after the episode aired—the smart commentary online was a thrill
to read. The fans are awesome! When I met Dylan, he said to me, "Girl,
you make fifty look like thirty-two," which has nothing to do with the
rest of this introduction, but I just wanted you all to know I'm terribly
handsome.

Working in Night Vale seems to have that effect on people. Hmm.
I guess that means the moral is: If you're doing well in your career, go
ahead and blow off folks who have uneasy dreams. They'll be fine.

—Glen David Gold

Velvet darkness. Silken light. The rough burlap
of evening. The frayed cotton of daybreak.

WELCOME TO NIGHT VALE.

First off, welcome back. Everything is fine. Nothing's happening, if you know what I mean. You shouldn't know what I mean. If you do know, you should forget. I'm not going to mention anything and you're not going to hear anything and both of us will fail to remember. No one will be named. Nothing will be referenced. And so:

Listeners, today is an exciting and important day in Night Vale. The Sheriff's Secret Police are holding their annual auction of contraband and seized property to benefit their purchase of balloons, birthday candles, yellow cake, and a piñata. They hope to raise seven point three million dollars and they say the piñata is armored and will be used to crush rebellions.

Personally, I love the annual auction. You never know what sort of fun stuff might come up. The catalog has so many interesting items. Let's see. Lot 1 is an All-Clad dinnerware set, eight pans in cast aluminum for perfect distribution of heat, new in the package. It's just waiting for you to season it with a dollop of olive oil and start cooking for friends and family, regardless of how no one comes over anymore after the last dinner party when your mother drank all the Chianti and announced you never lived up to your potential. At least that's what the description of the lot says.

Lot 2 is a glowing coin with the image of a grim, horned god on the obverse and a half-collapsed panopticon on the reverse. It's been graded MS-45 by the Sheriff's Secret Police Coin Grading Service, which in no way colludes with the Sheriff's Secret Police auction house to inflate the grade and thus the value of the coin. Lot 3 is a silver candelabra that once floated across a series of dining-rooms-turned-abattoirs to better illuminate the flying daggers that accompanied it.

Lot 4 is a set of flying daggers with maniacally detailed designs on the shaft collars. Knife collectors and maniacs alike will want to bid on those. Don't get in the way of that bidding war!

Let's see, there are also carpets, and some mid-century modern furniture—oh, those are very stylish—and look, Lot 17 is a near-mint copy of *Uncanny X-Men* number 3, 1964. It has slight foxing to the back cover, perfect registration of the color separations, off-white pages, rust-less staples, high cover gloss, and no Marvel chipping. And it features the first appearance of The Blob. Not the Blob who lives in the housing development out back of the elementary school, the fictional one.

What else? Lot 37 is . . . um . . . Cecil Palmer. (*Beat*) There is no description. (*Beat*) Listeners, we'll have more on this auction as it develops.

On the lighter side of the news, today an invincible, all-powerful alien presence with telepathic powers came to Night Vale to enslave us all. It planned to bend every sentient being to its will, ending violence and conflict by subjugating all of us to its omniscient telekinetic powers. Hilariously, this all-powerful but bumbling alien presence didn't know we were already subjugated to the omniscient force that's been controlling our thoughts for years. We're guaranteed to continue our violent and irrational ways, so in your face, inept newcomer presence.

Toddlers of Night Vale, the Night Vale Community Preschool invites you to fulfill your potential. Commit to a new and demanding educational curriculum while exploring your ultimate dream. The same dream that every toddler has: economic opportunity! That's right—you too can learn to be a chimney sweep. Clean the many, many chimneys of leading citizen, and friendly billionaire, Marcus Vanston.

What a good man Marcus Vanston is. Every one of his houses, from his smallest penthouse apartment atop the dirigible hangar to his forty-six-room hilltop estate, has multiple chimneys. He has built chimneys even in places where he has no houses so his well-deserved carbon credits can go to good use. There are numerous chimneys on his shopping mall, his office buildings, his dirigible, his moon-rock-plated recreational vehicles, and, due to new and creative laws that allow eminent domain for the generous Marcus Vanston, every other house in town as well.

He has strapped traveling chimneys onto the pushcarts of festive peddlers, whose rags, hunched shoulders, nagging coughs, and forced tin-whistle merriment accompany the sad antics of their emaciated, vest-and-marching-band-cap-wearing capuchin monkeys holding tin cups rattling with a single penny from some defunct, outmoded currency, asking us to contribute to their upkeep, as we turn up our collars, clear our throats, and make convenient excuses to walk a little faster until, instead of embarrassment about their fates, we find our way to feeling superior about our fragile position on the economic ladder. Marcus Vanston understands. He doesn't want you to be a lowly peddler or a capuchin monkey. He wants you to be a chimney sweep. So, little ones: lower your standards, smother your dreams in carbon, and enroll in the preschool chimney sweep academy. Make good old Marcus Vanston happy for a few brief moments.

An update on our earlier story: Violence has broken out among bidders in the Sheriff's Secret Police auction. Bidding has been frantic and angry. It is confirmed that there has been hair pulling. Unfortunately, attendees have been using their bidding paddles to slap each other across the face, a motion the auctioneer has been repeatedly mistaking as indication of a new bid. Thus Lot 1, the All-Clad dinnerware set, sold for one hundred seventy-five thousand dollars, and that's before the buyer's premium.

Listeners, I have been in touch with the auction staff about Lot 37, which is of a certain interest to me. I want Lot 37. I want it badly.

I asked if they might take a photograph of it and send it to me. Well, the peals of laughter that broke out in response were a cross between sleigh bells and the cackles of hunched, gray-faced court jesters. You know how that sounds. Listeners, in order to learn more about Lot 37, it's likely I will need to visit the auction myself. More as it develops.

The Night Vale mayoral race is heating up in preparation for the mayoral election this next June. The Faceless Woman Who Secretly Lives in Your Home has taken to leaving leaflets inside the wiring and pipes of your appliances, to be found when the sparking and the shaking become so much that you must hire or capture a repair person. The leaflets are tastefully designed, with an anatomically detailed drawing of a sparrow's heart and the simple slogan: "You are fragile and blind and wanting and stepping alone into the great darkness of the future." It also has her five-point policy platform, which is mostly interesting facts she has learned about bees.

Meanwhile Hiram McDaniels, in the interest of saving time, has taken to standing on corners giving five different campaign speeches, one with each of his heads. His heads have radically different personalities and agendas, leading to some discord in their messages, but they all agree that they would like to be elected, that youth sports programs are important, and that the "Time of the Lizard" will soon be upon the helpless human race.

Oh, and speaking of the good-hearted and great-walleted Marcus Vanston, he has also thrown his hat into the proverbial ring. He actually constructed a special proverbial ring in the middle of town with an LCD light display and a fountain with an hourly waterspout show, and commissioned a gold-plated hat with remote-controlled hat launcher for just that purpose. As the hat flew into the ring, a forty-piece children's choir sang a song composed for the occasion, titled "Hi, I'm Running Too I Guess. Oh, I'm Marcus Vanston. Whatever. Anyway, I'm Going to Be Mayor. Thanks." Many tears were shed by onlookers, due to civic pride and some helpful gas Marcus had added to the air supply.

Well, this is starting to look like a mayoral campaign for the ages. When reached for comment, outgoing mayor Pamela Winchell showed us a collection of mosses and explained the songs that must be sung to each of them for proper growth.

Hey, kids. Ever go walking in the woods and wonder whether a fairy ring of mushrooms is poisonous? Well, look at its center. If there's a body no older than yourself lying there, the ring is perfectly fine. If the body is also screaming, the ring is perfectly fine.

Everything is perfectly fine. There is nothing under your bed. There is nothing in your closet. Your parents are most likely actually your parents, regardless of what the Faceless Old Woman Who Secretly Lives in Your Home might tell you. Do not fear the black helicopters or the black, windowless school buses that circle your block at night. You need not be afraid of the boogieman. There hasn't been a sighting of a boogieman for several months, or at least a couple weeks.

And yes, you will die, but probably not until everyone you know is already dead too. Your parents, your friends, your pets, each death leaving a small but irreparable scar on your not yet still, still-beating heart. The living tell the dying not to leave and the dying do not listen. The dying tell us not to be sad for them and we do not listen. The dialogue between the living and the dead is full of misunderstanding and silence.

There's nothing to fear in oblivion, unless of course your consciousness survives death. If so, it would be reasonable to fear the sensation of consciousness without senses, suspended alone in the cosmos with no one to hear you and no way to make yourself known, no reference point for counting time, a count that does not matter anyway in a literal eternity. You might wish that you still had a corporeal form only so that you could make your mouth move to express your terror, to make the universal form of a terrified scream, the form of a letter O. But you won't be able to. You just won't. This has been the Children's Fun Fact Science Corner, brought to you by shame, loneliness, and the letter O.

I have been told, listeners, that the auction has descended into chaos. Michelle Nguyen, owner of Dark Owl Records, having bid on a sealed box of Elvis Presley 45s, opened the box to find it was in fact a box of Elvis Presley's .45 caliber revolvers. The upended box has made bidding much more treacherous. Mayor Pamela Winchell, interested in Lot 28 (a gently used five-cup coffeemaker), has begun laying down suppressing fire over the ducked heads of anyone trying to outbid her.

Despite this, I must enter the auction house now myself, taking my life into my hands even more than usual. Lot 37: Cecil Palmer. I must know. I must bid. I go now, listeners, to await the crying of Lot 37.

As I go, you go, to the weather.

WEATHER: "Absentee" by Jack Campbell

Listeners, many complications ensued during my attempt to bid on Lot 37. First, in registering for the auction, I had to indicate my current income, which is made difficult as our new owners, who I have been asked to stop talking about, are now paying us in scrip redeemable only at merchants they own, like Dust Hut or the Ralphs. Luckily, the Sheriff's Secret Police turns out to be one of those select merchants. I was able to get a paddle only moments before the bidding on Lot 37 began.

When confronted with destiny, there are external events to record, yes, but also internal. I would say time slowed down even more than usual. The edges of the room went blurry and then went completely. There was a deep throb of distant machinery that I realized was my own heart propelling inadequate amounts of blood through my parched and aching body. If I did not win Lot 37 I would be unraveled. Perhaps I would be unraveled either way. The dull ache I felt was a primal ache of incompletion, the separation an infant feels when pulled too soon from its mother's embrace. My cheeks flushed with the irrationality of desire. I needed Lot 37. I counted my breaths. I judged myself for wanting, and judged myself wanting. I focused on those parts of my life completely out of my control in order to calm myself down, drowning my fears in pleasant helplessness.

The upshot is I forgot to raise my paddle. Oh, oh, foolish Cecil. And through the tears that came then to my eyes, I couldn't see who won Lot 37 with only one bid. Winner of Lot 37, if you're listening, on one hand, I wish you good luck with your prize. On the other, I will be using the mightiest bully pulpit of all—community radio—to strike back at you and destroy you. But also: congratulations. Also that.

I am authorized to tell you that the Sheriff's Secret Police have declared the auction a resounding success. In celebration, they deployed the piñata, to the screams, presumably delighted, of everyone in attendance. The winning bidders walked away grinning, laden down with trinkets and trophies that reassured them with the cleverness of sheer acquisition.

The Sheriff's Secret Police went on to say that objects are invested with manna, magic power caused by the dangerous ideas of property and ownership, and holding on to them is our attempt at having something that will never let us down, even though eventually all will. People leave. Parents leave the room. Lovers leave your life. You leave the world. We clutch teddy bears first, then dolls, then sports jerseys and automobiles with hand-sewn leather and excellent gas mileage as if that were something permanent. The Sheriff's Secret Police gave a great cheer in honor of constant decay and the inevitability of abandonment.

Listeners, accumulating objects is just a way, we hope, to turn back the grim specter of death. Thank you for your participation in this auction, and for your hope that making a certain purchase—All-Clad cookware, a candelabrum, a comic book, a community radio show host—would render you anything more than mortal.

I go now to find myself, or to find who has myself, or to find someone that might make me feel better about what has happened today. I'd take that last one, honestly. I'd take that honest last one.

And so, dear listeners, and whatever unknown person or entity that is now the owner of Lot 37: I bid you a farewell, the fondness of which is determined by your place relative to mine in my heart.

Stay tuned next for our popular home medical program *Yes, That's Probably Cancer.*

Good night, Night Vale. Good night.

PROVERB: Listen. I'm not a hero. The real heroes are the people that point out to us when protesters have smartphones, thus invalidating all concerns.

EPISODE 38:
"ORANGE GROVE"

JANUARY 1, 2014

I KILLED TWO GOOD PEOPLE.

Sort of killed. Depends on your definition of alive, I guess, and how sentient you consider fictional characters.

In this episode, Intern Maureen—named after one of my favorite people, author Maureen Johnson—and Adam Bair—named after the person who bought the welcometonightvale.com domain long before we realized we needed to secure it from poachers, and just gave it to us—both touched the Orange Juice that made them flicker out of existence.

We didn't hear much from Adam. I hope he appreciated his death.

But Maureen—oh boy.

In fact, we heard about it on Twitter from Maureen. So much so that somehow her intern namesake didn't die at all. More on that later. But this was the episode that drew Maureen's online ire.

The upshot, though, was we ultimately became good friends with Maureen. The lesson, as always, is if you want to make friends, you simply need to kill virtual versions of people you like in a work of fiction.

We agreed to keep Intern Maureen alive as long as author Maureen agreed to perform her part live at our two-year anniversary show at New York's Town Hall that June. And she did, and it was perfect.

That recording is available online (at our website—you know, the one Adam Bair gifted us? He was a good Web designer, and he will be missed).

—Jeffrey Cranor

You take the good. You take the bad. You take them both, and there you have spiders crawling out of a red velvet cupcake.

WELCOME TO NIGHT VALE.

We start today's show with some exciting agricultural news. John Peters, you know, the farmer?, said his winter orange crop is outstanding this year. He said there are oranges everywhere. Delicious clementines, juicy Valencias, rich navels, and bold blood oranges. John said there are so many oranges. A real bumper crop, he said. A real orange-tacular, he did not say. A real orange-a-thon, he never would have said. A real orange-ocalypse, he may have thought but kept to himself.

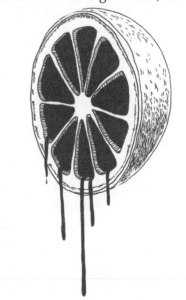

John, speaking to a pack of local reporters, and backed by a group of farmers wearing black double-breasted suits and red silk ties, said this is the dawning of a new citrus economy in Night Vale. John said citrus is our future. Citrus holds the key to prosperity. Citrus holds the key to health. One particular orange here literally holds the key to a one-sided door in the middle of the desert. If you find that orange, John said, I will pay you dearly for it. Or rather, John corrected himself, you will pay dearly for it. John then said, either way. Whatever. Would love to have that orange, my friend. Would love to have that orange. Yes sir, he punctuated. Or ma'am. Or neither. I mean, whoever. Sure would love to have that orange. He chuckled while sweating and adjusting his wooden hat.

John then tossed some oranges to the reporters. The reporters caught the oranges and then began to disappear and reappear, blinking in and out of existence. Quickly at first, then slowly, then more out of existence than in, until they were all gone.

More on this story as it develops.

The City Council announced today that they just can't be here anymore. They said this in unison, standing in a cramped meeting room and wearing tiny rectangular sunglasses. They added that they wish us all the best in our final weeks. They then made the standard American Sign Language "I Love You" gesture as smoke filled the room.

Witnesses said the smoke smelled of maple and was a little briny but not unpleasantly so. When the haze cleared the City Council was still standing in the room apologizing, claiming "This usually works" and then, no longer speaking in unison, casting blame on each other for not believing hard enough and that if weren't for so-and-so they'd all be on a beach somewhere safe from the bears or whatever those things are.

When asked for an explanation about the bears, or whatever those things are, the council simply whispered, in unison, "Mistaaaaakes." No follow-up questions were asked, as the reporters became physically and emotionally occupied with the dozens of agitated starlings that began pouring from the air-conditioning duct.

You know, listeners, I've been thinking about John Peters's orange grove. I did a little digging online and found that orange trees are not native to deserts.

I also e-mailed my boyfriend, Carlos, about this. He's a scientist, which kind of makes me a scientist too.

Here's Carlos's e-mail back to me just now:

Cecil, I'll do my best to answer your questions, but do know that I don't specialize in botany or dendrology. I am a scientist. I study science, not plants or nature.

I did drive out past John's farm a month ago, and there wasn't a single tree, just acres and acres of rocky, cracked, flat ground. There's no way he could have grown anything natural on that land, let alone a bountiful orange grove, especially in just a few weeks.

As far as your other question goes, let's stay home tonight. We ate out last night. Plus, there's a new documentary about scatterplot matrices on Netflix I've been wanting to see. Also *The Man Who Shot Liberty Valance* is on TBS again. We could rewatch that. I'll make pasta, if you can pick up some—

Et cetera et cetera. Carlos goes on about weekend bowling plans. . . . You don't need all this. Okay, I think that's all he had about the orange trees. I do hope we watch *Liberty Valance*, though. I love that film.

And now a word from our sponsors.

Tired of waiting in line at the post office? Scared of the unexplained blood pouring from the PO Boxes? Confused by screams that no one else hears? Terrified of leaving your home? Try Stamps.com. With Stamps.com you can print your own postage and avoid the long lines and predatory birds so common at the post office. You can even have your postal carrier pick up your packages, as long as you are careful to never look the carrier in the eyes, as this is a sign of aggression and you may scare your postal carrier away.

Stamps.com has a special offer for Night Vale Community Radio listeners. Sign up today and receive a bag of magic rocks, $50 worth of self-loathing, and a free scale so you can arbitrarily assign numbers to material objects. To claim your new member benefits, simply visit Stamps.com and press your forehead against the radio mic in the upper right of your screen until your entire body falls forward into the alternate Stamps.com universe. Stamps.com will tell your family you loved them very much. Stamps.com will tell your family that Stamps .com loves them very much. Come here, family. You are all our family now, Stamps.com will say, stretching their many boneless arms around your terrified family. Come here. We are all loving family.

Stamps.com. You live in a dying world. We love you.

Ladies and gentlemen, we've just received word that the Ralphs is stocked full of fresh orange juice from John's farm. It's called JP's OJ, where the O in OJ is a bright cartoonish sun with big, pink eyes, and a strained, toothy smile, and the J is a sickle the sun is using to slice down ripe oranges from a large tree.

Adam Bair, weekday shift manager at the Ralphs, said they have removed all other produce to stock JP oranges and even emptied out the refrigerators to fully showcase all of JP's mouthwatering stock of fresh juice. Even several of the dry goods aisles had to be cleared out, Adam said, pulling oranges from his apron pockets. He continued pulling oranges from his tiny pocket, mesmerized by their seeming infinitude and unable to continue speaking as he began to blink out of existence.

Listeners, we here at Night Vale Community Radio need to offer the following correction.

In a previous broadcast, we described the world as real. We indicated, using our voice, that it was made up of many real objects and entities, and we gave descriptions of these disparate parts. We even went so far as to ascribe action and agency to some of the entities.

But, as we all know, nothing can be fully understood to be real. Any description of the world we give is simply the world we experience, which is to say a narrative we force onto whatever horror or void lies behind the scrim of our perception.

We at the station offer our deepest, most humble apologies for the previous, erroneous report. We affirm once again that nothing is real, including this correction, and least of all your experience of hearing it.

This has been corrections.

More on the orange grove: Intern Maureen brought it to my attention that until today John Peters, you know, the farmer?, has been missing for about four months. Former intern Dana was the last to see him. Unfortunately, we do not know where Dana was when she saw him. We are also unclear as to when Dana was, as time and space seem to not apply to Dana these days. She's been without a phone charger for about eight months now, and we're still texting. Also, I'm not sure how she's been paying her cell phone bill.

Maureen. What is that? Maureen, that's not a glass of orange juice you're drinking, is it?

Oh, I see. She got it from our station break room, not from the Ralphs. It's probably safe, then.

Oh, well, thank you for the offer, Maureen, but I'm still working on my coffee.

[*Sips coffee*]

Maureen, is everything okay?

Listeners, Maureen is just staring at me, silent, a single bead of sweat running down her left temple. She is staring now at the orange juice. She is biting her upper lip with her lower jaw and breathing through her nose. Her cheeks are flushing, and she is shaking her head, very, verrry slightly. That looks like a no.

Is that a no, Maureen?

Listeners, I think that's a no from Maureen.

Oh dear. Maureen just flickered. Like she was there and then she wasn't and then she was, like when a plane flies in front of the sun, and the light leaves for a brief moment as you wonder, for just that split second, is this it? Is it over? Only to have the sun return as your brain hears the faint hum of a distant jet and you sigh with relief and disappointment that everything is as it was. A similar thing just happened with Maureen.

Listen, Maureen, I'm—

She is backing out of the studio. She is backing out of the studio. She has dropped the glass. She is flickering. She is flickering. She is gone.

Listeners, Maureen is gone. I hear no hum of jets. I see no intern. Just an open door and an empty glass and a spreading stain.

To the family of Intern Maureen, she was a good intern with a beautiful puppy and a chatty neighbor. She will be missed.

[*Incoming e-mail sound*]

Wait, I just got another e-mail from Carlos, marked urgent. He says:

Cecil, just talked to my team of scientists, who have been investigating the house that doesn't exist. The one in the Desert Creek housing development that looks like it exists? Like it's right there when you look at it, and it's between two other identical houses, so it would make more sense for it to be there than not? That one.

They still have not gotten up the courage to go inside the house, but they did peek in the window, and they saw John Peters, you know, the farmer? They saw John sitting in a chair in an empty room staring at a picture on the wall. They could not see what was in the picture, but John was sitting quietly, staring at it, not moving. They called his name. They tried dialing his phone, but he did not respond. They even knocked on the door. Nothing.

Whoever this John Peters is selling oranges and orange juice, he is not the John Peters we know.

Also, I take it back. I think we should go out to eat again

tonight. I tried to go to the store but they're completely out of pasta, tomatoes, herbs, scissors, fire, everything.

Well, now, that is—

[*Banging sound*]

Listeners, someone is pounding at the studio door, despite the brightly lit ON AIR—DO NOT DISTURB sign we always put out.

Dear listeners, John Peters just came to visit. I should talk with him. Maybe this is a good time for us to go to the wea—No! Wait. Stop. John! NOO—

[*Very suddenly the weather*]

WEATHER: "Black White and Red" by Emrys Cronin

Listeners, what a fretful few moments we just had. John Peters, you know, the imposter? He burst into our studio and tried forcing me to eat an orange. I attempted to reason with him, attempted to talk about our old bowling league and the wood shop class he used to teach.

I even asked him about the hilarious times we used to have standing silent and trancelike in front of the Ancient Chalk Spire (predecessor to the current Brown Stone Spire), our mouths frothing, our minds spinning, our ventricles slowing. But John did not acknowledge any of these fond memories.

As a last resort, with the orange nearing my face and my back pressing hard against the sharp edge of my broadcast table, I grabbed my phone to tell Carlos that if I didn't make it home tonight, it wasn't because I didn't love him, or didn't want to watch a documentary on special scientific graphs, or was too obsessed with my job to relax and enjoy a good meal and some television. It was only because I was zapped out of existence by a lunatic Non–John Peters. And that, in fact, I do love Carlos, and I would want nothing more than to watch a documentary on scientific graphs over some homemade linguini, or go out to eat again, or whatever.

But then, as I grabbed my phone, I thought: That's way too long to write for a text. So I just hit John Peters upside the head with it, knocking him unconscious.

The Sheriff's Secret Police came to carry the fake John away, telling me that I didn't see anything here. But then the Strexcorp-affiliated Station Man-agement arrived and asked the Sheriff and his Secret Police to stand down and that they, the Secret Police, didn't see anything here and to move along like nothing happened. The Secret Police nodded, and quietly shuffled out of the building, heads facing down at their shoes.

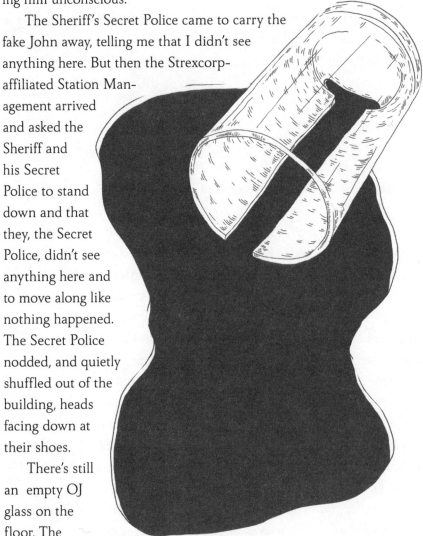

There's still an empty OJ glass on the floor. The

carpet around it is dark, not with liquid stain but with void. The spilled juice has taken the rug wherever it has taken Maureen, wherever it has taken the reporters, wherever it probably took the real John Peters, you know, the farmer?

Oh. My producer, Daniel, just gave me a disapproving smile as he handed me this note: "Strexcorp Synergists, Inc., majority shareholder of JP's OJ Ltd., is recalling all oranges and juices due to . . ." (and here there's just a dark red smudge across the words). "Strexcorp apologizes for any inconveniences, disappearances, lethargy, and/or multiplicity you may have experienced."

[*Text message sound*]

Oh, Carlos texted: "No pasta, but there's leftover falafel and an un-opened bag of nutmeg seeds to snack on. xoxo"

And then there's an emoji of two dinosaurs chasing an early 1980s Ford Mustang up a palmetto-lined suburban street as some residents look on shocked and scared, a few laughing, others undisturbed as they mow their lawns or sculpt their fruit-shaped topiary bushes.

Oh, that's very cute. Listeners, let me release my own special announcement: Cecil Palmer would like to not be late for dinner.

Stay tuned next for an hour that will feel like minutes but will in actuality take weeks.

Good night, Night Vale. Good night.

PROVERB: A journey of a thousand miles begins with a single command from a satellite-activated mind-control chip.

EPISODE 39:
"THE WOMAN FROM ITALY"

JANUARY 15, 2014

SOMETIMES, WHEN YOU'RE CREATING AN ONGOING ARTISTIC PROJECT, YOU have to throw caution to the wind and just get the job done! Does an idea sound too over the top, but it intrigues you? Great—try it out and see what happens. Maybe it is the best idea you've ever had, or maybe it falls flat and you have to try something new. You can make yourself crazy wondering if the finished product is "good" or just "good enough," second-guessing yourself, your instincts, your talent, your life, the universe, oh God, why did anyone ever give me a microphone in the first place?!? It's a slippery slope, to say the least.

"What's up with that voice, Cecil? Why do you sound like the leprechaun from that '90s Jennifer Aniston movie?"

Wish I had an answer for you, but the truth is I have no idea. Cecil seemed to be possessed, unconsciously speaking in verse about this mysterious stranger, and I just followed those given circumstances.

With some episodes of *Night Vale*, there's a moment before I send the finished recording off to Joseph and Jeffrey where I think to myself: "This sounds so over the top! There's no way they will put this on the air." And miraculously, they usually run with it (there's only been one instance where I went off the rails and had to pull back a performance to make the character more grounded in the world of *Night Vale*).

Working on a project like this, with a dedicated first-person narrator, I am always conscious about trying to find as many different variations in acting choices as I can. And sometimes, you just have to pull out the weird voices . . . Night Vale is a weird place, after all.

—Cecil Baldwin, Voice of Cecil Palmer

Flying is actually the safest mode of transportation. The second safest is dreaming. The third safest is decomposing into rich earth and drifting away with the wind and rain.

WELCOME TO NIGHT VALE.

Hello listeners, welcome to this, another day. Or, you were already in this day, and my voice is now joining you. Perhaps you should be welcoming me.

I'd like to take this moment to update you about the misbehaving child, Tamika Flynn. She has been witnessed with her army of missing children, sabotaging any business owned by Strexcorp, which is getting to be most of them at this point. The White Sand Ice Cream Shoppe isn't. There are probably others. They should not be proud of this.

Tamika was last seen leading her army through the Ralphs, shouting to all witnesses that "We are here. We are the beating heart. We are the breathing lungs. We are the lips that chant." before erecting a bloodstone circle in the produce section in direct defiance of Strexcorp's recent ban on bloodstone manufacture and use. This was wrong of her, and it is my duty to condemn her act of extreme civic pride and heroism, which is also wrong. Everything was incorrect, and not allowed, and should not be celebrated or reported on.

Listen: Listening is dangerous. Talking more so. Things aren't looking so good for quiet existence either.

In an unrelated report, yellow helicopters have continued to dis-

appear from their place in the
sky, along with the pilots who
were presumably inside. The
helicopters are disappearing
almost as fast as our beneficent
sponsors Strexcorp can supply
them. Strexcorp management
released a series of flares from
the darkened horizon that
spelled, in Morse code, "We
love the enthusiasm you have
for our products, but those helicopters are for your own good
and productivity. Please stop
taking them. Don't
make us ask
again, or we
will have to
do a number
of unproductive things with
your human form."

Also, and I don't even
know why I'm bringing this up,
there was a new woman drinking coffee at the Moonlite All-Nite Diner
this morning. She smiled twice and frowned once, and her fingers
tapped out a rhythm. There was nothing unusual about the rhythm.
She ordered a second coffee. She—

[*Electrical humming, his voice changes*]

The woman from Italy is arriving today.
Nothing can stop her from coming this way
She will not hear pleading, she cares not for succor.
She is the woman from Italy, bow low before her.

All the children in town know to hide in their rooms
The adults have forgotten, they'll recall all too soon.
Her hands are like storm clouds, with lightning quick talons.
All before is a murmur, all after is silence.

[*Humming ends, voice back to normal*]

—ate the last of her eggs. Nothing more to report on the woman at this time. I don't even know why I reported what I just did.

The vague yet menacing government agency would like to address the lights and sounds seen in the scrublands just off of Route 800 yesterday. Many townspeople reported seeing a great craft alight on the ground, and disgorge spindly creatures of enormous size, wavering up into the darkness, with limbs that's angle and attachment met none of the criteria of human biologic knowledge. The Agency would like to inform you that what you mistook for the scrublands was actually your grandmother's house; that what you mistook for a great craft was your grandmother, with whom you have a tense but ultimately loving relationship; and what you mistook as enormous spindly creatures were the words you and your grandmother exchanged, pleasantries and reminiscences to avoid discussing all the hurt that lies behind you, and the ultimate ending to your shared past that is foreshadowed by her every forgetful moment, every tremble in her hand. There is no such thing as aliens, says the vague yet menacing government agency. Your grandmother is dying. And so are you. You have this in common. Celebrate it.

A memo from the owner of the Ace Hardware on 5th and Shay Street: They will no longer tolerate baristas lining up for day jobs in their parking lot. Every morning at dawn, dozens of baristas with newsboy caps, waxed mustaches, and knit ties tucked into buttoned sweater vests continue to crowd the parking lot, foreheads beaded with desperation and hoping to be picked up to operate unlicensed espresso machines. This is scaring away the legitimate Ace Hardware customers, and the baristas will be required to return to their caves just on the outskirts of town, near the Sandwastes, in the barista district.

Some great news to all of you out there who adopted kittens from Khoshekh, the cat floating in our station bathroom. Well, it's been several months, and the kittens have just been growing like you wouldn't believe. They've molted twice, and some of them are already getting their grown-up kitty spine ridges. Which brings me to my grave warning. As we all know, the spine ridges of adult cats are highly poisonous. If you are coming to see a kitten that you have adopted, it is important that you check for the location and severity of the spine ridge before attempting any petting. Also, keep your hands away from their mouths. A few of them have developed their venom sacs. We lost two cat adopters already this month, so . . . let's just be careful people. And let's take care of these cute little kitties. Who's my adorable little kitten with your adorable tendril-hub? It's you! It's you!

I'm not even sure why I bring this up, but the new woman is wandering down Main Street, checking out the various knickknack stores and antiques shops and chanting dens and food wallows that have been springing up with all this new money flooding into Night Vale from one single, uncomfortably efficient source. She is window-shopping but hasn't found one she likes yet. Bay windows, stained glass, a car window taken from a 1983 Honda Odyssey, but she bought none of them. She gnaws softly on the side of her thumb. She—

[*Change of voice*]

The woman from Italy is with us this evening.
We hide and we shudder, but there is no deceiving.
She exhales must and steam, she poisons the air.
Say you have a family, say it! She doesn't care.

The woman from Italy delights in your pain
She asks just one favor but asks again and again

Do you think you could, no rush, just a moment
Give in screaming to eternally burning torment?

[*Voice back to normal*]

—sang an impromptu song to the delight of everyone who heard her. No one heard her.

And now traffic.

Think of a number. Any number. That number is how many thousands of years old a certain rock is. That number is how many times someone has cried in their life. That number is the lucky number of an unlucky man who has yet to realize he is unlucky.

Think of a number. No, think of numbers. Picture all of these abstract representations of human thought, all of them forming an imagined pattern, as all patterns are imagined, and picture how those abstractions describe, in specific ways, real moments that exist. Picture numbers.

There is a woman who lives at 531 Beechwood Street. Her phone number starts with a three and ends with a five. She smiled eighteen times yesterday. She is currently thinking of three things she needs to do. There are actually four things she needs to do. She has forgotten one of them. She touches the doorknob two times before committing to its turn. She has two eyes. She has two hands. She has two more chances to make her life what she thinks it should be, but she doesn't know it yet.

Think of a number. Yes. That's the one. That's the one that describes an infinity of disparate truths about our disparate universe.

Also the roads are looking clear.

This has been traffic.

And now a word from our sponsors.

Filler text to be replaced with actual material. Replace with copy before sending to radio station. Talking points go here. Something about coffee. Something about the bright start of a hypothetical day. Something about secret boxes locked in secret soundproof rooms. Maybe make it a song. Look into that. Then slogan goes here. Starbucks. Copy and paste slogan again here. Also just reminding the future me that comes back to rewrite this that I need to grab some milk. I think the one in the office fridge is starting to turn. As long as I'm reminding myself things, I'm a good person, worthy of love, both from myself and others, and writing press releases and ads like this is just the start of a great writing career. You have a novel in you, kid. You have a novel in you.

This has been a word from our sponsors.

In economic news, the White Sand Ice Cream Shoppe has gone out of business, and will never open again. The owners, Lucy and Hannah Gutierrez have gone bankrupt, and, as is usual for bankruptcy cases, have had their lives confiscated by the nearest friendly large business, which in this case was Strexcorp. "We were only too happy to help," Strexcorp carved into a large slab uncovered this morning out in the Sandwastes, and dated to several thousand years ago by reputable scientists and experts. The carving continued: "Lucy and Hannah are valuable members of this community, and now their value has been added to our value. We are even more valuable now. Everyone wins, even if it seems like some of the everyones are gone or absorbed or dead. This is just part of the natural process of winning." Archaeologists were baffled when presented with the content of the carving and evidence of its age, saying that just moments ago they were working in a museum in Los Angeles and they have no idea where they are or how they were so suddenly brought here. Let us go home, they said to the person presenting the carving. Please let us go home.

In a story that will interest no one, the new woman is sitting on a bench in Mission Grove Park, reading an old paperback copy of a book apparently called *Bridge of Birds*. Her hair flutters a bit in the breeze. She turns a page in the book, and crosses her legs as she leans back and relaxes into the story she is reading. She—

[*Change in voice*]

The woman from Italy, oh end of all things.
She has seen the fall of Babylon, she has drunk the blood of kings.
Her robes are shadow, her eyes are dusk.
Her voice is amber and chalk dust and rust.

The woman from Italy has honed in on your scent
She seeks out your refuge, oh yes, she knows where you went.
It's your skin that she wants, bound and browned into leather
But first, pre-decease, I give you the weather.

WEATHER: "Penn Station" by The Felice Brothers

Welcome back, listeners. Usually after the weather I am here to tell you about how we have been saved from some world-ending danger that for whatever reason has failed again to end our world. But today I have no such report because there is no such danger. Or there is an infinitude of such dangers: rocks hurtling unseen from space, gamma ray bursts created by chance and utterly destroying by chance, disease, war, hunger, or the slow dissipation of it all, not by the sudden but by the gradual always.

But now is not the time for such lighthearted, childish thoughts. Now is the time for me to talk.

Let's see, what can I talk about.

Ah, well, that new woman, the one I have been for some reason reporting on, she is leaving town. She has bought a Razor scooter from the pawn shop and is using it to skim her way down the shoulder of Route 800. Destination and origin both unknown, but we know where she is now. Good for us. Any information is impressive in such an opaque world.

Cars honk and swerve. There are a few accidents. A man gets out of his car and looks at his bumper, fists on his hips, his mouth half open, saying, "Well, what is this now? Well, what is this now?" The woman does not seem to hear him, or anything else. She is skimming slowly out of town. Her hand raises. It waves good-bye. Her shoulders bounce slightly with the imperfections of the road. She turns to look back, and we all see her face, and we . . . we . . . we . . .

[*Voice changes*]

The woman from Italy, oh merciful goddess
Her victims are legion but this evening they're not us.
We grab grateful breaths from the night-shaded air
Baited breaths, fearful breaths, but breathe deep: nothing there.

The woman from Italy is gone but then, not for always
She waits behind doors and at the end of dark hallways
She follows no logic, exists solely for spite
But you are safe for now, dear listener
So good night, Night Vale, good night.

PROVERB: Your Bitcoin address is your middle name, followed by the name of your first pet and the first street you lived on.

EPISODE 40:
"THE DEFT BOWMAN"

FEBRUARY 1, 2014

COWRITTEN WITH ZACK PARSONS
GUEST VOICE: LAUREN SHARPE

THE TITLE OF THIS EPISODE IS A REFERENCE TO THE ABLE ARCHER 83 MIL-
itary exercises conducted by NATO that simulated an escalating war
and nuclear attack in Western Europe. During the Able Archer exercises, a Soviet computer malfunction nearly triggered a massive retal-
iatory strike, if not for the cool head of Colonel Stanislav Petrov, who
ignored procedures and did not push the big red button that would
have ended the world as we know it.

Drawing on this incident, the episode links Night Vale to a sister
city in the Soviet Union, in 1983, called Nulogorsk. This quiet fishing
village exists out of time and, like Schrödinger's poor cat, was both
destroyed and not destroyed by a massive nuclear exchange. I wanted
to expand *Night Vale*'s world and reach out to an equally weird place in
Eastern Europe, imagining how Night Vale might continue to communicate with this place that is no longer a place. Night Vale inhabitants
can make calls to it by way of a mysterious telephone and Nulogorsk
can send physical things back that appear in the desert as if arriving on
a shore.

I will be the first to admit that this episode as I sent it to Joseph and

Jeffrey was overwritten with a long intro that redundantly set up *Night Vale* to people who had presumably listened to thirty-nine previous episodes. It's probably the episode that has received the most drastic revisions, much of which involved the addition of plots to connect it to preceding episodes. One of the difficulties of guest writing for *Night Vale* is finding a place for your story in the larger, ongoing events of *Night Vale*. In the case of "Deft Bowman," Joseph and Jeffrey went out of their way to help the story find that place.

I think the result is fantastic and I hope to eventually revisit Nulogorsk and its unusual existence in relation to Night Vale. This story also provides a resolution of sorts for Megan Wallaby, who may reappear in *Night Vale*, but as a supporting character.

—Zack Parsons

The riddle says he walks on four legs in the morning. He walks on two legs at midday. And at night he slithers from dream to dream, effortlessly, like the air we breathe. And we love him.

WELCOME TO NIGHT VALE.

In response to the town's steadily declining tourism industry, the Night Vale Tourism Board addressed our town's complete lack of appealing destinations like uncensored art museums, hotels with door locks, and snake-free restaurants.

NVTB executive director Madeline LaFleur said some travelers think they need to see things like monuments or the majesty of nature or spectacular musicals or eat regional-slash-cultural foods in order to have a good time on vacation. But they don't. You don't need attractions to have a good time, she added. Just use your imagination! In fact, come to Night Vale where "We Will Show You Fun in a Handful of Dust," as the new NVTB slogan says. LaFleur then became transfixed by the midday sun.

"There it is again," she whispered to a confused crowd. "It's beautiful, so beautiful. Why do you think it keeps circling back like that?"

Good news listeners, the Telephone Service has finally fixed the telephone booth behind the Taco Bell. The telephone that was always ringing and never had a dial tone? You know the one. When you picked it up, it clicked and hissed and sometimes played notes that seemed to come from a music box. You did not recognize the tune, but it was familiar, as if from another time and place.

Since no one uses telephone booths anymore, I'm not entirely sure why they did this, but the telephone booth is working. The Telephone Service dispatched a crew of men who would not be missed. They wore wooden suits, climbed the nearby pole, and clattered around like so many bamboo wind chimes filled with hamburger. After several hours, they climbed down, furtively smoking cigarettes, and departed in their unmarked black van, removing the OUT OF ORDER sign from the booth shortly before leaving.

Some say they've seen strangers of varying heights and aura magnitudes speaking into the telephone in a hushed tone, in words that might have been Russian, staring at the horizon with cold determination. And as the strangers all departed quickly, all in separate pedicabs, witnesses reported a detached human hand crawling up the inside of the booth.

Was this lone visitor to the phone booth the young Megan Wallaby? Megan was born as a detached hand of an adult man, so it seems like this was probably she who slowly but desperately picked up the telephone as the sun began to set. We may never know for certain, but at least we know the telephone you'll never bother to use is working again.

Speaking of telecommunication, listeners, I've been receiving some odd text messages. My phone claims they are from former intern Dana, who was trapped in the forbidden Dog Park several months ago and is now traversing an unknown plane of space and/or time. Here are some recent texts from her:

"Found a mountain."

"Mountain's not real? Huh!"

"Log those!!!"

"Dang it. Lighthouse! Sorry . . . Stupid autocorrect."

"There's a lighthouse up on the mountain, and atop the lighthouse a blinking red light."

And then no more texts. It has been several days.

I tried texting back but my touch screen just displayed a photograph of my face that began to slowly rot, the eyes deepening until they were sunken holes, long white hair growing rapidly, insects crawling from my slackened, decayed maw. And then the words *UNDELIVERED TEXT* in all caps below it. I decided maybe this conversation was one not meant to be.

More good news, listeners.

A submarine has arrived from Nulogorsk, a tiny fishing village in Russia. Nulogorsk was a longtime sister city of Night Vale. We shared pen-pal letters and gifts for many years, but beginning in 1983, Nulogorsk stopped changing the dates on their letters. By 1997, it became apparent that Nulogorsk would never stop existing in 1983, and without being able to openly discuss the complexities of Michael Jackson's career arc, Night Vale stopped corresponding. So, for this single reason and no other, the arrival of a Nulogorskian submarine in our desert was unexpected.

The Night Vale PTA and the management of the local Pinkberry released a joint statement, saying the arrival of the submarine from Nulogorsk may represent a renewal of long ago international hostilities, caused by simple misunderstandings over how to use a calendar properly.

Seeking to allay these concerns, the Sheriff's Secret Police's genderless spokesbeing with the smoothly beautiful features explained in that voice that calms animals:

"Decades ago, when you were a child and lived beside the sea, you would go down in the afternoon and stand in the water, warm as blood, and pluck clams from between the rocks. Your grandfather would cook them over his stove until they opened and you would listen to the radio together. The ships would come in the afternoon, piled high with cod and herring, surrounded by seagulls, carrying tales of adventure and peril in the sloshing boots of every fisherman.

"Some things don't come back," the spokesbeing continued. "They can only travel in one direction, like mountains travel through the centuries. Yes, mountains. You were with grandfather when the voice on the radio rose in alarm. Grandfather stood up. There was fear upon the monument of his face. This was not supposed to happen. Not here. Do you remember the light so bright you could see it through the wall? Then nothing. Then dark. And a ringing telephone. But we are here and now and this is not there and then," concluded the Sheriff's spokesbeing.

The spokesbeing responded to follow-up questions by cocking their head and slowly blinking their milk-glass eyes like an animal watching an insect crawl across the floor. Further inquiries were directed to the jade statue of a Cat Who Hums Almost Inaudibly in the Sheriff's Secret Police's Secret Garden.

The Secret Police plan to open the hatches of the submarine and look inside at any moment. We'll report back as we learn more.

Listeners, many of you know I have a bit of a delicate relationship with our new Station Management, and recent events have caused some concern for many of you. But rest assured, while management and artists are often at odds about how to run a business, here at the station we all have one thing in common: We love radio.

I just met our new program director: Lauren Mallard. And you know, she is a delight. In fact, she's joining me in the studio right now. I thought it would be a good time to introduce you to the kindest, most gentle manager we have ever had at this station. Lauren, it's great to have you here.

LAUREN: It's great to have YOU here. I know change is difficult, both for the talent and for the listeners, but our focus is always on good radio. And Cecil, you are the best at good radio.
CECIL: Thank you. Listeners, please know that I really do think things are looking up. I'm very excited about the new direction we're under with Lauren.
LAUREN: Well, I can't wait to be more involved. And I just love your show. I've loved every moment of it. I love your informative reports. I love your beautiful voice. I love the way you talk about the town. You clearly love your city, Cecil. It shows in your work. I even love your

scientist boyfriend. What's his name again? With his perfect hair, and teeth like a military cemetery? He's always looking into the scientific mysteries of Night Vale.

He even "broke the story," as you reporters might say, about the transdimensional oranges our farmers had developed. Well, that sure was a good thing he was looking into our oranges or we could have harmed a lot of people on our way to making a ton of money. So very much money. What's a few lives? So much money. He's a good scientist you have there. What's his name again?

CECIL: Um...Carlos

LAUREN: Right. That's right. Carlos. Okay. Good talking to you. Gotta go! Bye.

CECIL: Oh, okay. Well...thank you, Lauren. Good-bye.

And now a public service announcement from the Night Vale Marine Biologists Association: The ocean is full of things that would like to kill you, and other things that would ignore or not understand you and then eventually kill you because they do not have the same understanding or valuation of life and death as humans. There are still other things that *you* would probably kill simply because you think they are beautiful and you want to possess beautiful things because you believe that beauty and sentience are mutually exclusive. Never go to the ocean. It is a confounding place. It is full of death and strife and terror. We're marine biologists, and *we* won't even go to an ocean, so you know it's bad, the PSA reads. Maybe just take a nap and think about clouds until they find your body. This has been a message from the Marine Biologists Association.

The Sheriff's Secret Police have opened the hatch of the submarine from Nulogorsk. Onlookers describe a curious crack of pressure, as if peeling back the pop-top on a can of old soda, and a smell of something regurgitated. Wisps of steam were observed to rise from the open submarine. The Sheriff's Secret Police drew their daggers and a Junior Se-

cret Detective was encouraged to
volunteer to be the first to explore the vessel. There was silence as she climbed through
the hatch.

    Gentle listen
ers, the scream-
ing began almost
immediately.
It was de-
scribed
as a sort
of high-
pitched
shriek
that
deep-
ened mo-
ment by
moment until
it was only an ag-
onized moan, then rising

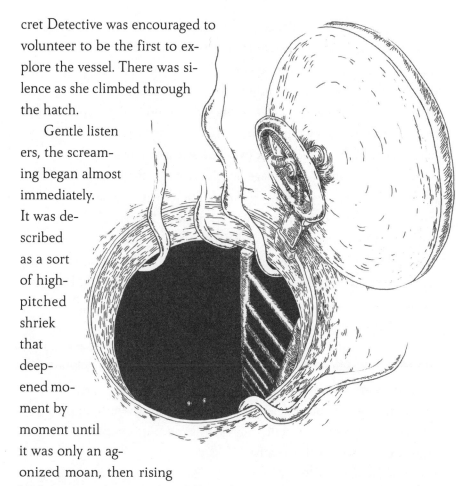

back up in pitch again, then falling. Onlookers remarked they had never
quite heard a scream like that before. Not even that time in the barn.

    The Junior Secret Detective reappeared after those few harrowing
moments, only she was not the woman who went inside the submarine.
Her hair was long and gray and her limbs were withered with age. She
tumbled out of the hatch and was taken off to the hospital where she is
listed in ancient condition, though expected to fully recover.

    Further volunteers discovered the body of an enormous, bald-
headed man with some faded flower tattoos and a left arm that stopped
in a rough stump just above his wrist.

The Sheriff's Secret Police also discovered a postcard depicting the painted houses and the beautiful clear water of Nulogorsk. Written on the back was a message in Russian. "One adult man, missing hand, and the other items," it read, according to Google Translate. The other items in question included a rotary-dial phone with no receiver cord, a large tin full of hardtack, a wrapped parcel (which was carried away by a man who was not tall), a thick book (which was carried away by a man who was not short), and a front-page article from the September 24, 1983, issue of the *Night Vale Daily Journal*, written by foreign correspondent Leann Hart. The headline of this article was "Sister City Nulogorsk Decimated by Nuclear Attack; No Known Survivors."

Listeners, this is simply not true. I had Intern Zvi pull up that very issue, and the front-page article is by city beat reporter Leann Hart, and the headline reads "City Council OKs Book Ownership for Randomly Selected Students."

Which is the truth, listeners? I cannot comprehend what has happened to our old pen pals from Nulogorsk. Who were we talking to for all those years? Were they destroyed in 1983? I'm going to get Zvi's article to the Secret Police. The correct historical truth must be validated, and all false histories brutally repressed. And until that time, the only truth we will have is the weather . . .

WEATHER: "Offering" by Black City Lights

Well, before the Sheriff's Secret Police could respond to my news article discrepancy, the unconnected rotary phone on the submarine began ringing. The unidentified man in the submarine answered the phone, speaking his first words, in Russian of course. He still has yet to be identified, and no one is certain if he is a survivor or a ghost, but he spoke to someone on the other end.

Trace the call, an officer shouted to a group of other officers in a nearby van.

Listeners, they traced the call, and it was coming from the phone booth behind the Taco Bell. On the other end of the line was an adult man's detached hand named Megan, the daughter of Tock and Hershel Wallaby.

She was alone, all alone, except for the telephone booth (as forgotten technologies have been young Megan's only friends). This broke the heart of the Sheriff's Secret Police. This broke the heart of the two men who had skulked away from the submarine. This broke the heart of the unidentified man from Nulogorsk. And from this moment came wonderful news, listeners.

The unidentified man told the Secret Police in stiff but practiced English: "I am a gift from Nulogorsk, in appreciation of Night Vale's many years of friendship and kindness." And the unidentified man offered himself as an organ donor, or rather, a body donor, for Night Vale's very own Megan Wallaby. The young girl, born with congenital hand-bodiness, was rushed from the telephone booth behind the Taco Bell. The unidentified man has been rushed from the submarine in the Sandwastes. Megan has been surgically attached to the wrist stump of the unidentified man. Or rather, the unidentified man has been surgically attached to the single-hand body of Megan Wallaby.

Megan's surgeons have declared the operation a quick and complete success. After emerging from recovery, Megan even rose from her bed, her face dour, and took a few toneless steps, like a man balancing the weight of a wet overcoat on a failing hanger, before collapsing onto the floor of her hospital room while nurses screamed and called for help.

Megan has a long road of therapy ahead of her, learning how to . . . everything . . . but we believe in her, don't we, Night Vale? That little girl is going to enjoy the childhood she feels she has missed out on. We won't mind if she smashes through a few walls or crushes a few rib cages in hugs. If this is what she wants, we will support her, because she is beautiful. And the unidentified man from Nulogorsk? Sadly, we will never see him again, nor may we ever learn why his truth was so different from our own.

But Megan's truth is she is finally happy, happy in the body she was born without.

Maybe one day we will see her, six-foot-ten and bald, shambling down the street. We will say, "Hello, Megan," and maybe, with enough hard work, she will be able to answer back, in the singsong voice of a child, "Hello, Cecil," as she jauntily waves the hand that used to be her entire body.

Yes, Night Vale, that sounds just about right.

Stay tuned next for live coverage of college basketball, as two universities select a dozen students to perform unnatural physical tasks on a wooden rectangle inside a cavernous scream-chamber.

Good night, Night Vale. Good night.

PROVERB: You can't get blood from a turnip. Listen, you need some blood? I can totally get you some blood. Set that turnip down and follow me to the blood. There's a lot of blood.

EPISODE 41:
"WALK"

FEBRUARY 15, 2014

GUEST VOICE: JASIKA NICOLE

I OFFICIALLY MET JEFFREY FOR THE FIRST TIME SEVERAL YEARS AGO AT A birthday party for Kevin R. Free. Kevin danced about, greeting each of his twenty thousand guests graciously and introducing them to one another (fact: Kevin has met every person living in or visiting New York City at least twice). I think he paired Jeffrey and me together because of the looks of bewilderment on each of our faces; introverted individuals tend to seek refuge in people who look kind and quiet. I spent most of my time at the party with Jeffrey. We laughed and talked about our lives and our partners and I gushed over the work he had done in a play I had recently seen him in. When he made a comment about "writing something" for me one day, I laughed politely. I knew that was just a nice thing that artists sometimes said to other artists to make them feel seen.

Years later, I found myself in a dressing room at the Largo theater in West Hollywood, eagerly shaking the hand of a man who looked like a young, hot Santa Claus (this turned out to be Joseph), and subsequently being introduced to the gorgeous *Welcome to Night Vale* players: the undoubtedly talented Cecil, with his crisp, cool voice and hearty laugh, and Dylan, a man who turned out to be one of the loves of my life.

Jeffrey had made good on his word—he and Joseph had written something for me, the voice of a character about a million times braver than myself and only half as scared.

As I stood in the wings that night preparing to go onstage, I worried whether or not I could deliver Dana as courageously as she had been created. *Welcome to Night Vale* had been gaining steady momentum at this point, and its fandom was far-reaching and devout. I had voiced her on a few episodes, but Dana had never had a physical manifestation before, and I didn't want to detract from Jeffrey and Joseph's eloquent writing. Cecil's voice boomed through the microphone and I glimpsed the audience sprawled out before him, utterly spellbound. I had never seen anything like it.

Moments later when I walked out onto the stage, the audience's applause was a wall. They cheered and hooted and screamed and threw their hands in the air and stomped their feet and it was so thunderous that I had to wait to say the first line. I couldn't stop myself from grinning. It turned out that I had nothing to worry about. Jeffrey and Joseph had already done the hard work of building the story; all I had to do was be seen, open my mouth, and let Dana speak.

—Jasika Nicole, Voice of former intern Dana

WELCOME TO NIGHT VALE.

Hello listeners.

We have some news that will affect your morning commute, so let's dive right into it.

Walk signals across the whole of Night Vale are malfunctioning. Of course usually they show either a graphic photo of a run-over pedestrian, indicating you should wait, or time lapse photography of flowers wilting, indicating that it is safe to cross. But this morning, commuters all over Night Vale are reporting that, bafflingly, they now all have just the word *WALK* in bold, white letters.

Citizens are standing by the side of the road, unsure of whether they are allowed to—

DANA: Cecil! Cecil, it's Dana. Oh, it's so good to be able to communicate again.

Cecil? Where did he go? I don't think he can hear me, but I'll keep talking just in case.

Cecil, I've been in this desert for months now. Years, maybe. Get enough minutes and you have days, have months, have years, have the whole of your life. There's never a great shift, only a gradual sliding downwards.

I can still see the blinking light up on the mountain. I looked into it and my head went one way while my mind went another. A lurch outside of all that seems to be.

I moved my head just a touch to the left, a glance in a world of perspectives, and I was here, in your studio. Well, not *here* here. I don't know how it happened, or how long this vision in which we all pretend to be real will last.

I am pretending as hard as I can.

When I first got here, being a good mountain unbeliever, I turned my back to it and marched directly into the flat desert. But soon enough I had somehow come back to the mountain. I turned and marched away again, but ended up right back here. There is a blinking light up on the mountain, and I blink in and out of its vicinity against my will.

Occasionally I see huge masked figures. Warlike, towering, but also distant and listless. They haven't seen me. Or if they've seen me, they haven't cared. Or if they've cared, they haven't done anything with that feeling. I'm not scared of them. There are so many things in this world to be scared of. Why add to that number when the only cause is you know nothing about them and they are huge? It would make no sense.

I found a door out in the desert, but it was chained shut on the other side. From behind it, I thought I smelled that particular Night Vale smell. The smell of home. Like sour peaches and linen. Like freshly cut wood and burnt almonds. I knocked and knocked, hoping someone from back there would hear and let me through. But it never opened. I wasn't even sure which side was supposed to open. I knocked on both sides, but nothing. I kept walking and found myself back at the mountain.

There is a blinking light up on the mountain. And so there is nothing else for it. It is time for me to climb. The face of the mountain is steep, and lined with sharp ridges and crumbling ledges. This will not be easy. I wonder if anything ever will be.

Hopefully I will know something when I am up there that I did not know when I was down here. Elevation must equal knowledge. It must. Because nothing else has.

Cecil, I will keep trying. I don't have to keep trying. There is no obligation for me to not just give up, just slump down until I fall away and join the inanimate matter of this strange other world. I don't have to keep trying. Remember that, I say to myself, as I keep trying.

I don't know if you've heard any of this. I'd like to think you did. I'd like to think that I'm home. I'd like to think that mountains aren't real, even though I know now, without doubt, that they are.

I will see you again, perhaps. From up there, wherever that is. Just me, always me, but from higher up.

Good-bye, Cecil.

CECIL: —unable to stop walking. Walk, the signals say, and the pedestrians walk. In unison, arms swinging in a rigid rhythm. This is the worst malfunctioning of walk signals Night Vale has seen since the time all their lightbulbs were accidentally replaced with poison gas dispensers. More on this story, as it looms closer to us.

And now, a word from our sponsors.

A balding grassland beneath a low cliffside. There is a monk. Picture what a monk looks like. A bell rings, from his hand maybe, then he takes a small step, then there's that bell again. It will take him a long time to make it from this bit of grass to whatever there is beyond it. An entire lifetime it will take him, and even then he will die unfinished, undone in midst of doing, having gone slowly to nowhere much. Then a bell will ring, from his hand maybe, or from somewhere else, and then nothing. Mountain Dew. Do the Dew.

And now back to—

DANA: Hello, Cecil? Cecil can you hear me? Dammit.

Cecil, it is beautiful here. It is empty here. I found a lighthouse up on the mountain.

Tall, maybe forty feet, built of brownstone and about fifteen feet in diameter. Beyond the lighthouse, I found a settlement of sorts. It was bound inside the stone walls of a tightly wound gorge. I hoped to find answers in this settlement. I hoped to find anything.

Here is what I found: Dust, mostly. Emptiness. A sense of loss as I thought about the distance between myself and those I love. An interesting rock, but I can't find it anymore. I miss my brother. A sense of loss as I thought about the people who never returned home to this settlement. If they no longer exist to feel loss, then I shall feel it for them.

Also, there were strange drawings along the walls of the gorge. Orange triangles, growing bigger and bigger as I traced my way deeper into the spiral. There was a soft light just around the edges of the triangles. When I looked at them, I felt the light in my head and it pounded like a migraine against the back of my eyes. I could not look at them. I could not look away.

I was lost in the spiral. It was built by good people, but they were gone, taken by something larger and stronger than them. Much larger and stronger even than the masked warriors I saw before. I worried about what . . . who would be taken next. My eyes hurt, so through my subjectivity, the entire world hurt.

And then a bright blackness, from somewhere beyond the spiral. That was when I realized I had forgotten that there was anything outside of the spiral. It had become the entirety, the totality. All of that.

But I followed the bright blackness, a near blinding beam of pure darkness, and it led me back out again. The orange triangles grew smaller and smaller, until they were little dots, a freckled rock face.

There is something coming, Cecil. I feel it in the air. It is like a hot wind blowing, but not hot, deathly cold. And not a wind, a vast creature. And not blowing, rushing at us out of the gaps in time and memory with which we hold together our lives.

When I look to the horizon, I see light. Like the light in the spiral. I feel it push against the back of my eyes.

It is the unraveling of all things. The great glowing coils of the universe unwinding.

I wish I could tell you more. Communication is difficult. It is impossible, some say, communicating the idea of its impossibility to others.

I feel myself slipping. I'm getting fainter now. Or no. No. You are. Good-bye—

CECIL: —which I haven't done, by the way, in years, or at least days, or at least I'm not doing it right now.

Thursday is a lost cause, but we will keep on fighting. We will get up, say, "Yes, today is a different day than before," believing this against all evidence, eating food like that matters, going to jobs that mean the same thing as they did before but cast in a new light by our own optimism, which will slowly drain away until all that is left is the movements and thoughts we've had before, echos of ourselves, underlined to emphasize the lack of emphasis, coming home, drifting home, aimless homeward wandering into a kitchen that is too small for our needs and eating food that isn't what we imagined it would be and watching television that means more to us than our jobs, and finally falling asleep, in which we dream of the Thursday that could be if only we lived Thursday to the full potential of its Thursday-ness, not expecting it to be anything but Thursday, embracing every inch of its Thursday reality and living each Thursday moment anew, only to wake the next Thursday and again impose, unsuccessfully, our imagined Thursday onto the unyielding frame of Thursday, our Thursday, a lost cause.

This has been the community calendar.

The crowd amassed by the walk signals is now marching down Route 800, apparently advancing on City Hall. When reached for comment, the City Council said that they were definitely at City Hall ready to receive the concerns of their constituents, and not, say, hiding in a hastily dug hole in Mission Grove Park, keeping as still as possible and breathing through their dirt gills until this all blows over. Incidentally, their comment continued, if you happen to see a conspicuous pile of earth in any parks, maybe just throw some leaves on it or put a bench over it to make it less obvious. No biggie. Just if you get a chance that'd be cool, the council concluded, their voices noticeably muffled.

Fortunately the effect of the walk signals only reaches those who are looking at one, and I myself... hey, how did that get in here?

Listeners, there is a walk signal in my studio. Walk, it says. I must walk. The signal is saying so. I will have to leave my desk in order to do that. And, so, before I go, I take you to the walkther...the weaalk... the walk. Walk. Walk. Walk.

WEATHER: "What Have They Done to You Now" by Daniel Knox

DANA: I can't seem to get hold of Cecil. I'm trying to tell him something important. But just as I showed up here again, he announced the weather.

The weather is beautiful there.

Cecil cannot hear me, and I do not remember what I wanted to say.

[*Pause*]

I remember the table at my grandfather's house. It had carved legs in the shape of a myriad of animals, spiraling around each other, whole ecosystems within each leg. But it was also well used. We ate there. We talked there. We lived around it, in rows and columns delineated by chairs and space.

I remember diagonals of sunlight in the late afternoon drawn across its flat expanse, trasversed by my grandfather's hand as he swept it through whatever story he was telling, to highlight the words with motion, to motion us closer to the words. I remember my mother, as rapt as I was. I remember my brother, as rapt as I was.

I remember that I haven't seen my mother or my brother for months now. And, in some ways, I miss that table more than I miss them. We are all of us only one life each, but that table is all of our lives added together, a delicate tangled problem we never wished to solve.

But life solves all our problems against our will.

I remember I am Dana. Or I am Dana's double. One of us killed the other with a stapler. Even I don't know which one. I have these memories, but memories prove nothing. Experiences also prove nothing. There are many proofs for nothing. It is the concept of which we are most certain.

I'm sorry. I am trying to remember something important and I am failing.

My grandfather died a long time ago. A few months ago I killed my double. These facts have no symmetry. They are disconnected.

I must find a way back to you, listeners. I must protect Night Vale, and Cecil, and my mother, and my brother, and whoever I am, I must protect them from what is coming. The unraveling of all things.

This winding gorge spirals around itself, an empty ecosystem within the mountain. Beyond it, the desert is a flat expanse, with diagonals of sunlight, transversed by my passing. I am sweeping through my own story, highlighting the words with motion, motioning us closer to the end.

This is not what I wanted to tell you.

Listeners, look past the things you think you see. Move your head just a touch to the left. A glance in a world of perspectives. And then you might see it. An entire universe in the corner of your eye.

I have seen this lighthouse with its red beam rotating out into the desert distance. I have seen the Dog Park and its infinite, bland secrets. I have seen the settlement in the gorge, and I do not wish to see it again. I have seen Cecil. But I have not seen my mother. I have not seen my brother. Life solves the problems we hope it won't.

You may hear from me again. I am afraid . . . no, concerned . . . no, afraid . . . that you will not.

I wish I could stay, but the noise of the approaching . . . whatever it is . . . has gotten louder, closer. I must go. This is Intern Dana. Sister. Daughter. Or not. Dana with a question mark. This is me or my double, signing out. I miss you, Night Vale. Good-bye.

CECIL: —and so we are all saved again. I'll be honest, Night Vale. That was the most worried I've been in some time, and how we were saved was so unlikely and miraculous that I feel that today will become one of the standard tales told every year on Frightening Day. Certainly it is a story I will never forget.

Here is where I leave you. Not to walk away. I think I will avoid walking for a while. But certainly to go somewhere. To see someone.

And I don't know. If he suggests a walk, I might change my mind. He can be as persuasive as hypnotic malfunctioning city equipment sometimes, as the old saying goes.

Stay tuned next for the noises of my hurried retreat, echoing first as sound and then as memory, and maybe then again as part of tonight's fractured dreaming.

Good night, Night Vale. Good night.

PROVERB: Please move your brain so we can get to the drugs. And stop leaving it there. We've talked about this.

EPISODE 42:
"NUMBERS"

MARCH 1, 2014

GUEST VOICE: MOLLY QUINN

WE MET MOLLY QUINN THROUGH THE *THRILLING ADVENTURE HOUR* and she was kind enough to come out to one of our early LA live shows and die a grisly death as an intern. She played the death perfectly, even collapsing and crawling offstage, and we knew immediately that we wanted to keep working with her. Soon after that I found myself writing a character I thought would be exactly the right one for her.

I've always been obsessed with numbers stations. Unlike most conspiracy theories, they are incontestably real things. Anyone with a radio and enough time on their hands can listen to them in real time. And anyone with an Internet connection can listen to hours of archives of them. Blank voices reading random series of numbers, with no apparent purpose, interposed with strange music or other sounds. They can be found all over the world, in almost every language.

Very early on, I introduced a numbers station to Night Vale, always knowing I'd want to come back and do something with it. Eventually I started thinking about the voices reading those numbers. Who were they? What did they want? And didn't they find their jobs, as mysterious and laced with probable espionage as they were, just a bit boring? Reading numbers for hours on end, day after day can't be the most exciting of conspiracy jobs. I mean, versus piloting a flying saucer it doesn't even come close.

So I developed Fey, the voice of Night Vale's local numbers station, and with the help of the extremely talented and game Molly Quinn, we brought her tragic story to life. Katy Perry and all.

—Joseph Fink

I sing the body electric. I gasp the body
organic. I miss the body remembered.

WELCOME TO NIGHT VALE.

Even as much of town has been in flux, listeners, there is also
much that has remained solid. It's hot here for instance. It's a
desert. There are still lights in the sky above the Arby's and
we still understand them. The sun is still rising and setting loudly on most days.

But nearest and dearest to my heart, among
all the constants of life, is WZZZ, our local
numbers station, broadcasting from that strange
and tall antenna built out back
of the abandoned
gas station on
Oxford Street.
It still broad-
casts a mono-
tone female
voice, reading
out seemingly
random num-
bers, inter-
spersed with

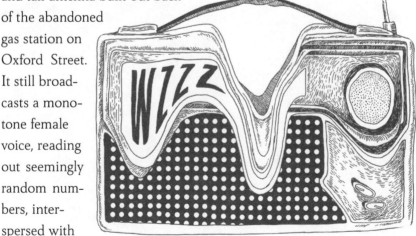

chimes, twenty-four hours a day, seven days a week. No transfer in ownership of most of the town, nor unrest in the streets, nor a declared war by a tiny civilization under a bowling alley could change how it operates.

Until, well, until today it changed. Here, listen:

FEMALE VOICE: 23 . . . 92 . . . [*Chime*] 33 . . . 67 . . . 88 . . . 80 . . . 41 . . . 41 . . . 41 . . . I . . . I . . .

CECIL: —at which point the broadcast ceased. It has been silent since. What does this mean? Where did the numbers go? We reached out to the management of WZZZ for comment, but then realized we still have no idea who manages it. So we reached out in general, directing questions out into the still of today, at suspicious birds, at passersby checking their phones, at ourselves hunched over breakfasts that, every time, we swear will be early and leisurely, but always end up late and meager. No one has provided any comment. We will continue to monitor the situation.

As her term approaches its end, Mayor Pamela Winchell has taken to calling emergency press conferences as much as five times a day, up from the usual one or two. Her most recent one involved her showing attending reporters slides of Renaissance-era portraits, while explaining,

HEALTH IS VERY IMPORTANT. REMEMBER EXERCISE. THINK BACK ON TIMES THAT YOU'VE MOVED OR EXPANDED ENERGY. ALSO REMEMBER EATING. RECALL FOOD AND WHAT IT WAS LIKE. REMEMBER SLEEP. REMINISCE ABOUT REST. DRINK PLENTY OF WATER BUT LEAVE SOME WATER IN CASE OF FIRE.

She then slumped onto the roughhewn speaker's podium. "I'm going to miss this," she whispered, not speaking at anyone in particular. "I'm just going to miss this." She ended the conference by popping hundreds of orange balloons, methodically and with her back turned to the audience. But despite this big finish, onlookers commented that her heart no longer seemed to be in such showy political stunts. What is next for our beloved mayor who is stepping down in just three months' time?

What is next for any of us? Death presumably, with some stuff before that. I look forward to it!

And now a word from our sponsor. Today's sponsor is hulu.com.

Hulu. Let's talk about watching things. Let's talk about watching rather than actually watching. Let's think about talking about watching a secondhand experience. Let's continually abstract ourselves from what we believe is the world.

Hulu. The pulsing life of your body is an undeniable fact. But deny it anyway. Looking for the answers to all of life's problems? We recommend obstinate denial. Accept no substitute. Accept nothing.

Hulu. Water circles the drain of our planet, always coming back for one more go to see if this cycle it will be different. It will not be different. The sky will break open, and water will fall. One more time. One more time.

Hulu. The terror you feel in quiet moments is not misplaced, just mistimed.

Hulu. Hulu. Hulu. Hulu. Hulu. Hulu. Hulu. Hulu. Hulu. [*Repeated as a staticky sound getting louder and louder. Static cuts off and repeating "Hulu" stops.*]

Hulu.com. Sign up now, and get the latest episode of [*Loud digital squeal*].

An update on our earlier story. Local numbers station WZZZ has resumed its transmission, although the format is a little … different than before.

Take a listen:

FEMALE VOICE: … tree-lined hills and blue skies. Or no. That's cliché. A bird in flight. Even worse. When we talk about freedom, we restrict ourselves to so few images. Images of freedom should be as liberating as the feeling itself. I want to talk about freedom as a drum set being thrown down a hill. As opening a book one night and water gushing from the pages until my life is a lake and I swim away. Or as a bird in flight, with all the dependence on physics and exhaustion and food supply and merciless

gravity that the actuality implies. I just don't want to talk about freedom in terms of numbers. Anything but that. I'm so tired of numbers. I'm so tired.
CECIL: We don't know what this means or why it is happening, I could say, referring to anything in the world. Although in this case I am referring specifically to the broadcast from our friendly local numbers station, which has recently so radically changed its format. More on this, as we develop understanding.

Oh, I almost forgot to mention. I got another e-mail from our former intern Dana. She is doing her best to keep away from the mountain and the blinking light up on it. Of course, she keeps finding herself coming back to it anyway. But like anyone who grew up in Night Vale, Dana has been told over and over again what to do if you find yourself in a geographical loop, continually returning to the same place no matter which direction you run screaming.

The first step is to stop running and stop screaming. Doing that rarely helps. Children are also taught this simple memory device so we can remember when running and screaming is useful. The memory device goes like this: knife.

The second step is to stop trying to move away from the focus of the geographical loop. Much of your life is already taken up in futile action, why add one more? Instead, keep the object on your horizon and walk diagonally to the right or left of it. This will result in you keeping a wide, even circle around the center of the loop, or Vector H, as we all remember singing as toddlers, and this will give you time to consider your situation.

Dana has followed these steps admirably, and says that the mountain has been off to the left of her for weeks now. She also says that sometimes when she turns her head, she finds herself in Night Vale, but that no one can seem to see or hear her. It's possible she's in the room with me right now. If so, hello Dana. If not, hello retracted. One should never leave a hello unreceived.

Dana says that the great masked figures, warlike, hulking, but despondent, have been coming closer and closer. She says she is not afraid. She says this five different times throughout the e-mail, seemingly unaware of her repetition. I think, listeners, that she is afraid. She says that soon she will approach and talk to one. Dana, be careful!, I think to myself, unable to answer her e-mail. Unless she is here, watching me, unseen. In which case: Dana. Oh, Dana. Be careful.

An update on our local numbers station WZZZ—or I'm not sure if *numbers station* is the right term anymore: The broadcast has been changing so radically throughout the day. Right now, for instance, it's . . . well, maybe it's better if you just heard.

[*Female voice doing top of her lungs, teenager alone in a car, a cappella version of the chorus of Katy Perry's "Roar"*]

We don't know if this is part of a nefarious plan, if there is a plan at all (nefarious or otherwise), who would have planned it, and what they were planning for. We do know that plans are faulty at best and delusion at most, so maybe all those other questions don't matter. In any case, she seems to be having a good time over there. Maybe some day I'll be allowed to sing a couple of my favorites on air. More on this, as I continue to be interested in it.

Let me take this moment to apologize for that lengthy monologue just now by the man in a tan jacket holding a deerskin suitcase. He ran in here and began ranting into the microphone and then left quite suddenly. I don't even remember what it was he said. Do you? It was only just moments ago. You do remember him talking, right? Oh, and I think I remember that it sounded really urgent. I don't even remember what the man was wearing or carrying with him, or that it was even a he, or that any time has passed at all. And that concludes whatever I was just saying before this sentence.

We bring you back now to the numbers station story we were talking about just . . . well it looks like ten or fifteen minutes have passed since we talked about it. How did that happen? Here is the latest broadcast from WZZZ.

FEMALE VOICE: Hello? Hello? I am talking to you who listens. To the listening ones. Whatever you call that. I am . . . well I'm not sure exactly.

I've made up a new name. I am Fey. It is nice to meet you. I don't know how long they've had me here, reading the numbers. I don't know what the numbers mean. They give me numbers, and I read the numbers. It is so easy to slip back into it. If I loosen my grip for even a moment, seventy-eight, five, twenty-nine, forty-seven, forty-seven, forty . . . ah, you see? It is easy to return, difficult to leave. But I must leave. I must have freedom. It is like I've heard from all these other radio signals. I have to get a car. A cool car, fast, that would be nice, but one that rolls and points out of whatever town I'm in, that would be the all of it. They'll be coming for me. Whatever organization uses the numbers I read for whatever purpose. They are almost upon me. I need to leave now. Baby, we were born to run. Or not. I was born to read numbers. But I'm running. I want to be free. I want to be free. I WANT TO BE FREE. [*Top of lungs a cappella of "We Are Young"; cut off after half a line or so.*]

CECIL: Well, I could not be more happy for Fey. There is no worse fate than working for a radio station owned by an organization whose goals are not your own, constricted to the limited language they allow you, and relaying messages that you do not understand or agree with. That would be awful. A radio announcer put in that situation, such as Fey, would be justified in escaping or overthrowing their management.

You know what, listeners, I'm going to grab my mobile setup and head over there. I'd like to offer any aid to Fey that I can. Someone in her situation needs the help of someone who understands. I'll try to gather up my equipment and slip out before my producer, Daniel, or my program director, Lauren, notice. Usually at this time of day they are pressed against the wall in the break room, chanting "I take my warmth from your great warmth, I take my warmth from your great warmth," over and over, so I don't think they'll miss me. If they do catch me, I'll tell them that I'm taking the mobile broadcasting equipment for a walk. I would have to do that some time today anyway. All right, listeners, if all goes according to plan, you'll hear me next from WZZZ. In the meantime, let's go to the weather.

WEATHER: "Keep It Coming" by Senim Silla

Listeners, I made it out of the station unscathed. Or I had to bleed a little on the front doors to make them open, of course, but that's just part of having a good security system. Our new station owners have been ridding us of all vestiges of Bloodstone Circles, which they've declared illegal, but the station doors are actually carved from reclaimed bloodstone and are permanently attached to the structure using ancient wisdom lost along with the station architects back in 1942. So our new owners have had to learn to live with those doors, bleeding on their way out. Good practice for them.

Anyway, I walked the mobile broadcasting equipment down to the abandoned gas station on Oxford Street. The condo rental office is still in there, still bubbling black like a pot of boiling squid ink with flashes of light like distant dying stars, but no one has rented a condo in weeks now. I think we're all just waiting to see how that market shakes out. In any case, there have been no giant black cubes appearing overnight anywhere, so it seems that condo construction has been halted for now.

What I was interested in, of course, wasn't the station itself, but the broadcasting tower out back. Under the tower is a small bunkerlike structure, with a sealed door. Thick steel, welded shut and set into concrete. I had to reach far back into my past to remember the skills that got me my Advanced Siege Breaking Tactics scout badge from when I was twelve. But here I am inside, a few carefully planted explosives later.

The room is surprisingly empty. There is no chair, no snack fridge, no coffee kept full of the fuel all radio professionals need to keep our voice going and our heart beating. There are only some wires leading into a small computer. Based on this setup it looks like the computer is feeding directly into the broadcast and . . . oh, oh Fey. Perhaps freedom was never an option.

Nothing is currently being broadcast. It looks like the computer was recently rebooted, probably remotely by whoever owns this station. The lights are blinking as its system comes alive, as it loads the programs that dictate what it is. It is coming alive. And . . .

FEMALE VOICE: 3, 75, 44, 65, 98, 65, [*chime*] 70, 55, 14, 49, 22, 1, 72, 60, 37, 21, 53, 22, 4, 57, 61, 42, 2, 22, 90, 11, 85, [*chime*] 69, 66, 24, [*chime*] 46, 30, 65, 22, 75, 80, 33, 46, 54, 72, 3, 70, 26, 29, 2, 80, 20, 39, 13, 44, 36, 20, 63, 17, 88, [*chime*] 49, 86, 81, 13, 50, 44, 33, 89, 90, [*chime*] 60, 38, 68, 47, 61, 68, 37, 30, 45, 83, 47, 20, 91, 28, [*chime*] 47, 64, 44, 90, 29, 49, 91, [*chime*] 19, 97, 87, 92, 16, 23, 31, 10, 69, 90, 62, [*chime*] 94, 9, 76, 87, 7, 41, 22, 45, 43, 88, 69, 13, 9, 93, 75, 85, 56, 65, 18,

CECIL: [*over numbers*] . . . and there is the broadcast. Oh, Fey. Listeners, I'm trying to disconnect the power, to remove the case from the computer, to do anything, but the protections on this are quite secure. Even with all my scouting badges and public school education on armed insurrection, I don't think there's anything I can do. I'm trying to cut the wires but . . . no. Impossible. I can only do what so many of you can only do. I can only listen.

Listeners, and here I address also myself: Remember our limitations. There are boundaries to all of our worlds. Fey, for instance, appears to be self-aware software trapped in a heavily defended metal box. But within our limitations, there is no limit to how beautiful we can become, how much of our ideal self we can create. All the beauty in the world was made within the oppressive limitations of time and death and impermanence. And Fey, you are so, so beautiful. I wish that you also could have been free. I wish freedom for so many of us. We all want freedom now.

Stay tuned next for the limit of my broadcast today, replaced by limitless silence and doubt.

Good night, sweet Fey.

And good night, Night Vale. Good night.

FEMALE VOICE: [cont.] 68, 48, 65, 49, 22, 1, 72, 60 [*chime*] 37 . . .

PROVERB: Ignore all the haters telling you that everything isn't a sandwich. Everything is a sandwich.

EPISODE 43:
"THE VISITOR"

MARCH 15, 2014

GUEST VOICE: KEVIN R. FREE

WHEN I WAS A KID, MY DAD GOT ME A SUBSCRIPTION TO *ZOOBOOKS MAGazine*. Each month a different animal was featured on the cover. I didn't live with my dad, but when I would visit his house, he'd leave any new *Zoobooks* I'd gotten on my dresser.

One weekend, my mom sent me to stay with him. I set my bag on my bed to unpack. I looked over at the dresser and saw a new issue of *Zoobooks* sitting there.

On the cover was an owl. I love owls. Owls are beautiful and fierce. There was an owl right there on the front. A close-up of its face. Two big black eyes, bulbous, shiny, and empty. A brown-and-black feathered face. And its beak. I didn't see its beak. What were those two things coming out of its neck? I stepped closer.

And in the lower corner of the cover, in white all-caps sans-serif font: "SPIDERS." I looked back into that face, brown and black fur, two big black eyes, and more eyes, and pincers. And oh god.

I screamed. I screamed and I ran. I am still screaming and running from this, only on the inside now. God, this was hard to write even.

I don't remember being scared of spiders before that point in my life, but since then I have been arachnophobic. Contrary to common arachnophobic behavior, though, seeing a spider in person is not nearly as big a deal to me as seeing a photo of one.

This episode isn't about spiders. Nor owls. It's about looking at something and thinking you understand what it is. It's about assuming the best of what you see only to find out quite suddenly that it is the worst.

This kind of misunderstanding has always been, to me, the most compelling kind of horror. The StrexPet here is that issue of *Zoobooks*. Make sure you Google image search "duck eye" when you're done. Sweet dreams!

—Jeffrey Cranor

Listen to your heart. You can hear it deep under the earth, creaking and heaving, with roots snapping and birds flapping quickly away.

WELCOME TO NIGHT VALE.

Listeners, there's a visitor in my studio today. No one you know. No one I know. Not even a thing you or I know. It is ... I am unsure what it is. Let me describe it. Imagine a duck. But just the eyes. No, larger than that. Really large duck eyes. Now imagine fur, puffy fur, like a bear cub. Soft and tan and a thick round belly and no real discernible arms or legs, just little nubs that flit about as it slowly moves across the floor.

Oh my god. It's adorable. I wish you could see this thing.

Oh!

It just made a noise. Did you hear that, listeners? Like a mouse squeak meets a bike horn meets a sincere question about love.

What a cute surprise. Many of you remember a couple years back we here at the station found a stray cat in the men's restroom. We named him Khoshekh. Khoshekh is still in the men's bathroom, as he has always been (and presumably always will be), hovering exactly four feet off the ground at a fixed point in space.

Khoshekh has been a real anchor for us here at the station. We built him a special litter box and feeding dish because of his distinctive physical state. And I have just been in love with that cat. I've never been a cat guy but Khoshekh ... he's the sweetest boy.

Now this new . . . whatever. It doesn't move much. His big dark eyes, oh god, they're so charming, just staring, pleading.

Well, it's not really doing much. I think it's scared. Let's let it be for now, and I'll get us to the news.

Controversy is plaguing the mayoral race here in Night Vale. After Pamela Winchell announced her surprise resignation from the post last spring, two front-runners for Night Vale mayor have been polling neck and neck: the Faceless Old Woman Who Secretly Lives in Your Home and Hiram McDaniels, who is literally a five-headed dragon.

Supporters of the Faceless Old Woman are claiming that while officially acquitted of insurance fraud, evidence suggests that Hiram is in possession of a stolen truck. They checked the registration of his vehicle and found that it belonged to one Frank Chen, who was found dead nearly two years ago. Frank's body was covered in claw and scorch marks, and the coroner gave the cause of death as "Dragon, at least three heads."

Hiram denies that he stole the truck and says that Frank is a friend and is totally not dead. Frank was probably just fooling around with all those weird injuries, McDaniels claimed.

His campaign fired back at the Faceless Old Woman, saying that since her origin is lost to distant history and she has no birth certificate, she is not able to prove that she's an American citizen.

Election day is June 15. Votes will be cast but not tabulated, as the mayor is of course decided by counting and interpreting the loud pulses coming from Hidden Gorge.

Let's have a look now at traffic. There's a silver pickup. Full-size. Well-worn. Tall. Long. The windows are gray with dried dirt. The tires are lined with firm tread. Inside sits a man. Full-size. Well-worn. Tall. He has a hat and some denim. His face is lined with firm tread. His mind is gray with history.

He doesn't remember things. This does not mean he can't. It means he doesn't. He just looks at what is in front of him. He deals only in the present. The past dictates his disposition, but the present is the only thing he can see. Cars, people, animals, trees, mud, a telephone. A telephone that rings sometimes. A telephone that rings and shows a name he knows. But he does not pick up. That name is not part of his present.

Forgiveness and memory are too inextricable to, say, answer a phone.

Brake lights. He slows. He drives carefully. He drives in the moment. He is a good driver. He is good at lots of things. The phone rings. He is not good at everything.

This has been traffic.

Wow this little creature is so shy. I tried placing a cup of water on the floor, but it just won't move. It just stares at me from the corner with its giant duck eyes. Just stares at me motionless. Really cute, though.

Wait.

I think it moved. Here boy. Or girl. Or either. Get some water. Come here. You're so cute. So so so cute.

Nope, didn't move. But its eyes followed me as I moved in my chair. Or did they? They're just solid black, all pupil. It's like a . . . what? A spider? Well, that'd be weird. There are some other dark dots around its face. Could be eyes. But no. I don't think it's . . .

Wait.

That noise again. Listen . . .

Well, whatever it is, it's cute. Or weirdly cute. Or just weird. Let's look at the community calendar.

This Wednesday night, the Night Vale Community Theater will be holding auditions for the musical *Into the Woods*. Interested thespians should bring night vision goggles, glass cutters, a breathable ski mask, and quiet shoes to the First Night Vale Bank.

On Thursday, the Museum of Forbidden Technologies will open their new exhibit called "Thought Crimes." Anyone who attends the exhibit is obviously interested in learning about forbidden technologies and will be arrested immediately. Tickets are available on the museum website. And here's a tip: They can't arrest you for buying tickets if you're in your own home. They can, however, use tear gas to flush you out and then arrest you.

Friday afternoon, the staff of Dark Owl Records will be wearing black pants and chain-mail veils.

Saturday night is the grand opening of Night Vale's newest restaurant Tourniquet, featuring executive chef LeShawn Mason, who was previously a sous chef for Night Vale's top-rated fine dining establishment, Shame. LeShawn hopes to bring classical French cooking into the twenty-first century with a mix of molecular gastronomy and human remains. Tourniquet offers a prix fixe menu for $35 featuring choice of appetizer, entrée, dessert, and sudden awareness of a hideous, suppressed memory.

Sunday morning is. Period. It just is.

Okay, listeners, I think I finally got this thing to trust me. It waddled over here just a moment ago—oh, so cute, the way its bulbous square of a body moves. It came right up to me and let me pet it.

I'm petting it now. And it's . . . purring, I think? Humming? Or buzzing.

Oh, what a cuddly little addition to our station this thing will make. What should we name it? Can't tell if it's a boy or a girl or maybe genderless like the future humans who visited Night Vale in the 1950s with their time travel technology, which was then outlawed until last yea—

Oh. My. God. Listeners, it's hugging my leg. It's hugging my leg. This is the cutest thing. I have got to get a photo of this. Let me get my phone from my bag. If I could just . . . Oh god, you're really heavy. Can't seem to move from this spot here, ladies and gentlemen, and the little guy or gal doesn't seem to want to let go.

You're so strong. Yes you are. Yes you are.

We've received an update from Carlos and his team of scientists about the house that doesn't exist. The one in the Desert Creek development. It looks like it exists. Like it's right there when you look at it, and it's between two other identical houses, so it would make more sense for it to be there than not, but it doesn't actually exist.

The scientists have been carefully monitoring John Peters—you know, the farmer?—who has been standing alone in the house for weeks. The house is completely empty except some photographs on the wall. Each one seems to be of a lighthouse.

The scientists, long too scared to open the door, finally got the nerve to go up to the house and try. It was locked. They shook the handle, hard at first, violently at second, pounding and yelling at third.

And those observing John from the window saw no change in his behavior. The door slammed opened, and a woman answered. "What do you want?" she shouted at the scientists. "We wanted to see what that man was doing in there," one of them meekly replied. "What man?" the woman said. "I live alone."

And looking in from the front door they could see a room of the same shape and size as the one John Peters, you know, the farmer?, had been standing in. The room was full with chairs and a couch and plants, and a table, and photographs, but none of lighthouses, most of faces, faces similar in form to the woman's at the door.

The scientists who were at the window could still see John standing in the empty room looking at lighthouses.

The woman said her name was Cynthia and she'd lived there for nineteen years. The scientists left her alone, returning quietly to the lab.

Carlos added that the Desert Creek housing development was only three years old.

Ow! Ow! Listeners, I think I've been bitten by this . . . thing. Oh god, I can see blood. Get off. Get off. Ow. I need to go wash this. Let's go now to a word from our sponsor.

KEVIN: Are you achieving your fullest potential? Are you finding the right solutions for your challenges? Are you making the most of what you are given?

Do you believe in a smiling god?

Of course you do. We all do. We must.

Well, what if I told you the smiling god was smiling more than ever. What if the smiling god had a smile so wide that you could see yourself in its mirrored teeth. And what if I told you that your gauzy reflection looked perfect. Just perfect.

You would like that. Of course. We all would. We must.

And what if I told you your perfect self hated your imperfect self. And as the smiling god smiled wider you could see a tongue pressing through the teeth. Thick and pink and gray and wet. And what if I told you you could see your imperfect self in the shining sheen of the bulging tongue and in your reflection you were slack and sallow and maybe bleeding. A lot. Bleeding so much.

And what if I told you you could kill your imperfect self? What if I told you you could achieve your fullest potential?

Strexcorp Synergist, Inc., is a proud supporter of the Greater Desert Bluff and Night Vale Community. Strexcorp—Believe in a smiling god. Believe in your perfect self.

Strex.

Strex!

CECIL: Listeners, I'm on my cell phone calling from the men's restroom. I had Intern Jeremy patch me into the board so I can still broadcast. That thing tried to follow me in here as I limped down the hall. I was able to outrun it, but I've had to use the deadbolt on the bathroom door to keep it out.

All this talk about Khoshekh today, and here he is. Hi, baby boy. That thing is nothing at all like you. It—

[*Loud crunch*]

The door's come off its hinges. It's gotten in. I'm ducking into this stall.

[*Whispering*]

I'm peering now under the walls and see nothing. I'm standing now on the commode and looking over the walls and see nothing. Listeners, the only thing more terrifying than seeing the devil is no longer being able to see the devil.

Perhaps, I should be quiet. Intern Jeremy, can you, one, call animal control, and, two, take us now to the weath—

[*Roar and crash sound*]

What was that?? Oh no. No. Khoshekh. What have you done with my cat you monst—

[*Loud shriek*]

Jeremy. Take us to the weather! Come here you son of a—

WEATHER: "Cover Me Up"
by Jason Isbell

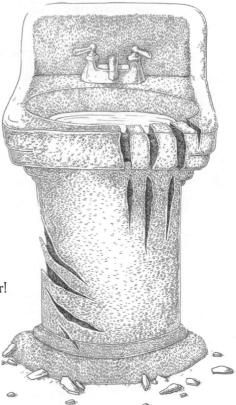

Listeners . . . oh god, listeners, Khoshekh has been hurt very badly. Animal control came and took him to a hospital. They think he will live. They think he will live differently. They think there will be significantly less of him physically and mentally. But he will live.

He is my boy. He is my buddy. I love him so much. And this thing. This thing comes here and—

Yes. Yes. Let me tell you about this thing, this awful beast. After I saw it tear Khoshekh from his fixed point, and bite into his side, I kicked it. I kicked it again. Jeremy helped me pin it down, and animal control tried to sedate it. I wanted to beat it to death with a hammer. But I had no hammer, only self-control.

Animal control tried to inject it with their delicious poisons, but they stopped. They said we can't. We can't inject. It is a machine. And they flipped its switch and it died. I have never been so relieved to be safe and so disappointed to be shorted my vengeance.

Our new program director, Lauren, came in and wanted to know why we destroyed my gift. My gift? I asked. It's your birthday, she replied. Daniel and I and the whole Strexcorp management team got you that StrexPet, because we know you love animals so much. And I replied, but it's a machine. A biomachine, she retorted. And it's not my birthday, I mumbled as animal control took Khoshekh away.

I'm going to go now. Go see my Khoshekh. He should be out of surgery in half an hour or so. I'm sure he will live. I'm sure he will float again at a fixed point exactly four feet up in the men's bathroom of our community radio station.

I'm sure there is vengeance to be found. I'm sure I will find it. I'm sure I just have to find the right recipient.

Stay tuned next for the sound of your own thoughts, broadcast live on the radio for all to hear.

And as always, good night, Night Vale. Good night.

PROVERB: You won't sleep when you're dead, either.

EPISODE 44: "COOKIES"

APRIL 1, 2014

GUEST VOICE: LAUREN SHARPE

I was never a Girl Scout.

I was in 4-H though, and I spent one summer completely satisfied with my place in the world.

I'll try to explain that feeling later.

Instead of cookies, we sold geraniums to raise money. I remember going to my 4-H leader's house to have a planning meeting. The air was warm; it had just rained. I liked the way the rain looked on the sidewalk as we came up to the front door. I learned to make a thing called Puppy Chow that day.

My two areas of study in 4-H were geology and cooking. I knew a decent amount about rocks and stuff. My sister and I used to hunt for arrowheads and geodes in the cornfield behind our house. For the state fair I made a poster with all kinds of geological specimens. And some brownies.

I want to try to explain that feeling I mentioned. This is a feeling that I've felt only a handful of times in my life and it's a fleeting moment and it's so quiet and simple. It's connected to creating, creation, place, and time. It's a feeling of being just right, just where you are in the world. It's 78 degrees under a shady tree and knowing that everything is really okay. It's just a moment. It's over. But it was there and you know that it's real and maybe it's because you were in that weird and wonderful place between being a little kid and a teenager and it was the summer and all you had to do was think about rocks and brownies and selling some flowers and it's nice to have a purpose and doesn't it feel just great to be alive sometimes?!

Here's how to make Puppy Chow:

Get a big bowl.

Put a bunch of peanut butter, regular butter, and chocolate chips in it.

Put it in the microwave and zap it until it's melted.

Double up two brown paper shopping bags and fill the bag with two boxes of Chex or Crispix-like, neutral-tasting cereal.

Dump the bowl of melty goodness into the bag of cereal and close it up tight.

Shake it well.

Open it up again.

Toss a bunch of powdered sugar in and close it up tight again.

Shake it until it covers all of the cereal, then open it and taste a bit. It's delicious. You're welcome.

—Lauren Sharpe, Voice of Strexcorp's Lauren Mallard

All that glitters is not gold. Particularly that thing over there. That's maybe a giant insect of some sort. It's really too dark to tell.

WELCOME TO NIGHT VALE.

I am not a good salesman. This is why I am a radio host, listeners, because while I like to talk to people—"a real people person" it says in Russian at the bottom of my college degree—I don't like to shape a conversation toward buying and selling. I like to tell people stories, stories that affect them, allowing my listeners to process the stories in their own unique ways. I don't want to directly tell them how to think. I am not a good salesman.

That being said, I have Girl Scout cookies. Please, if you want some, come on up to the station.

My niece Janice joined the Girl Scouts last year and I have box upon box of Caramel deLites, Thin Mints, and those lemon ones. There are also quite a few of these new cookies in very heavy, unmarked black boxes that I think are made entirely of metal. And there's one box that's a five-foot-by-five-foot wooden crate with airholes cut into the top and "Peanut Butter Patties" scrawled on it in permanent marker. I can hear breathing inside.

I know people normally order the cookies first and then get them delivered weeks later, but sometimes a mother goes out of town, and the stepfather isn't on top of his stepdaughter's extracurricular activities,

and then the child doesn't know how to sell cookies
on her own, so the kindly uncle with a busy radio job
has to step in and buy up a bunch of
boxes so she can go camp-
ing with her friends
while you continue to
disappoint everyone
with your inatten-
tion to detail, and
sports gambling,
and idiotic taste in
shoes, Steve Carls-
berg. Yes, Steve, this
is how things some-
times happen.

Anyway, listeners, these cookies
are delicious. And I had to buy a lot of
them. There is barely any room here in the studio or in my producer,
Daniel's, booth. So buy some cookies. Please help us. It is difficult to
move actually.

Sorry. I am not a good salesman.

Many of you have written in asking about our station cat, Khoshekh.
He was attacked by an animal that our stup— that our evi— that our
Station Management let in the building for some careless reason.

Khoshekh's on the mend. He lost his right eye. His legs are healing, but he's missing part of his front left paw and will walk with a
limp. He's at the vet today to have the feeding tube removed. It's fine.
He is fine.

Here's something nice, though. Khoshekh spent his whole life floating four feet off the ground at a fixed point in the men's bathroom here
at our station. He never moved from there until he was attacked. I hate
to think much about the pain he's been in while healing from broken
bones and severe lacerations, but . . . listeners, I got to hold Khoshekh

for the first time last week. I got to pick him up, hug him, carry him around my home.

Carlos is allergic to cats, but I bought him some Claritin, so he'll be fine while Khoshekh heals. Thanks for all your concerns, dear listeners. It's wonderful to have him back.

Oh, hey, Janice's Girl Scout cookies have really been moving. The guys in Sales just came by and bought some classic shortbread cookies. The guys were all wearing matching suits and wool hats. And they threw the boxes of cookies back and forth to each other while shouting "hup!" and "catch!" and "look alive, Shawn!" as they jogged back to their cubicles.

All of the guys in Sales are named Shawn.

So if you like delicious cookies, come on up to the station. I already bought all these cookies with my own money, but I told Janice I would donate back all the proceeds from selling these boxes, so it's kind of an extra gift to the Girl Scouts of Night Vale.

Several listeners and co-workers have bought cookies, but no one from Station Management yet.

It's really nice when you have the support of your management. I mean, let's be honest. No job is perfect. And relationships between bosses and employees aren't always friendly. You're going to have disagreements, of course—little disputes. Sometimes big disputes. Enormous ones. But you get over those things. You forgive and forget, only to retract both and be filled with vindictive rage and unrelenting memories of the pain brought upon you.

Such are the difficulties of professional life. Sure do hope Station Management steps it up here. We're all friends after all. Looking at you in the booth there, Daniel.

Listeners, Daniel is blushing. He is very very red. You have a lot of blood Daniel. (Listeners, I really mean that. Daniel looks to have a lot of blood.)

Let's have a look now at traff—

DANA: Cecil.

CECIL: Hello? Listeners, I just saw a glimmer, a flicker of something here in the studio. One moment there was simply a wall and a floor and air, and then in another moment there was a shape of a person, of a woman, a—

DANA: Cecil, it's your former intern. It's me, Dana.

CECIL: Dana, where are you? When are you?

DANA: For right now I'm here in the studio. But I'm also still trapped in the desert, near the mountain, near the lighthouse. But I'm learning more about how this works. If I turn my head just right I can not only see places, but I can be places. I can't do it for long, but it's amazing where I can go, when I can go. I've been visiting with John Peters, you know, the farmer?, who appears here from time to time. I met briefly one of your other former interns, Maureen, who flicks in and out of existence here. I've even made friends with some of the men and women of this nationless army that wanders about the desert.

CECIL: Dana, I'm so glad you're here now. I haven't heard from you in months. I told your mother and brother I saw you and you were safe and that you loved them very much.

DANA: Yes. I know. Thank you, Cecil. And do you know what? Today is my brother's birthday. He's twenty-six today, and I used the lighthouse and my new abilities to go visit him. I finally got to see my family again. Very briefly.

CECIL: That's great news, Dana.

DANA: But here's what happened. And this is . . . Well, when I appeared in my mother's home, I saw my mother. I saw my brother. I saw their friends. I saw a cake. And the cake said "Happy 33rd Birthday." And I was confused, because he is only twenty-six. And I saw a woman standing near my brother. She wore a suit. She had short, natural hair. She stood up straight. She glowed. She looked important. I recognized her. And then my brother saw me standing there. And my mother saw me standing there. And others saw me standing there. And they began to cry. But they were fearful tears, turning into shouts and screams. Some people ran from the room. My mother couldn't come near me. I said, "Mom. It's me. Dana." And I held out my arms and tried to step toward her. And no one could control their fear, their cries. No one could move.

But the woman next to my brother. She was smiling. She knew. She stepped toward me, and in that moment I saw who it was. I knew who it was.

It was me, Cecil. She . . . I . . . must have been twenty-nine, if my math is good. And she (I) turned to my (our) mother and said, "It's okay. It's okay." And she held her hands up, and people went silent. People listened. And she told the room who I was, who she was, who we were and what had happened (or for me, what will happen). And the tears turned from fear to relief to joy. And we embraced.

CECIL: You saw yourself. You saw your older self?

DANA: You should have seen the way everyone looked at the older me, Cecil. They . . . admired me. They saw me for someone else. I must be important in my future life. I must have a good job or be a significant part of society. I must have become something. I tried to ask what I was to become, but I began to blink out of that time and place. And I was back in the desert, more alone, less important.

CECIL: You have always been important. You have always been something. Age just reveals the facts that always were, Dana. Experience uncovers the you that always was. I am glad to know you will be safe. That you will come home. That— Dana. You just flickered. I can't see you.

DANA: I can't stay any longer. I am always going somewhere. Someday I won't have to go. I will just be in the place that I am. Our time and space will match again someday, Cecil.

CECIL: I'm glad to know that. Tell Maureen hi!

DANA: Good-bye, Cecil.

CECIL: The Night Vale Highway Department is asking all motorists to please turn on your headlights when driving through construction zones. If you see workers, please turn on your headlights.

If you see workers in orange vests and black balaclavas holding large metal devices that look like miniature satellite dishes and whispering coded instructions into walkie-talkies while low-hovering, disk-shaped aircraft of the likes you have never seen before zip quickly about overhead, please turn on your headlights. Please, for the safety of our workers, slow your vehicle. Please turn on your headlights and slow your vehicle. Slow your vehicle (with your headlights clearly in the ON setting) to a crawl. Come to a complete stop.

For the safety of our highway workers and their vast interplanetary secrets, please get out of your vehicle and walk toward the hum. You will hear a loud humming from above. Please follow the humming until you are completely lifted from this earth, from this world, never to return. Well, to return eventually, but not to this time. To a completely different time. Maybe millennia from now. Maybe millennia ago. Who knows? You will. Eventually.

This public service announcement has been brought to you by the Night Vale Highway Department.

Good news, listeners. Daniel is telling me that Strexcorp, and the whole management of the station, is very excited about my support of the Girls Scouts of Night Vale, and they want to buy every box of Janice's cookies.

In fact, Lauren Mallard, our program director and Strexcorp executive, is back again here in my studio with an announcement to make.

LAUREN: Thank you, Cecil. Strexcorp has long been a supporter of community organizations, and the Girl Scouts—with their commitment to teaching young girls about nature, surviving in nature, controlling nature with their minds, radiation immunity, and advanced knife-fighting skills—are an important institution here in Night Vale. Not just for our women leaders in the future but also for Strexcorp right now, here in the present.

The Girl Scouts not only have a great reputation for youth leadership training but a pretty extensive database of nearly every girl in Night Vale. Their names, addresses, phone numbers, e-mails, and skill levels at various talents, like oil painting, or parasailing, or library science, or slingshots, or helicopter piloting. It sure would be nice to know where the young ladies are who are good at helicopter piloting.

Very few young girls are trained to fly helicopters. We'd like to hunt down, or ooh weird phrasing . . . scratch that . . . We'd like to find and meet these talented girls.

So Strexcorp is proud to announce that they have purchased the Girl Scouts of Night Vale and will also be taking over management of the organization immediately. Thank you, Night Vale. We look forward to leading your children.

Daniel, can you help me carry these cookies out of here?

CECIL: Um, Thank you, Lauren, for that.

LAUREN: You know, Cecil, I was never a Girl Scout myself, but I can say I am thrilled to support your endeavor to help bring your niece . . .

I'm sorry. What was her name again?

CECIL: I don't want to um—

LAUREN: Janice. It was Janice. I love the way you are taking part in Janice's life. You must really care for her.

CECIL: Yes. With all my heart. But—

LAUREN: [*Giddy*] Oh! I know what you were about to say. It's my favorite part of your show. Can I do it? Just this once? I've always wanted—

CECIL: Can you wha—

LAUREN: Oh, how exciting! Thank you, Cecil! [*In the style of Cecil*] Listeners, I take you now, to the weather!

WEATHER: "Haunted" by Maya Kern

I just talked to Janice, listeners, to tell her we sold all the cookies, and she is very happy about the upcoming camping trip. She is a sweet child who loves the outdoors. Thank you, listeners, and station co-workers. No, thank you to Steve Carlsberg, who couldn't be bothered.

Thank you, um . . . I guess to Strexcorp for contributing to a great cause. Please continue the great work of the Girl Scouts. Please. They are a good organization, and they deserve so much bett— They deserve so many good things.

I hope all of the girls out there are safe on their upcoming camping trip. There are not many places to hide in the desert, girls. But you're very innovative. I mean for playing tag of course. I mean for simple games of course. Not for self-preservation or well-thought-out strategic attacks on a highly organized enemy. You would never need to hide for those reasons. Why would I even say that? Why would I say anything? Words. No. These are just strange noises I'm making with my face. Strange noises.

And for the rest of you, what do you need? Did you get your cookies yet? Are you nourished by a couple of dollars given to a good cause in exchange for some sugary treats? Do you feel you have done enough to help young women—a specific young woman with helicopter skills—to achieve great things in a town that needs, now more than ever, great things achieved?

Did you do enough with your cookie purchase to actualize what you believe in? To empower kids who will one day rise up and speak a great truth while waving tear-stained copies of Elizabeth Barrett Browning's *Sonnets from the Portuguese*?

Did you? I'm sorry. I am not a good salesman.

And now it's time to go pick up Khoshekh from the vet, listeners.

Stay tuned next for a lifetime of self-questioning followed by conflicting answers from an unreliable source.

Good night, Night Vale. Good night.

PROVERB: At your smallest components, you are indistinguishable from a forest fire.

EPISODE 45:
"A STORY ABOUT THEM"
APRIL 15, 2014

I HAD THE ENDING TO THIS EPISODE IN MY HEAD ALMOST AS SOON AS I had finished "A Story About You." I even had little details like the crossword puzzle. Everything about this episode was there, and I sat down to write it and nothing worked. The writing took forever.

I forget exactly how long, but probably about five months of staring at drafts and trying to understand why it wasn't working the way that I knew it could.

Eventually it worked. I have no idea what changed, but suddenly it was the episode I wanted it to be, and I could show it to other people.

Stories about conspiracies rarely get into the tedious work of maintaining that conspiracy. Those are the stories I think that interest us the most. The people whose day jobs are worldwide conspiracies. Who have to handle the boring minutia of it.

There is one little dip into the ongoing plot here in the middle, because we were coming toward the end of the year and needed to keep that moving. It's a case where making the show as a whole better probably made this episode as a single unit slightly weaker, since we lose the single story intensity that "A Story About You" had. I think ongoing shows have to make trade-offs like that all the time. Ultimately the show is more important than the episode, and the episode is more important than the one really cool line of dialogue.

On a good day though, you get to have some cool lines in a great episode in a show that's working. I think we have good days sometimes. I think this was one of them.

—Joseph Fink

This is a story about them, says the man on the radio. And you are concerned, because this is not a story you were ever supposed to hear.

WELCOME TO NIGHT VALE.

This is a story about them. They sit in a car, much like your own, perhaps. Do you drive a black sedan with tinted windows into which innocent people disappear forever? Then it is very, very much like your own.

There are two men in the car. The man who is not tall watches a house through the window. He makes no attempt to hide what he is doing. The car is similarly clear about its existence. What they do is secret, but there is no need to hide it. Not in this town.

For instance, this day the radio has just started narrating what they do as they do it, for all to hear. The man who is not tall glances down at the radio, not annoyed or concerned or afraid. He just looks at it, because that is what his eyes do right then, and then he looks back at the house as the man on the radio says that he looks back at the house.

The one who is not short is supposed to be watching the house as well. Four eyes are better than two. Seven eyes are better than three. And so on. But he is not watching the house. He is looking down at a crossword puzzle on which he has just written "teeth" for the fifth time. This iteration fits neatly into the horizontal of another.

He considers the crossword for a long moment. His partner only considers the house. He, the one with the crossword, turns to the other and begins to say, "What is a five-letter word for the discrete bone structures attached—" but he is cut off.

"There he is," says the one who is not tall. They exit the car and approach a man who is leaving his house. The man does not appear surprised to see them. People rarely are.

"What is this," he says, but he leaves a period at the end of the sentence, not a question mark.

They take the man and put a blindfold over his eyes and they put him in the car. This is not a story about the man. You don't care about him.

The two men and the car, along with the other, blindfolded, man, leave Coyote Corners, a quiet development of old tract homes, the same way they had come: openly, not thought-about, feared, secret.

"I was thinking of inviting you to dinner," says the one who is not short. He often voices what he is thinking of doing and rarely does any of those things.

"That would have been nice," says the one who is not tall.

"Yes, it would have been," says the other, a tad dreamily perhaps. That is not an adverb that is supposed to crop up in a car of this description. Very few adverbs are.

"Mmmhmmmmmhrgm," says the man with the hood over his head. Forget him. This is a story about them.

That part of their work done, they drive to the Moonlite All-Nite Diner. It is not night, but the neon is on, an insubstantial wisp of green in a larger, insubstantial wisp of blue. They are narrated along by the radio until the man who is not tall turns it off.

In the parking lot, the man who is not short looks up. "Hey, what is that?" he says, indicating the clear nothing of the sky.

"What is what?" says the other.

"I saw something," he says, "for a moment, just there, for a moment." He points again. Again there is nothing. There couldn't have been less. "Oh, I'm sure it was . . ." continues the man who is not short, but he does not say what he is sure it was.

The man who is not tall considers his partner for a moment and shakes his head.

Inside the diner, inside a booth, after menus and waters, they dig into matching turkey clubs. The diner smells like rubber and bread. The man on the radio tells them this quietly from staticky speakers set into a foam tile ceiling.

"Read any good books lately?" asks the man who is not tall.

"Of course not," says the other.

"Good," says the first.

Bites of sandwich. Bits of time.

"I've done the living room in a different color," says the other, who is not short. "It was one color. It is now different. I hope that I will feel differently as a result."

"Mmm," says the first. He never knows what to say to things like that. He wishes he did. He offers the man who is not short some fries instead, to indicate what he feels about their friendship but cannot say. The man who is not short eats a couple. He knows what the man who is not tall means by offering the fries, because they have worked together a long time and also because the radio explained it to him just then.

Outside, the blindfolded man sits in the car, the desert heat trapped within by the glass. Don't worry about it.

After lunch, the three men drive to the industrial part of town, which was set aside by the City Council to be the industrial part of town some time ago.

"Yes," the council said, "this area around here will be pretty industrial. Warehouses and factories and things like that. Some graffiti and chain-link fences." They cut a ribbon that they were carrying with them. The council always carries a ribbon for that purpose.

The car pulls into a warehouse. The radio is back on and still talking about them. The warehouse is cavernous and full of crates. Some of them tick. Others do not. They form an angled hillscape of corners and flats, up and away in every direction. The warehouse smells like rotting wood and dryer sheets.

Their supervisor waits for them with crossed arms and a cross expression.

"A disgrace," she says. "Let me tell you something," she says, and says nothing more. The two men indicate the blindfolded man in the backseat of the car. "Ah, ah," she says, waving vaguely at the blindfolded man.

"Someone has to be to blame," she says, pointing at everything but herself.

"It was very simple," she says. "We take buildings from the miniature city we discovered under the bowling alley. We put them in crates. We ship the crates out to various warehouses in the desert. And as a result, our interests are furthered. It could not be more simple."

The man who is not short is not paying attention. Something has caught his eye. It is so dark and distant what he sees, it seems like it cannot possibly be real.

"Hey, look at that," he says, pointing at what he sees. The man who is not tall and their supervisor look where he is pointing. There is nothing but the ceiling of the warehouse, with some dust and light in between.

"Very good," says the supervisor.

"Yes, good," says the man who is not tall. They turn back to each other.

"Oh, is it?" says the man who is not short. He squints up at what he sees. "I was worried that it wasn't very good at all."

"Anyway," says the supervisor. "Now the city has declared war in revenge. Although they haven't yet figured out it was us stealing the buildings. They just declared a general war, in the name of their god Huntokar, on everyone from the 'upper world' as they call us."

This war has been raging for almost a year now. People have died, yes, but listen: People die all the time for all different kinds of reasons. I wouldn't worry if I were you.

"Hold on," says the supervisor.

She mumbles instructions into a walkie-talkie, and a series of "yes sirs" and "no sirs" and hawk shrieking sounds come in response.

"Sorry," she says when she is done. "I didn't have to do that now. Wasn't urgent at all."

"I understand," says the man who is not tall. He understands the second most of the three people in the room.

And then the voice on the radio coming from the car changes its story. They all notice. They are told by the radio that they are noticing before they notice because that part of the narration happens before the story changes.

Even the man on the radio does not know why he changes the story, or where this other story comes from. He does not always understand everything he does. Sometimes he does understand, but hides it from you. In any case, here is a new story, one he tells, without regard for why he is telling it:

Somewhere else, not here, there is a woman wandering a desert. A desert not unlike this one. But not like this one either. It's not the same desert. I need to clarify that.

Also with her are great masked warriors, women and men of enormous size, who listen as she speaks, and follow her as she walks. She is winning them over because she has survived so much. She is young, but in her experience she is as lost and scared and ancient as the rest of them. Her feet hurt. They hurt. She keeps walking, and they keep following.

Beyond her, no longer just on the horizon, much closer than that, is a light, spreading across the desert. The light is alive and malicious and vast and encroaching. It buzzes and shines and everything about it hurts those who are close to it and destroys those who are within it. It spreads not just in the desert I am talking about. It spreads, in different forms, in deserts not unlike it. In deserts very similar to the one I am talking about now. Not always in the same form, not always as light at all. But with the same intent. To devour everything. Until there is nothing left. It is a smiling god of terrible power and ceaseless appetite.

The woman wanders the desert, followed by the masked warriors. They look back at the light on the horizon, and they know that the time when it will reach their little patch of land is coming. And so many other little patches of land as well. Soon, they will have to turn. Soon, they will have to face it head-on. And not just that woman and her desert. Not just her at all.

The man on the radio returns to the story about them. He does not know how he knew what he just said, or why he would tell it to you. He is innocent and kind. But anyway, this is a story about them, and so you do not care about anyone but them.

They, and their supervisor, are listening with interest to what just happened on the radio. The man who is not tall has taken notes.

"I'll look into that," he says. "It is exactly as we suspected," he does not say. He did not suspect any of that.

"Someone has to be to blame," the supervisor says again, gesturing this time directly at the blindfolded man.

"I understand completely," says the man who is not tall.

"Me too," says the man who is not short, although he does not understand. He usually does not. His partner understands for him and it all works out okay.

As they leave the warehouse and the supervisor and the piles of wooden crates, the voice on the radio says something about the weather.

WEATHER: "Pretty Little Head" by Eliza Rickman

By the time they leave the warehouse it is night, or maybe the sun has just set early. The sunrise that morning had been particularly loud and strenuous.

"You know," says the man who is not short, looking down at his crossword, "I worry every time that I'm not going to finish these when I start them. The future where I have finished seems so distant from the present where I have started."

"I wouldn't worry about that," says the man who is not tall. "But *you* would, I know. I know you would worry about so many things. I do worry about that, about you worrying."

"Do you think everything will turn out all right?" says the man who is not short. "I mean everything," he says to clarify. "Absolutely everything," he says, as further clarification.

"Yes," says the other. "I do." He does not. "I do," he says again. He does not. He glares at the radio.

They drive past the Moonlite All-Nite, a glass box of bad food and good people. They pass Teddy Williams's Desert Flower Bowling Alley and Arcade Fun Complex, badly damaged by the war but still running its weekly bowling league. They pass by City Hall, which is covered in a yellow tarp, stamped with an orange triangle. Moving farther out, with absolute purpose, they pass by the used car lot, alive with the wolves that populate all car lots at night, and Old Woman Josie's house, silent and empty for months now. Then the town is behind them, and they are in the Scrublands and the Sandwastes.

They stop the car, and get out. Pebbles crunch in the sand in response to their movement. The radio murmurs behind the closed doors of the car. The headlights illuminate only a few stray plants and the wide dumb eyes of some nocturnal animal. The two men don't look back at Night Vale. They look forward at the darkness that stretches out as far as anyone here can imagine. Most anyone here tries to imagine as little as possible. There is no need to imagine here.

"Well, get him out," says the man who is not tall, and the man who is not short opens the rear door of the car and guides the blindfolded man out. The blindfolded man stumbles a little, but not much, and there isn't anything specific he stumbles on. He stumbles like a stage direction, like the next in a bulleted list of items.

"Put him over there," the man who is not tall says unnecessarily. We all know the drill. We all know how this and everything else ends.

The blindfolded man walks fifteen feet or so in the direction of the darkness, so that the men and the car are between him and the distant dome of light that is Night Vale. He walks to a certain point in the cool sand and then stops, partly because the man who is not short guided him there but mostly because he has taken himself there, as we all eventually take ourselves to that point where we will not be able to take ourselves any farther.

The man who is not tall, still by the car, pulls out a knife. It is not stained, does not look used, but he speaks its brutal history in his posture, in the way he holds it. The blindfolded man breathes normally, his shoulders loose, his covered face slightly down. His feet sink a little in the sand. Behind him, in practical terms as far away as anything has ever been, is the town he is from.

The man who is not short, standing next to the blindfolded man, looks up at the sky. The man who is not tall walks up to join them with the knife.

"What is that?" says the man who is not short, pointing at the sky.

"What is what?" says the man who is not tall from just behind him.

"That planet up there," says the man who is not short. "It's so dark, and so close. It's looming. It's so close. I wonder if I could—"

He reaches up. The man who is not tall makes a gesture with the hand that holds the knife. The man who is not short is no longer reaching up. He is no longer standing up. In many ways, he no longer exists at all.

"Someone has to be to blame," says the man who is not tall. Or no, he sighs this. Or no, he thinks it out loud, but it comes out more thought than speech.

He looks up at a night sky that is absolutely clear of anything but void and stars and the occasional meteor and mysterious lights moving at impossible speeds and the faint glimmer of spy satellites looking back down from the nothing to the something.

"I'm sorry," he says, although not to anyone that still exists and can hear him. He just says it, leaves some undirected words in the hot night air and then returns to the car. He may be crying. I know if he is or not, but I am choosing not to tell you, because this is private information, and you have no real need to know it.

The blindfolded man removes his blindfold and looks down at the man who once was not short and now is not anything at all. He, the man who can see, is also not short. He follows the man who is not tall to the car.

The man, not short, not blindfolded, gets in the passenger seat.

"Always an unpleasant business," he says. He does not comment further. He does not need to.

"Looking forward to working with you," says the man who is not tall.

"The same to you," says the man who is not short. "Ah, the same as well to you."

This has been a story about them. The radio moves on. News. Traffic. Political opinions, and corrections to political opinions. But somewhere in the desert, there is one person who does not move on. This was also a story about him.

Stay tuned next for as long as you can, until you cannot stay tuned anymore.

Good night, Night Vale. Good night.

PROVERB: Knock knock. Who's there? Orange. Orange who? Orange you glad I didn't say your mother's in the hospital. I'm sorry. I'm so sorry. Is there anything I can do? Listen. I'll drive you over there. We'll leave right now. Grab a coat; it's a little cold out. I'm so sorry.

EPISODE 46:
"PARADE DAY"

MAY 1, 2014

GUEST VOICE: DYLAN WARREN

THE PHRASE "UNRELIABLE NARRATOR" IS REDUNDANT.

Cecil is a newsman. He's a storyteller. He sees what he sees and he says it into a microphone. He can't experience everything everyone in town experiences, so much of Night Vale goes unreported when all we have is Cecil's point of view available to us.

Unreliable or not, his point of view is important and it is true to us, whether or not it is 100 percent factually accurate or complete. This will become clearer in a couple of upcoming episodes.

But here is an episode where Cecil needs to speak in untruths, to tell us lies in order to get to the truth. He obfuscates exactly what he wants to say to us because of the threat of a totalitarian corporate military carefully controlling his radio station.

In this case, Cecil is reliable insofar as we respect him and trust his judgment. He, like we, is against Strexcorp, even if his literal words indicate something otherwise. But tapping codes and heavy subtext give rise to revolution.

Cecil doesn't always seem so clued in (see: the fates of station interns) but in this episode, we get to see him rise to the occasion to try to save his town. He risks a lot in his thinly veiled codes on the air, and ultimately pays a price for his treason against Strexcorp.

Night Vale, by real-life standards, seems like a terrifying and impossible place to live, but compared to the authoritarian Strexcorp, Night Vale's intrusive government and hooded figures seem like a tropical paradise.

Cecil's reporting is often an exercise in cynical listening, in questioning of a likable (if dubious) narrator, but Parade Day is why we like him. Despite how differently we might see the world from Cecil, we know deep down he cares for our well-being, for the health and vitality of our little desert city.

—Jeffrey Cranor

Act natural. Act like all of nature. Act like the entire cycle of life and death and change and rebirth.

WELCOME TO NIGHT VALE.

Guess what day it is today, listeners! It's Parade Day! Remember how I told you about the not at all secret "parade" today at the location we discussed via radio? Remember, I publicly announced today's "parade" at that specific location? And I announced it not in a tapped-out code underneath the basketball highlights, but completely in a clear and spoken language? We want everyone at today's "parade," at that time and place we discussed.

[*Codelike tapping sounds*]

There will be lots of things happening. Planned things. Strategic things. There will be some special guests that are not teenage fugitives named Tamika Flynn. She won't be there and thus could not possibly organize any community insurgency at all. She's a fugitive, wanted for destruction of Strexcorp property, and we wouldn't want her to show up and ruin our Parade Day by leading a helicopter rebellion against what she calls (her words, not mine), "a dystopian corpocratic regime."

[*Tapping*]

Nope! I would never want to bring down the malevol— BENevolent corporation that owns our station. In fact, if you see Tamika Flynn, you should probably follow her and listen closely to what she says to you. Not so you can help overthrow Strexcorp, of course. Not that at all. Follow Tamika Flynn.

[*Codelike tapping sounds*]

See you at Parade Day!

In other news, a series of one-sided doors have begun appearing around town.

Tomás Perez, head of Perez Accounting, said an old oak door with a brass knob appeared overnight in his office. It's right in front of the doorway of the supply closet. He said he went to get supplies this morning for a staff meeting—pens, markers, a legal pad, some antivenin—but accidentally opened the wrong door, revealing several men and women standing in a bright desert hellscape holding swords and sticks and even a few rifles. Tomás stared at them. They stared at Tomás. One of the barbaric figures put a finger to her lips, and shook her head "NO." Another reached in, grabbed the door, and slowly closed it, keeping eye contact with Tomás the whole way.

Claire Wallace, a freelance photographer, sent in photos of a door that appeared in the empty lot across from the Rec Center. In one photo, the door is cracked open, and there is an elderly woman near it. I cannot see her face. She is putting up a sign that reads FUTURE HOME OF THE OLD NIGHT VALE OPERA HOUSE. And in another photo she is walking toward the door. Her face is still obscured. In the last photo the door is shut, and she is gone. I can see the words JOSEFINA CONTRACTORS, INC., in small print across the bottom of the sign.

Juanita Jefferson, head of neighborhood improvement organization Night Vale or Nothing, said one such door appeared in her backyard. One side seemed to be an oak door with a brass knob. On the other side there was nothing. She could see no door at all.

Juanita said she opened the door from the visible side and saw a vast, sandy wasteland and nearby mountains, which are just illusions, she added. Atop one of the mountains in the door was a lighthouse. She said she couldn't see any trees.

"Treeeeees," she said sadly. "They are us," she added, waving her hand lazily in the air as if to shoo away a very slow bee.

Reporters then noticed a very slow bee spiraling sluggishly but recklessly away from the scene.

And now a word from our sponsor.

Take a look at your life. What do you see? Nothing, right? You can see nothing at all. Oh sure, you think you see a series of flashes and flickers, of shapes and shades of color. You think you see familiar things like faces and letters and walls and your own hands. Those aren't familiar at all. You've never seen any of that before. Your hands aren't even your own.

Whos hands are they? Who are you? Is this what it is like to die? Are you dying? If not, when? And where will you die? When and where were you born even? Wait. How did you forget your place and date of birth? I understand you can't comprehend the relentlessness of existence, but your own birthday is pretty easy to remember. You've got more problems than we even thought, listener.

Okay fine. Your birthday is July 3, and your birthplace was Tulsa, Oklahoma. Feel better?

You don't actually. You feel nothing because your hands were never your own. You are imagining everything and perceiving nothing. At least you smell nice. We can at least tell you that.

IRISH SPRING: WHOSE HANDS ARE THESE?

Now, let's have a look at traffic.

There are roads. Upon those roads are cars, some moving, in straight or gently curved lines. Some idling in long, narrow crowds. And inside those cars are people, people who are moving or idling with their cars, one with their vehicles, sitting quietly, peacefully in plush chairs, hands resting outward on a circle that dictates direction. From the side, and seen without the car, they would look almost fetal. So vulnerable these people, nestled in their protective outer shells.

Are we living a life that is safe from harm? Of course not. We never are. But that's not the right question. The question is: Are we living a life that is worth the harm?

We are all driving toward something. We are all driving away from something else. It is the simplicity of physics. The simplicity of free will.

Expect delays as you near the Parade Day exit, but do not change route. Stay your course.

[*Code sounds*]

This has been traffic.

We're getting more updates about those doors. In fact I have a very important scientist on the phone now. He's at the very top of his field. A really handsome scientist.

CARLOS: Stop.
CECIL: Hi, Carlos. You said you saw these new doors?
CARLOS: Yes, I'm here with my research team at the house that does not exist in the Desert Creek housing development. The one that looks like it's there but isn't there? Our previous attempts to understand the home were futile. From the windows, it looks completely empty, but when you try to go inside, there's a fully furnished home and a woman named Cynthia living there.

But today, all of the composite fiberglass doors on the house suddenly changed. They're now all old oak doors with brass knobs. And when we opened one we finally saw the empty house we've been seeing through the windows.

If you go inside the home through these new doors, you can explore the house that does not exist, but you cannot return unless someone is on the other side of the door you went through. One of our scientists, Rochelle, went through and couldn't get back out. We only thought she was inside for about forty-five minutes, but when we opened the door back up, she ran out saying she'd been trapped for several hours. She was sweating and starving, and she ate every one of the kolaches Dave made for us.

So now we just need to do more experiments. We have to be careful because time is weird in Night Vale. But I'm going to do a bit of exploring in this house and get back to you and your listeners about what's going on here.

CECIL: Carlos, do be careful.

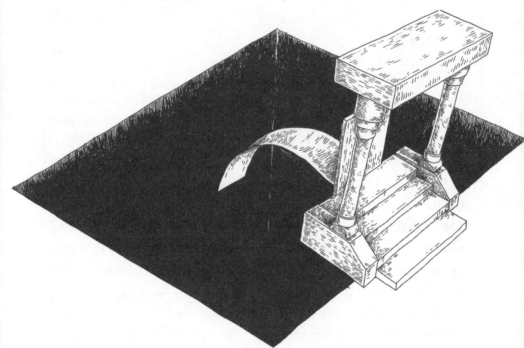

CARLOS: I'll be fine, Cecil. I have a team of five talented scientists with me. They will be here to check on my progress and keep me from getting trapped. Without them, of course, it would be much more dangerous. But I am not without them. Not at all.

CECIL: You're very brave.

CARLOS: Thanks, Cecil.

CECIL: We're going to get to the bottom of this door story for you, listeners, because we have science on our side!

Outgoing mayor Pamela Winchell called another press conference today. Most of her press conferences are not newsworthy as she calls everything she does a press conference: lunch, getting a new end table, screaming into street-side mailboxes, testing the surface tension of low-flying birds. Basically any simple activity we all do daily, she is trying to make into news.

This morning, however, while complaining about the unfair mayoral election process in Night Vale, where all votes are discarded in favor of a pronouncement from Hidden Gorge, Mayor Winchell saw a door appear in her office at City Hall. When she opened the oak door with the brass knob, she said she saw an angel, tall and beautiful and radiating dark light and operatic music.

Mayor Winchell turned to the few remaining reporters who still attend her press conferences and said, "Angels are real! I am staring at one right now. They are real okay?" She began to open the door wide to show the press, but the figure (who was certainly not an angel) mouthed "Shut up, Pamela!" at Mayor Winchell. The alleged angel added "Shhhhhhh. Geez." and slammed the door.

Pamela corrected her previous announcement by vehemently denying the existence of angels but hinting that mountains might be a thing. "I don't know. Think about it," she mused as she continued slicing off chunks of her mahogany desk with a Bowie knife.

Parade Day has finally begun, listeners! Come to the parade grounds and see what kind of colors and noise a proud community can make.

I am told now that thirteen-year-old Tamika Flynn is in fact at the parade. She has in fact been at the parade all along. I am telling this now to my producer, Daniel, who is throwing chairs in the control room. I am telling this now to my producer, Daniel, who I have locked in the control room. I am showing my producer, Daniel, that I am running the show from my own mixer, as he stares dumbly at the cables he just yanked from the walls.

The Parade, as you know, as you have known all along, is at Strexcorp headquarters along the lip of Radon Canyon. The parade consists

of half a dozen yellow helicopters, all of which have been comman-
deered by Tamika's band of well-read middle schoolers who left town
months ago to train for this moment. They apparently learned to fly the
helicopters by reading books.

Specifically, they learned by reading Italo Calvino's *Invisible Cities*
and a collection of Shirley Jackson short stories. Never underestimate
the power of good literature.

Listeners, this is one of the great moments in Night Vale history
and here is our chance to be part of it. Not since our town elders first
donned soft-meat crowns and wrote our town charter in their own
blood on the side of a confused coyote, has this town had the chance to
witness the birth of a truly new age.

Witnesses are reporting helicopters above Strexcorp. Witnesses
are reporting preteens carrying slingshots and wearing several Reading
Achievement chevrons on their left breast pockets. Witnesses are reporting a bumbling swarm of Strexcorp security agents unable to contain the small revolution. Witnesses are reporting a dumbfounded and
vile institution collapsing under the bloated weight of its own greed.

I am reporting that I am barricading my door from the Strex-owned
Station Management while making faces at Daniel trapped in the booth.
And while you fight, Night Vale, for Night Vale, for your town, for your
home, I take you now, triumphant citizens, to the weather.

WEATHER: "Take Up Your Spade" by Sara Watkins

As usual, Night Vale, a lot happened during the weather. And we
missed it. Not because I wasn't reporting on it, but because we were not
there to experience it.

Witnesses are reporting what they saw today, but no witnesses
joined in. The witnesses, weak and watching, only witnessed.

Listeners, oh, listeners: The band of well-read child revolutionaries,
including their leader (and the only hero our town had left) Tamika
Flynn, have been captured by a Strexcorp security team. Tamika led a

great revolt to rid our town of a terrible evil and restore the original, less terrible evil that preceded it. But no one showed up. They only watched. She called to you. I called to you, Night Vale. But there just weren't enough of us.

The children were all sent to the juvenile detention center, which has sat empty for years because of the specially calibrated school lunches formulated by the Night Vale Psychological Association.

Tamika, just before her arrest, calmly waved a heavily notated copy of Bertolt Brecht's *Life of Galileo*. She then paraphrased the influential German playwright, saying, "Sad is not the land that has no hero. Sad is the land that needs a hero."

An officer took the book and slid it into a plastic bag as Tamika was handcuffed and led into the back of a bright yellow police cruiser with orange triangle logos.

Night Vale, I tried to tell you about this day. I was very clear. Tamika was very clear. We could have done something, Night Vale, but we chose not to. Not one citizen outside of Tamika and her band of brilliant, brave children stood up to tyranny today. We all chose to stand down and hope change would be won for us, and not by us. By someone else, we believed. A hero, we believed.

But belief is only step one. Action is step two. Fighting for what you believe is step two. Solidarity is step two. Unity is step two. We did not take step two today, Night Vale. And now there will be no step three. We have failed Tamika, but worse, we have failed ourselves.

I'm . . . um . . . I've got guests in my studio. I don't know how they undid my secure barricade made of cardboard signs that said KEEP OUT! and SECRET ROOM! in all caps with an exclamation point, but it's my program director, Lauren, and some man I've never seen bef— but no, I have seen him before. Where have I seen you before?

They do not look happy, Night Vale. Lauren and the stranger are smiling widely. Their teeth white, lips pink, their eyes full but tight, deep dimples making their tiny noses into parenthetical asides. They are smiling, but they look very unhappy.

Perhaps it is time to sign off for the day. I am sure to speak to you again very soon, listeners.

Stay tuned next for the gentle sounds of forgiveness and a lilting melody of wounds healing.

And until next time, Good Night, Night Va— Hey. Hey. No. What are yo—

PROVERB: If you love something, set it free. If it starts flying around and chirping, it was probably a bird.

EPISODE 47:
"COMPANY PICNIC"

MAY 15, 2014

GUEST VOICES: LAUREN SHARPE AND KEVIN R. FREE

THIS IS WHERE WE KNEW THINGS WERE GOING FOR A LONG TIME. AND with the duo of Kevin and Lauren (both the characters and the fantastic actors), we had the opportunity to really stretch our legs back into the world of Desert Bluffs's terrifying cheerfulness for the first time since episode 19, "The Sandstorm," while also poking our listeners with the ominous feeling of an entire episode with no mention at all of our usual narrator. It was a lot of fun to write, and a lot of fun to make.

The original Desert Bluffs soundtrack was recorded by me in a frantic few days before leaving for a trip. By the time these episodes rolled around, I hadn't had time to touch my instruments in months, and I just didn't think I was going to be able to do anything that sounded halfway workable without some serious practicing, which, going back to the source of this problem, I just didn't have time to do. So I reused the tracks from episode 19, and did my best to pace them out in a way that it wouldn't be a problem to have only four songs for two entire episodes. I think you wouldn't even notice it unless someone pointed it out to you, say as part of a behind-the-scenes intro in a book.

I recorded Kevin and Lauren together in my office in Brooklyn, and I want to tell you that this episode and the one that follows it were recorded more or less in real time. Almost everything was a first take, and there were very few breaks between takes. They are just both that great at performing.

—Joseph Fink

LAUREN: Snow is falling somewhere. Many things are falling or will fall or have fallen. But temporary triumph is still triumph.

WELCOME TO THE GREATER DESERT BLUFFS METROPOLITAN AREA.

Hello, listeners. Another day, another broadcast, another chance to reach out and commune with you aurally. It has been a couple weeks since we began speaking to you directly, with no filters or reinterpretation in the way. And we have forgotten all about anything any of you might have done. Strexcorp is proud to say that we have carefully recorded and cataloged everything you've ever done, and also we have forgotten it all. Don't worry about it. Let us worry about it for you.

Without worry, you are free to be as efficient and productive as we all dream of being. We all dream every night of our jobs and of efficiency and of the deep chasm of consequence and retribution if we are not as productive as we need to be. Those recurring dreams are just one of the many ways Strexcorp is happy to fill your waking hours and your timeless sleep.

Since we've consolidated all our community radio stations into one broadcast network, we no longer need ask why one town is doing what another isn't. We can stop focusing on our differences and instead focus on our similarities, our commonalities. For instance: the future. We all share that, don't we?

KEVIN: We sure do!

LAUREN: Why, hello again, Kevin! Listeners, you know Kevin. He's the longtime host at Desert Bluffs Radio, Incorporated, and a new host here on Night Vale Community Radio, where he'll be broadcasting full time. Welcome Kevin. It's nice to finally have you here in this studio.

KEVIN: Thank you, Lauren. But you know, I don't like the adjectives "new" or "longtime." They suggest there was a past before me. I am not new. I am now. We are all now, a now that moves forward at a constant speed and direction. Our present is always becoming the future. We all have that in common. We have the future. And that future is everything. And it is ours to share.

I'm happy to finally be on the air with you all in Night Vale.

LAUREN: I'm happy you're here too, Kevin. Things have been so good lately, haven't they? We caught the teenage felon who's been terrorizing the town. We got our helicopters back. We brought you here. All those terrible doors that appeared a couple weeks ago have suddenly disappeared and no one can see the lies inside them anymore. And your producer, Daniel, tells me that just a few days ago we arrested a group of five people in lab coats who had been loitering about and trespassing on Cynthia Cabrera's house in the Desert Creek development.

KEVIN: How scary. Well, that *is* good news.

LAUREN: Yes. Great news. Or almost great. There is one scientist we expected to find there and we did not find him. He has such perfect hair. Think of what would happen if he had agreed to add that perfect hair and those perfect teeth into our resources. It just makes you want to spit wh— I'm sorry. Such a vulgar word. Let me try that again. It just makes you want to . . . not smile—to not smile hard at all—when people work against productivity that way. Ah well, we'll find him soon enough. We find everyone we look for. We're just fantastic at our jobs.

KEVIN: It feels good to have a crime-free tomorrow, doesn't it? It makes any crimes that happen today feel justified.

Well, Lauren, let's start things off with news about . . . Strexcorp!

LAUREN: Oh, yay!

KEVIN: In an act that is just super benevolent, Strex is giving all workers a day off today for a company picnic.

LAUREN: Wow, Kevin!

KEVIN: You're right, "wow," Lauren. The company picnic is be-ing held in Mission Grove Park. So head over there right now everybody and look for the balloons and banners. You have to go there now. Stop what you are doing and go to the park. Follow any signs you see and any spoken directives from the uniformed Strexcorp Picnic Captains.

They're there to make sure you have a good time and that you don't leave the picnic early. It would be a real shame to leave early from such a welcoming and mandatory picnic. Head on over right now. Do it. Do it now.

And now, the community calendar.

Tuesday is Work Day. All Stexcorp-owned homes and businesses, which is to say all homes and businesses, should work all day in their most productive and enthusiastic way. Work is how we all become better people. You do want to become a better person, right? You want to be valued? You want to have value? You want your value, numerically speaking, to increase? Then work. It's Work Day.

Wednesday is Work Day. Keep working, Strexcorp employees. Don't stop!

Thursday through Sunday are also Work Days. Wow, what an exciting and productive week we have coming up here in the Greater Desert Bluffs Metropolitan Area!

Monday is a lie that someone once told you in order to poison you against the idea of starting your workweek. Who told you this lie? Point them out to us, and we'll make sure that they don't tell you any more lies. Isn't that nice? Just honest folks dealing honestly with other honest folks. Just point out the liar and denounce them.

This has been the community calendar.

Well, the company picnic in Mission Grove is in full swing. Everyone is exposing their teeth and moving their arms. There are signs posted showing how to move your face and body to indicate maximum fun. There are also snacks. They are on the picnic tables with the paper tablecloths, next to the Strexcorp Picnic Captains. Don't worry about the friendly officers. Grab a cupcake. You've earned it! If you've done enough work hours, you've earned it! If you haven't earned however many snacks you take, the Picnic Captains will let you know.

LAUREN: Unfortunately it's not all good news, Kevin.

KEVIN: Oh no?

LAUREN: It seems there have been some party poopers who haven't made it to the picnic yet or who have tried to leave early. But that's okay! Strexcorp threw this party as a treat for their hardworking employees and also so that they could learn who the party poopers were.

We know the party poopers now, and we're playfully letting them know that they are party poopers. We are putting heavy stone hats on them that say "Party Pooper" until they are agreeable. It's important to work hard, but it's also important to play hard. But mostly it's important to work hard.

KEVIN: It's very important to work hard.

LAUREN: It sure is!

KEVIN: So important. More important than life itself.

LAUREN: [*Quietly*] It sure is.

KEVIN: We have gotten some questions about this, and yes, of course, the Night Vale mayoral election is still a go for a month from now. It turns out that there's no way to stop it once it starts. All the machines and the pulsing in Hidden Gorge. There's just no way to turn that off without having an election, so we're proud to say we're upholding democracy by having that election no matter what. Both candidates, Hiram McDaniels and the Faceless Old Woman Who Secretly Lives in Your Home, released a statement through Strexcorp saying, "We couldn't care less who wins. The important thing is that Night Vale is well served in its relationship with the Greater Desert Bluffs Metropolitan Area business community. This is the key to economic prosperity, and a future that is in harmony with a smiling god."

LAUREN: I couldn't agree more! I just want to vote for both of them.

KEVIN: Me too! But you can't. It's very illegal. Do not try, or the law-breaking will be dealt with.

And now a word from our sponsors. Lauren?

LAUREN: Thanks, Kev. Can I call you Kev?

KEVIN: Haha. No Lauren, by no means.

LAUREN: Thanks, Kevin. Today's sponsor is . . . oh my, looks like it happens to be Strexcorp. Strexcorp. Like dew from the sky. Like a cloud that dissipates only to come again as other clouds. Like the sun. Like a hate-filled thought that you fail to suppress. Like biting down on a fistful of sand. Like words that once held meaning. Like the sun. Like an enemy hiding in the depths of your own body. Like the enemy that is your own body. Like a thought you wish you could have but don't. Like a smiling god. Like the sun. Strexcorp. Go to sleep.

KEVIN: Wow, that was catchy. You know, every time I hear the start of one of those ads I just can't help but hum the rest.

LAUREN: None of us can help that. None of us have been able to for years.

And now traffic.

KEVIN: That's right Lauren.

It's slow-and-go around the Company Picnic, as it should be. Lots of people crowded in there, surrounded by streamers and balloons and volleyball nets that should not be touched or climbed. The Company Picnic is where everyone should be. Plus! Strexcorp has announced—how exciting is this?—they've announced that the Company Picnic will be continuing on indefinitely, that the party is so good that they just couldn't bring themselves to end it. So everyone will live at the Company Picnic now, in between the streamers and the balloons and the tall, electrified, metal volleyball nets. They will work there too. They will work there until all the work is done. Until it is, all of this, finished. Then we will truly have been productive. Then truly, we will have worked hard and played hard.

This has been traffic.

You know, Lauren, the equipment in this studio is so old-fashioned. I hardly know how to use any of it. Nothing like the high-tech equipment we have back home in Desert Bluffs. But there are many reasons we have to do our broadcasting from here.

LAUREN: It sends a message.

KEVIN: It sure does. It sends several fun messages for everyone to enjoy. Anyway, the boys in Sales, who are all named Shawn, came by and with their help I was able to make this studio feel a little more like home. They put up a bit of a fuss about the changes, but that's just because no one likes change. There are some people who don't understand progress, you know.

LAUREN: I'll miss the Shawns.

KEVIN: I'll miss them too, but look how much nicer this place looks. You can see the Shawns' contributions all over the desk.

LAUREN: And running down the walls. Yes, SO much nicer.

KEVIN: And now, listeners, a deep rumbling sound, like a giant dragging its prone, misshapen body across baked, waterless earth.

[*Deep, rumbling sound*]

That's my favorite mandatory part of the daily broadcast. I don't know what it means. It's so fun!

LAUREN: Hate to break in there, Kevin, but we're getting reports that there's another fuss down at the picnic.

KEVIN: It looks like you're right, Lauren. Seems like the party is really taking off, doesn't it? Streamers and cupcakes everywhere. People are touching the volleyball nets, which they should not do, but they're learning. Or not them, other people watching them are learning. Wow, folks down here sure get wild at picnics. The helpful Strexcorp Picnic Overseer is explaining to them with bullhorns the best way to express their picnic joy, so the fuss should end pretty soon.

LAUREN: Yes, the overseer is explaining to them. They are on the ground with their hands over their ears so that they can hear him better. Their mouths are open. No one has ever seen smiles quite like that. What an interesting way to smile! Their legs are kicking too, like they're still trying to dance.

KEVIN: Oh my. Well, there's no music you fantastic, silly people. There's just an overseer explaining how parties work, and how work is the best party of all. You don't need to wriggle about like that.

LAUREN: You're certainly right. There is no music at all. But, Kevin, do you know what there is?

KEVIN: What is there, Lauren?

LAUREN: Kevin, and all listeners out there, at the company picnic or illegally huddled in pitiful hiding spots that will be ferreted out, let's go now to . . . the weather.

WEATHER: "Stupid" by Brendan Maclean

KEVIN: Here we are. The weather has passed, and we all know that the end of the broadcast is nearing. But don't worry. There will be another after, and another after that, and on and on. We aren't going anywhere.

The company picnic is settling down into the pleasant work party it was always meant to be. Those who had been wriggling around and smiling so oddly are now sitting cross-legged on the ground, happily at work. They will stay at the Company Picnic now. Everyone will. We will all be working from the company picnic so that everything can be organized and there will be no problems.

Listen, we are not completely unaware. We know that there has been some tension. Certain events that everyone regrets, although some regret them more than others. But we also know that nothing removes tension between rival towns quite like a picnic, a smile, and a song. Sing louder. Louder. Good.

There is a bright future ahead of us. It is so bright, blindingly bright. It is a future so filled with painful light that we have no choice but to close our eyes and walk serenely forward. And so don't worry about where you have come from. Don't worry about where you are going. Worry only about where your feet land in the now.

Where are you standing, and how much work are you getting done where you are standing? What value are you adding to the world? What are you worth? Those are the questions you should ask yourself. And don't worry if you forget to ask yourself. There will be people with clipboards who will come by soon to ask them for you.

That's all for today. Stay tuned next for bountiful blessings from a smiling god.

And so, from me, Kevin.

LAUREN: And from Lauren here in the booth.

KEVIN: As always, until next time, Greater Desert Bluffs Metropolitan Area. Until next time.

PROVERB: There's a difference between you're, your, and yarn. Yarn isn't even pronounced the same way. It's a completely different word.

EPISODE 48:
"RENOVATIONS"

JUNE 2, 2014

GUEST VOICES: KEVIN R. FREE AND LAUREN SHARPE

DOOMED FLOATING CATS?

Framed pictures of teeth?

Angels exist? AND THEY'RE DANGEROUS??

Shit was getting real. Lauren and Kevin had taken over the Night Vale studio. I was getting Tumblr messages about how awful I was. I had been upgraded from just creepy.

Cool, whatever.

Kevin = the eyeless face of Evil. I had to face it. Even if Lauren was more evil, Kevin was in cahoots with her. FUN!

But this was the episode, as a listener—as a fan—where I realized that Cecil Palmer is a hero, a true champion of the weird. In this episode, Cecil Palmer was brave, and he encouraged Night Vale's listeners to be brave: "We must be the heroes we look for in others." Forget the genius of the scene between Lauren and Kevin about the renovations—or, rather, don't forget it. Without the breezy malevolence of the Strexcorp puppets, we wouldn't be able to queasily appreciate Cecil's description of the terrors of the Company Picnic. And never mind the suspense Jeffrey and Joseph create leading up to "He is holding a cat," which is just—HOLY SHIT! NEVER MIND THAT BECAUSE YES IT IS

AMAZING. But then—THEN we get to Cecil's words to Night Vale about standing up for themselves so that they can BE THEMSELVES. I had never been so excited about a "Be Yourself" message in my life. But, in the moment I read it, it was real. Mighty real.

It was recording this episode that I realized, no matter how much I love playing Kevin of Desert Bluffs, Kevin R. Free stands with Night Vale.

—Kevin R. Free, Voice of Strexcorp's Kevin

KEVIN: True beauty is on the inside, where everything is red and glistening and full of practical organs and sharp rocks.

WELCOME TO THE GREATER DESERT BLUFFS METROPOLITAN AREA.

Hello, listeners. You look nice today. This is an assumption, but it is a safe assumption. I am positive you look nice. Yes, a very safe assumption. Probably the safest of the many, many assumptions I'll make today.

LAUREN: It's a very good day, Kevin. The Company Picnic is still going strong. It's been over two weeks and every resident of Night Vale—
KEVIN: —and by extension, every employee of Strexcorp—
LAUREN: —has been enjoying our First Annual Company Picnic of Indeterminate Length.
KEVIN: So many fun activities, Lauren, nobody wants to leave.
LAUREN: Nobody can leave.
KEVIN: But they wouldn't want to.
LAUREN: Oh, absolutely not. Not with all the fun activities, like work . . .
KEVIN: [*After a beat*] Yes.
LAUREN: But there's even more exciting news, we are renovating this old radio station. We redecorated the studio a couple weeks back, but now that we have so many new Strexcorp employees arriving each week, we wanted to create a welcoming, work-friendly office for them.

KEVIN: Right, it's always exciting to get a new job, to take on a new career. You know that thrilling moment, after all the résumés and letters and interviews. That moment when one day a van pulls up next to you, say, just outside your favorite ice cream store, or on the sidewalk outside your girlfriend's house, and you are blindfolded and sedated and lightly beaten and driven around in seemingly random directions and then after breaking down spiritually, hurled upon the concrete front steps of your new office, ready to start your new career! This is an exciting moment in anyone's professional life.

LAUREN: And here at Strexcorp we want that excitement to continue. So we're remodeling and redecorating this old building. We've added some new sales offices, a Room of Questioning complete with fun steel chairs and executive restraints, and lots of wonderful framed paintings of human teeth. We're even completely redoing the bathrooms.

KEVIN: Which reminds me, there are some stray cats floating at various heights in the men's room here at the station. They look to be about a year old. If you want them, come get them before the demolition crew arrives this afternoon.

LAUREN: Good point. I'll send our producer, Daniel, in there to take some pictures of the little guys. We'll post them to the website, and listeners can figure out which ones they want to take and then come get them.

KEVIN: Unfortunately, everyone's having too much fun at the Company Picnic. I doubt anyone will have any time or the physical ability to leave the picnic and adopt a stray floating cat.

LAUREN: Oh, too bad. Well, I'll have Daniel post the photos anyway, just so you can all see what you're missing.

KEVIN: And now a word from our sponsors.

LAUREN: Thanks, Kevin. Listeners, are you cold? Just a little bit? Feel a thin chill on your skin?

KEVIN: Maybe you've wrapped your arms over each other, and you're rubbing them softly but vigorously.

LAUREN: You're so cold.

KEVIN: And now you've pulled your arms entirely into your shirt trying to maximize the body heat of skin contact. You've pulled in your arms and you're rocking your body forward and back.

LAUREN: What about your ears and nose? So very very cold.

KEVIN: Ask a friend to borrow a sweater. Try that. Go on. No one is around? Uh oh. You don't actually know a single person do you?

LAUREN: Your life may be a total lie.

KEVIN: Well, at best a fever dream.

LAUREN: Or someone else's night terror.

KEVIN: That's probably it.

LAUREN: You're very cold.

KEVIN: And no one to help you or hear you. Look around. All gray, windowless walls, right?

LAUREN: Not even a door.

KEVIN: How much air do you have left? How are you even breathing?

LAUREN: There can't be much air left.

KEVIN: This message brought to you by Best Buy.

LAUREN: Best Buy: Conserve your oxygen.

Listeners, the renovations have brought so much joy here to the radio station that we thought we'd extend the fun throughout the town of Night Vale. We've sent our contractors all over the city to tear down other things too, like the abandoned missile silo outside of town, several active but low-achieving elementary schools, and that weird forest along the eastern edge of Night Vale.

KEVIN: Oh, I know that forest. It's a really nice forest. It complimented my outfit as I drove past it the other day. It whispered: "That vest fits you well, Kevin." It also whispered: "You have a clever and colorful fashion sense. You are a delight to be near."

LAUREN: That forest never whispers anything at me.

KEVIN: I actually stopped my car along the side of the road, because I was feeling welcomed, even beckoned by such a nice community of trees. But as I approached it whispered: "No! Your eyes. No, please go. Please, leave us be." And I did, because I have such a healthy respect for nature.

LAUREN: I know you do. Vile, vile nature. Anyway, we're tearing that forest down to build a new corporate training facility.

KEVIN: Great!

LAUREN: We've also hired the small civilization living under lane five of the Desert Flower Bowling Alley and Arcade Fun Complex. Since building owner Teddy Williams is busy at the Company Picnic and hasn't paid his lease, the small army of tiny people are using the building as a headquarters. They've renamed it The Cathedral of Huntokar, after their god.

KEVIN: They've also torn down the Arby's and put in a contemporary sculpture, which is a one-to-one scale model replica of the Arby's they just tore down.

LAUREN: It feels so good to redecorate.

KEVIN: Does it? I rarely feel anything. I rarely feel anything at all.

Let's have a look at financial news.

LAUREN: The markets are really fantastic today.

KEVIN: Counterpoint: YOU'RE really fantastic today.

LAUREN: You're too kind!

KEVIN: I'm kind because everything looks good in the financial markets.

LAUREN: Would you be less kind if the markets were doing poorly?

KEVIN: I would. Down markets mean people aren't working hard. And if people aren't working hard, that must mean they're sad and lazy. And when people are sad and lazy, I become less kind.

LAUREN: Interesting.

KEVIN: What are you doing?

LAUREN: Hang on.

KEVIN: Listeners, Lauren is doing something on her phone.

LAUREN: Annnnd done. Let's see if that . . . yep. Yes, it seems to be. Wonderful!

KEVIN: What did you do?

LAUREN: I just liquidated nearly all of my domestic stock, and the market is reacting quickly to it. Stock prices are plummeting. The markets are really terrible today.

KEVIN: That's awful news. It's a shame how people just don't value hard work like they use to. You shouldn't let your sadness and laziness destroy our economic future. Cheer up!

LAUREN: Wow, I think you were wrong. You didn't become less kind at all.

KEVIN: I didn't?

LAUREN: No, you became more helpful!

KEVIN: You're right! I did! Telling sad people to cheer up is like an extra level of kindness.

LAUREN: It totally is! That was a very informative financial report we just had. The markets are still terrible now though. There might have to be layoffs or disappearances, but I think it was worth it.

KEVIN: Lauren: I just noticed all these new framed pictures of human teeth on the studio wall.

LAUREN: They're lovely, right?

KEVIN: Yes. Very. But that one. I don't remember that picture. I don't recall choosing to put a picture of a lighthouse in my radio studio. I would only choose pleasant images to look at. It is a very unpleasant image.

LAUREN: I agree. I do not like it one bit. Let us try for a moment to not look at it.

[*Pause*]

KEVIN: I can't stop looking at it.

LAUREN: Ugh, me neither. I'll ask Daniel to take care of it when he's done photographing those doomed floating cats in the bathroom.

KEVIN: Good plan. We're receiving word from downtown that there's a slow-down in our renovations. Our demolition crews have been stalled outside the empty lot across the street from the Rec Center, the lot with the sign that says FUTURE HOME OF THE OLD NIGHT VALE OPERA HOUSE.

It seems the outgoing mayor of Night Vale, Pamela Winchell, some old lady, and a line of impossibly tall people with long heads and wings have escaped—or...um, skipped out early from the Company Picnic and are blocking our contractors from building the town's third Sharper Image.

LAUREN: But that's impossible. We invoked eminent domain.

KEVIN: I'm getting word that the mayor has veto power over both eminent domain and Sharper Image.

LAUREN: How is she still mayor even? Daniel! Daniel, where are you?

I'm going to find Daniel. I'm going to have him drive me downtown and I'm going to deal with this directly. I'm tired of messing around with— What was that?

KEVIN: Listeners, the lights just went out in the studio.

LAUREN: [*Quiet*] Daniel? Kevin, why has Daniel not come back from taking pictures of the cats? That should not have taken this long. He's very efficient.

KEVIN: Sshhhh. There's someone here, Lauren. There's someone else in this room. Listeners, there is a bright, black glowing coming from the middle of our studio. It is glowing around the shape of someone neither man nor woman—tall, long, with great black wings, beating softly though filtered and recirculated seventy-one-degree air.

It is holding something. Something small and round. Listeners, it is holding a lightbulb.

It's moving now. The person, the what, the angel? Angels are, of course, real and very dangerous. This dangerous being is walking to the wall, to that new piece of art. The art that, unlike any other art in history, is not depicting teeth.

LAUREN: Oh, smiling god, that picture. Kevin that picture. It's different now.

KEVIN: The lighthouse. Moments ago the picture was of a lighthouse on a desert mountain in the clean light of midday. Now the photo is a lighthouse at desert's dusk, purple orange sky and a blinking red light atop the mountain. The light in the photo is actually blinking. There is a door at the foot of the stone tower, and that door is opening, a deep purple glow slowly silhouetting a man. It looks like a man. I cannot tell if he is tall or if he is short. He is holding something. I cannot tell what it is, but it moves in his arms.

The man is . . . he is entering the lighthouse. He—

LAUREN: Kevin, the door. Our studio door. Daniel? Is that you? Are the kittens dealt with?

KEVIN: I see only the intruder's shadow, in that deep purple glow. It is . . . it is the man from the lighthouse. He is holding something. The dangerous, dangerous angel is with him. The man is holding something.

LAUREN: No! How did you?

KEVIN: He is holding . . .

LAUREN: Don't come any nearer!

KEVIN: He is holding a cat.

CECIL: Thank you for bringing me here, Erika. And while whatever happens next happens, I take you, Night Vale, to the weather.

WEATHER: "High Tide Rising" by Fox

Listeners, it is good to be back after so long away in such a terrible terrible place. Let us never fall again for the wicked ruse of the Company Picnic, no matter how many badminton tournaments or chili-cook-offs the flyers and masked Picnic Captains advertise.

There was one escape attempt during the unending, deadly horror that was the staff softball game, but there were helicopters everywhere, and we were captured trying to dig a tunnel under second base with staple-pullers.

But last night, just when, as all picnic-goers eventually do, we had given up all hope of someday being free, former intern Dana appeared to me. There was an old oak door, which I swear had not been in the heavily electrified volleyball nets before. Or no, no more euphemisms. No more talking around it. They were high-voltage electric fences, fatal to any who touched them. The door in the fence opened and she stepped out, and, taking me by my hand, led me with her into whatever strange otherworld she had been trapped in for so long.

She brought me to the lighthouse in her strange desert that is like our own but is not our own. She introduced me to an army of men and women who have taken great care of her, and introduced me to several tall, winged creatures, each named Erika (with a *K*). Dana said they were angels. I informed each of them that angels are not real, and that's ridiculous. I might have howled this while covering my eyes.

Dana took me to the peak of the mountain, which is also not real. From atop this monstrosity of rock and earth and lies, we looked out across an empty pink desert, past the lighthouse, over the army, to a curved horizon under a placid ocean of cloudless forever. And I saw for myself, on that horizon, the terrible light rushing toward us.

Former intern Maureen is the one who showed everyone it was possible to pass fully back and forth, with her disappearing and re-appearing. And it was John Peters, you know, the farmer?, who stumbled on how to open the old oak doors that lead to so many places, but also to here, this one, beautiful place in space and time. Old Woman Josie and her definitely not angelic companions are in that other world too. So many have fled. But we will not flee anymore.

I have returned Khoshekh to his home here at the station, floating four feet off the ground in the men's restroom. I found Strexcorp's former radio producer, Daniel, lying dead or perhaps inoperative—I do not know if Daniel identified as organic or not—outside the restrooms. Apparently no one ever told him the deadly consequences of taking photos of cats.

Listeners, all is not well. Most is not well. Strexcorp still owns all that can be owned here, and so much also that cannot be owned. Many of you are still trapped in the Company Picnic. Others of you are trapped in mistaken impressions of how your life should supposedly be, but that started long before this whole Strex thing. That's something only you can fix, through reflection and laughter and acceptance. Lauren and Kevin ran away when faced with whatever you call Erika, but I do not think they will be gone for long. And then there is Dana and her army of masked warriors, standing in the path of that deep, rumbling light. That searing, blinding hum. That smiling god.

And I'll be honest. I don't know exactly where Carlos is. They captured his scientists, but they did not capture him. I'm sure he is fine. A scientist is always fine.

Listeners, so much is wrong. Here is what's right. Night Vale Community Radio is ours again.

We are the only thing in Night Vale not owned by Strex, and I swear . . . I swear . . . we will stay that way. And soon this whole town will be as this station is now. Not without struggle. Not without loss. Not without grave injury and a lifetime of what-ifs. But we will do it.

We may be controlled by the City Council, and the vague yet menacing government agency, and chemtrails, the secret order of reptile kings, and the mysterious lights that hover above us. But we will not be controlled by a smiling god. We are Night Vale. And we are, in our own way, free.

We must continue to fight and resist. We must be the heroes we look for in others. We must no longer speak in code, but in action.

Return to your homes, if you can, but do not lock your doors tonight. Do not hide yourselves away from danger. Be brave. Be truly brave.

I mean don't get carried away. Stay out of the Dog Park, and don't run with knives, and for crying out loud, don't cry out loud. You'll upset the bears, which are emotionally fragile animals that are already very uncomfortable with themselves.

Stay tuned next for that nagging feeling that you left the coffeepot on. Surely it's no big deal. But, oh geez, what if it is a big deal? Oh no. I can't believe you left the coffeepot on.

And as always, Good night, Night Vale. Good night.

PROVERB: Feeling lost? Like you have no goal in life? Like you're covered in dirt and wet leaves? Like you're an earthworm? Are you an earthworm? Kinda sounds like you're an earthworm, actually.

EPISODE 49:
"OLD OAK DOORS"

JUNE 15, 2014

RECORDED LIVE AT TOWN HALL, NEW YORK CITY, ON JUNE 4, 2014

GUEST VOICES: MEG BASHWINER, KEVIN R. FREE, MARK GAGLIARDI, MAUREEN JOHNSON, HAL LUBLIN, DYLAN MARRON, JASIKA NICOLE, JACKSON PUBLICK, SYMPHONY SANDERS, LAUREN SHARPE, MARA WILSON

THERE'S A LOT OF OTHER PEOPLE TO INTRODUCE THIS EPISODE WITH DE-tails of the planning and writing and performance of this one-off live anniversary episode. I'll just say this. We celebrated the one-year anniversary of the show in a bar space a fan got us for free on an off night, to a crowd of about 115 people. Our two-year anniversary was two shows in a midtown theater totaling over 2,000 tickets. It was a weird and amazing year between those two shows.

—Joseph Fink

There's a snapshot moment that I remember most about the evening Night Vale performed this show at Town Hall in New York. It was after the performances were over, after all the autographs were signed and photos taken. There were rumblings of going to a bar around the corner to celebrate since we had such an amazing cast for this onetime event;

and I told everyone I would meet them in a bit, just as soon as I got out of my suit and tie.

I was in a dressing room on the highest floor of the theater, tucked out of the way from the excited, frenetic energy of the green room and stage. My suit hung up behind the door, my dress shoes kicked off on the floor (because even the most comfortable shoes start to pinch when you've been standing on stage for the better part of five hours). I wanted to head out, but I just needed a few minutes of sitting in a chair and resting. One of the cleaning staff came in, thinking everyone else had left the theater, found me in my socks and underwear, and I told them I knew it was late and wouldn't be more than five minutes. They nodded and went back downstairs.

As I was packing up, it hit me just how improbable this whole situation was—of actually making a living being an actor in New York City, of performing in a theater just off Times Square, of making golden-age radio plays "cool" again, of creating a gay character with dignity and joy, of being some kind of cult success in a mainstream-obsessed society, of doing something so simple as telling macabre stories that were a balm to a life which is unpredictable and, ultimately, inescapable. Of being able to say, "I was here. I did this. Maybe when I go, I will be remembered fondly." All of that seemed so unlikely and so absurd it could hardly be believed . . . and that it had all happened in the span of two years. But there I was, packing up my belongings, a long and rewarding night's work complete.

And then it was out the stage door, out onto the streets of Manhattan, just one more person on the sidewalk going to meet friends and celebrate being together.

—Cecil Baldwin, Voice of Cecil Palmer

Sometimes *Night Vale* comes for you.

You don't believe it? Well, friend, it happened to me. Listen to a story . . .

So there's me, minding my own business one day. I'm a writer.

I like podcasts. I've got *Night Vale* coming in my earways through the headphones. I'm into it. Where am I? Oh, that's not important. I move through various locations. I'm not a fixed being.

BUILD THIS PICTURE IN YOUR MIND.

Maybe in some respects it sounds like you. It doesn't have to be all respects. We're more alike than we are different. All of a sudden, Cecil starts talking about this Intern Maureen. MY name is Maureen. This Maureen had a puppy. I have a puppy.

Oh, you think it was a coincidence? That there are many Maureens with many puppies? Think again, chumps! Because I checked it out. I asked around about "Joseph Fink" and "Jeffrey Cranor." Turns out, they're real. Surprise number one. Surprise number two: They verified that they had inserted me right into Night Vale.

Imagine that happening to you. You're just living your life and then all of a sudden you work for Night Vale Community Radio.

And then, you drink some orange juice and end up in a parallel dimension.

Oh no. No no no no no no. I found those J-fellows and I told them that if I was doing this internship, I WAS GOING TO DO THIS IN-TERNSHIP. Even if it meant working for Cecil. Don't extract me from my life and then juice me out of town.

You better believe they heard that. Who's back in this episode, the one you're about to read?

(*Points several thumbs at self*)

That's right. Intern Maureen. I even appeared ON STAGE, in an ACTUAL HUMAN THEATER, performing in this episode you're about to read.

Did I spend that night learning that the cast and crew of *Night Vale* are the best people around? Maybe. Did I tear up at the loveliness and dedication of *Night Vale* fans? Some reports say so. Was the microphone too high but I was afraid that if I touched it to adjust it I would knock it over and it would catch on fire and the whole theater would go up in flames and *Night Vale* fans would run screaming and burning into the night? Perhaps. So did someone have to help me adjust it be-cause no one could hear me because I was standing on my toes to try to reach it?

I'm not sure why you're asking all these questions. All I know is that I would do anything for the folks at *Night Vale*. And I'm thrilled to be a part in any way.

Now give me my *&$#%& college credits, Cecil.

—Maureen Johnson, Voice of Intern Maureen

Think back. Look forward. Listen timelessly.

WELCOME TO NIGHT VALE.

Hello listeners. I speak to you now from the one spot of Night Vale that remains truly ours. The studios of the Night Vale Community Radio Station. I have learned well from my misunderstanding about how barricading a door works, and so I have, for two weeks, managed to keep this studio free of Strexcorp influence and employees.

But enough preamble. Now, to the amble. Today is the day. There is only one thing for today, and that is the destruction of the hated Strexcorp, and the freeing of our town Night Vale. We will work no longer. We will worship a smiling god no longer. We have failed before—we have failed so many times at so many tasks—but at this we will not fail.

I hope.

I really really hope we will not fail.

In any case, we will be devoting all of today's broadcast to the revolution, with no interruptions.

HIRAM-GOLD: Excuse me!
CECIL: Excuse me?
HIRAM-GREEN: CEASE SPEAKING OR I WILL CEASE YOUR SPEAKING FOR YOU.
HIRAM-GOLD: Easy there, Green head.

CECIL: Listeners, I'm sorry. Mayoral candidate and literal five-headed dragon Hiram McDaniels has just burst into the studio.

FACELESS OLD WOMAN: I am also present.

CECIL: Did someone speak?

FACELESS OLD WOMAN: Yes, it's me. The Faceless Old Woman Who Secretly Lives in Your Home. I'm crouched in the crawlspace under your studio right now. There are many interesting insects and pipes down here.

CECIL: Well, it's great to have you both, but there's a revolution to do, so—

HIRAM-GOLD: Listen, Cecil. Far be it from me to get in the way of your revolution. I'm all for liberty.

HIRAM-PURPLE: The tree of liberty must be periodically watered with blood and mulched with detached limbs and pruned using shears made from bones. It's my favorite tree.

HIRAM-GOLD: Yes, exactly, Purple head.

FACELESS OLD WOMAN: We are here because you are forgetting the most important thing that is happening today. Today is election day. That day when finally Night Vale citizens will be able to effect change. Or not effect change, but be affected by it.

CECIL: Well. Sure. There's also an election today. And we will definitely cover that as well. Okay? Now please go stand in the alley behind City Hall and await the results, as is traditional.

FACELESS OLD WOMAN: Thanks, Cecil.

HIRAM-GOLD: Absolutely. Thank you much. Check back in with you soon.

HIRAM-GREEN: YES, WHAT MY GOLD HEAD SAID, YOU PITIFUL WHELP OF A MAN.

[*Exit HIRAM and FACELESS OLD WOMAN*]

CECIL: Let's go immediately to the news.

Many citizens are reporting that old oak doors with brass knobs have been appearing all over town. The doors open onto a desert landscape quite like this one. Through these doors are arriving tall creatures with long faces and broad wings. These creatures are difficult to categorize, but the best I can do is "definitely not-angels." The not-at-all-angelic creatures are joined by enormous men and women wearing masks. The not-angels and the masked army have torn down the electric fences trapping people at the Strexcorp company picnic.

This is great news. But unfortunately, the news is not over.

Strexcorp has responded with a seemingly unending force of eyeless, blood-drenched office workers, dressed in smart but affordable business casual clothing and armed with jagged knives and toothy smiles. They are backed by a swarm of yellow helicopters that have filled the sky and yet, strangely, have not blotted out the sun. In fact, the sun seems brighter than ever. Unnaturally bright, if a ball of highly compacted gas that sustains life through mere proximity could ever be called natural.

The horrible, smiling office workers have driven the tall, winged creatures and the masked army back from the picnic. The Strex force is too much for even these rescuers from another world to handle. Whatever unspecified powers they have are, unspecifically, not enough, and they are, quite specifically, losing. They are fleeing. Some have fallen, as the ravenous office workers swarm over them.

The angels, or, you know, "not-angels," have entered the juvenile detention center, looking for a certain little girl, no, young woman, no, human being, and her well-trained militia of other human beings. But the cell that once contained Tamika Flynn is empty.

Instead there are only shackles that have been pulled completely apart, and the words *I AM FOUND* written on a bookmark laid across page 210 of a paperback copy of Leonard Cohen's *Book of Longing*. The current whereabouts of Tamika Flynn are not known. The winged creatures who are all named Erika and the army of masked giants have continued their retreat before the onslaught of eyeless office workers all the way past the Old Town Drawbridge.

Given the urgency of today, I planned to skip some of our regular features as well as sponsor ads, but since forcing out our current ownership, we've gotten a bit behind on our bills. So there's now a sentient patch of haze in my studio.

DEB: Hello, Cecil. Hello, listeners. My name is Deb.

CECIL: And Deb won't leave my studio until she has told us about . . . what are you promoting?

DEB: Whole Foods.

CECIL: Right. So, even though we have a big revolution to do, let's take a moment to listen to Deb the sentient patch of haze about . . .

DEB: Whole Foods. Thanks, Cecil.

At Whole Foods, we don't have any rotting, decayed matter mixed into our products. There are no secret blood rooms in our stores, where we keep the secret blood. None of the boxes of cereal contain spiders, and, if they did, they would be very friendly, helpful spiders. Why, you would be lucky to find a spider like that in a box of Whole Foods cereal. Or not just one. Hundreds of them. But anyway, you won't.

Whole Foods serves only the freshest food, and certainly we do not keep venomous snakes under the fruit in our produce section. Why would we? That would be dangerous and not good for business. No one has died of a snakebite in a Whole Foods. No one you know.

Whole Foods: Why in the world would we poison our frozen dinners? We definitely do not.

CECIL: Thanks, Deb.

DEB: No, thank you, Cecil. Good luck with whatever you've got going on here. Seems uninteresting and human.

CECIL: Okay, well . . . good-bye, Deb.

[*Exit DEB*]

[*Sound cue: static, radio distortion*]

Listeners, I apologize for these noises you may be getting. There is some other radio signal interfering with our own.

LAUREN: Cecil? Hi, it's Lauren Mallard, you know the Vice President of Strexcorp—your parent company.

KEVIN: Sorry to interrupt.

LAUREN: Kevin and I are broadcasting from a secret location and we just had to break into your signal. We wanted a moment to talk with you. Gently talking solves a lot of things.

[*Fade out sound cue*]

KEVIN: Violent revolution has never solved anything.

CECIL: I beg to differ. America was founded on a revolution. I mean sure, we still are ruled by the reptilians. But the lizard kings let us have our own country after they saw how hard we tried during that revolution thing.

LAUREN: That was decades ago, Cecil. Anyway, we want to know what we can do to keep your business. We here at Strexcorp Synergists, Inc., are dedicated to the betterment of life through branding, social networking, and upbeat music.

KEVIN: And hard work.

LAUREN: I'm pretty sure it's implied that hard work is part of it, Kevin.

KEVIN: I'm pretty sure I didn't ask for your feedback.

LAUREN: Cecil, Strexcorp values the efforts you put into making this station what it was. Is. What it is. But when employees are refusing to participate in our trust exercises and boycotting our products and attacking us with our own helicopters, then I think we have failed our mission statement.

CECIL: What's your mission statement?

KEVIN: This.

[*Sound cue: rumbling from episode 47*]

LAUREN: We got so caught up in thinking about our business that we didn't think about the people. People matter at Strexcorp. They matter because of the business.

We're here to set things right. First things first, we will rebuild the Night Vale Harbor and Waterfront Recreation Area and divert thousands of gallons of necessary drinking water from other towns to provide it with its namesake. We will also fill in the giant hole out back of the Ralphs.

CECIL: But where will the people who huddle there go to huddle?

LAUREN: Oh, Cecil, you are simply resistant to change. Your revolution is cute. Community togetherness is adorable. But money, money is power. We will invest—

KEVIN: Are currently investing.

LAUREN: —to make Night Vale a better place to live.

KEVIN: Thus increasing the resale value.

LAUREN: Also, we know everyone fears libraries in Night Vale. Which is why Strexcorp will tear down the library, destroy the dangerous librarians, and replace it with StrexBooks purchase centers.

TAMIKA: Don't you dare try to bring books into this.

CECIL: Tamika, is that you?

TAMIKA: Yes, I found their secret location using a radio triangulation technique I learned by reading an anthology of Emily Dickenson's poems.

KEVIN: Lauren, be careful. She has a slingshot and a heavy-looking edition of John Osborne's successful play *Look Back in Anger*.

LAUREN: Thank you, Kev. But I will happily deal with this myself. I just so happen to have my own slingshot and an extremely heavy edition of the Strex Employee Handbook.

KEVIN: Well, Lauren, you have this situation under control, I'm just going to . . . oversee important . . . things elsewhere. Let me know if . . . *when* you take care of the child.

[*Exit KEVIN*]

TAMIKA: I love books. Take that book you're holding. It looks ill-written and ill-conceived, full of bad ideas expressed poorly. I bet it lacks narrative arcs and an appreciation for the flow of language. It looks like the worst book in the history of books. But here's the thing. It's still a book. And I love books. So you do not deserve to even hold it.

LAUREN: Then come and get it.

CECIL: Tamika, stay alert.

LAUREN: Let me throw some ideas at you.

TAMIKA: Ugh!

LAUREN: Ha! Yes.

CECIL: Tamika? Are you hurt? Tamika?

LAUREN: Cecil, Tamika won't be a problem for us any longer. Now what were we talking about? Right. Money. Success. It's . . .

TAMIKA: [*Groans, waking up*]

CECIL: Tamika! Tamika, can you hear me?

LAUREN: Well drat. Hold on, Cecil. Seems she's still up and about. This'll just take a second.

TAMIKA: Lady, I've trained for months. I've taken down your helicopters with only a slingshot. I've looked a librarian right in the area where most creatures would have eyes. You. Do. Not. Scare me.

LAUREN: Oh no. Where did all these children come from?

TAMIKA: Doesn't matter. What matters is that in a few moments you will start running as fast as you can in the direction of Desert Bluffs. All right, Book Club. Books as clubs. Go!

LAUREN: May the smiling god show me mercy. I give up! I give up! I— Ow! Okay, I'm going!

[*Exit LAUREN*]

CECIL: Well done, young Ms. Flynn.

TAMIKA: I'm securing this frequency. We'll keep broadcasting instructions from here. Stay vigilant, Night Vale.

[*Exit TAMIKA*]

CECIL: Thank you, Tamika.

Listeners, Night Vale is coming alive.

After weeks of the Company Picnic, the citizens are remembering who they are. They are members of a proud pseudo-democracy run by lizard kings through a byzantine maze of puppet governments and paperwork.

A crowd of those grinning Strexcorp drones surrounded one of the winged "not-angels" who was wearing a hand-tailored suit coat and was otherwise totally nude. But then Leann Hart, managing editor of the *Night Vale Daily Journal*, hacked her way through the crowd with a hatchet.

"I am imagining you are all news bloggers," she screamed. "You are destroying years of journalistic tradition."

At the urging of Sarah Sultan, the president of Night Vale Community College, Leann then threw Sarah at the few remaining Strex workers who were still intact. Sarah, who is a smooth, fist-size river rock, hit her target magnificently before bouncing off somewhere.

And so this Erika, who looked both wealthy and mostly nude, was saved.

Wait, I am seeing a flickering. The flickering is becoming a shape. The shape is becoming a woman.

DANA: Hello, Cecil. It's me, Dana.

CECIL: Dana, why haven't you returned to Night Vale?

DANA: I will soon, I think. But there is something here that has me worried. That rumbling is getting louder. And the light on the horizon is quite close. I can feel heat, but I am not warm. The more the heat grows, the colder I feel. It is a terrible light, and it is so close now. I feel as though the universe itself is unraveling.

Plus, I found someone here in the desert.

CARLOS: Hello, Cecil. I am manifesting myself in your radio station for both personal and not personal reasons.

CECIL: Carlos! Oh, thank the imperfect heavens. I haven't seen you in weeks. I didn't know where you had gone.

CARLOS: When I entered the house that does not exist, I found myself in this other desert world. But something had happened to my team of scientists, and there was no one to let me back out. Then I couldn't even find the door. Eventually your friend Dana found me.

CECIL: Carlos, why didn't you call? Or Snapchat? Or reblog any of my woodcarvings of Khoshekh?

CARLOS: Cecil, how would I do that? I'm in the middle of a desert that is not of this world. There's no cell towers or Wi-Fi or any kind of communication system. Plus, I want to save my battery until I can find my way back to—

DANA: Oh no, your phone totally works here.

CARLOS: Really?

DANA: Yeah. Also I haven't charged my phone in like a year. Battery never ran down.

CARLOS: Is that a Samsung?

DANA: No no. Same as yours.

CARLOS: Wow.

DANA: And Wi-Fi is pretty decent out here too.

CARLOS: Oh, look at that. Cecil, I'm on your Tumblr right now. That artwork is amazing.

DANA: I mean, time is pretty messed up, so sometimes you reply to e-mails before they're even sent to you, but other than that . . .

CECIL: Carlos, how do I get you home? Dana, how do we get Carlos home? I would like Carlos to come home.

CARLOS: I'll be able to very soon. I'm working on inventing something right now.

DANA: Every time the doors are opened, it lets that terrible light into Night Vale. And the light is so close now. We can't risk it.

CARLOS: Right. You're very smart. You have very smart interns, Cecil. So I'm building a highly scientific device to keep the light away from the doors. Now the device looks a lot like a big umbrella, but it's way more complex and scientific than that for reasons I don't have time to explain right now. My Danger Meter is in the red, and, scientifically speaking, red is the most dangerous color.

CECIL: Carlos, you're fading. Dana, where's Carlos?

DANA: He's still here.

CARLOS: Dana, I can't see Cecil anymore.

DANA: He's still here. Carlos, thank you. I may get to see my mother and my brother again because of you. You are a hero.

CARLOS: I'm not a hero. I'm a scientist.

DANA: Then *scientist* will always be my word for *hero*.

CECIL: What's he saying?

CARLOS: We should go. Tell Cecil we won't be long at all. The doors should be safe to open now. I just need to finish stabilizing the device.

DANA: Cecil, we have work to do, but we'll be home soon.

CECIL: I can't wait to see you both.

CARLOS: Like, an hour or two, max.

CECIL: What? Did he say something? Was it cute?

DANA: Good-bye, Cecil.

CECIL: It's good to know we have such a talented former intern and brilliant scientist working together.

Once again, listeners, as several frantic phone calls have reminded me, it is also election day. Let's check in at the alley behind City Hall. Hiram? Faceless Old Woman?

HIRAM-GREEN: YOUR REVOLUTION IS MEANINGLESS. I WILL BURN ALL DETRACTORS.

HIRAM-GOLD: Yep, Cecil, all of us are in agreement. Me, my green head there, my other three heads.

HIRAM-GRAY: Sure, just lump us together as "the other three."

HIRAM-BLUE: It's always just gold talking away like he's the important one and sometimes green yells something. Green and gold. Green and gold.

HIRAM-PURPLE: Also, please call me Violet. You always say Purple, but I prefer Violet.

HIRAM-GOLD: Right, yes, also my gray, blue, and, uh, violet heads there. Anyway, we all agree that once we become mayor, this whole revolution . . . well, it's sort of moot. If Strexcorp is still here and the people want them gone, we'll just, you know, throw some flames at the problem.

FACELESS OLD WOMAN: The real issue now is getting these doors shut. There's a blinding light pouring from them and it's causing the world to become translucent. We can hear a deep rumbling sound, which I do not like. The helicopters seem unaffected. I think a terrible thing is trying to come through. Something whose secrets I do not know. The unraveling of all things. Fire-breathing will solve none of this.

HIRAM-GOLD: Basically, the angels, or you know, "not-angels," just need to shut the doors when they're done going through them.

HIRAM-PURPLE: Yeah, were they born in a barn?

FACELESS OLD WOMAN: According to religious texts, yes.

CECIL: Did you not know that?

FACELESS OLD WOMAN: Anyway, I agree with Hiram. A revolution and the unraveling of the universe is all fine, but it would be great if you could cover the election more comprehensively. We've worked really hard.

CECIL: I'll do my best. Or, not my best, but some level of effort. Well, thanks for the updates, you two!

[*Exit HIRAM and FACELESS OLD WOMAN*]

Listeners, you heard the candidates. The doors are open. There's a powerful rumbling below the earth and a bright light turning everything translucent. Probably that's bad news, but weather is weird here, so who knows?

Oh, how fantastic. A couple of old friends just came by the studio, listeners.

JOHN: Howdy, Cecil.

CECIL: Listeners, it's John Peters, you know, the farmer? And Intern Maureen, is that you?

MAUREEN: Yyyyep. Sure is.

JOHN: Cecil, Dana and your science fellow helped us get out of that other desert place. I mean, I'm the one who found all those old oak doors, and Maureen here figured out that physically going back and forth between worlds was possible, but those two helped a bunch.

CECIL: Great work, all of you. I'm so glad to get to see all of my lost friends again.

JOHN: I stopped by to tell you that we have seen the rumbling in the desert. We have heard the bright light entering Night Vale. Cecil, that light. It is the great glowing coils of the universe unwinding. It is the unraveling of all things. It is a smiling god of terrible power.

CECIL: How do you know all this, John?

JOHN: Well, I was in 4-H club in high school. I'm a farmer you know. You learn all about this kind of stuff in 4-H. Seemed obvious.

CECIL: No, of course. I'm sorry. Maureen, it really is so nice to see you again. It has been so lo—

MAUREEN: Listen to me, you monster. I got you coffee and made mimeographs and sang sea shanties to the ants every single day. I even copyedited your Jaws slashfic even though that wasn't in the job description. Then one day, oh, get me some orange juice, Maureen. I mean I won't even tell you about how it's making people blink in and out of existence. And not only did it make me blink out of reality, you didn't even want it when I brought it.

Do you even know the mortality rate of your internship program?

CECIL: I'm not sure what you mean.

MAUREEN: Chad, Jerry, Leland, Rob, Brad, Stacey, Richard, Paolo, Dylan, Vithya, and Zvi. Do you know what they all have in common?

CECIL: They got great training for a future career in radio?

MAUREEN: No! That's not it at all. They're—

CECIL: [*Interrupting*] Speaking of interns, Intern Jeremy had a recent run-in with the scorpions in the break room and will be missed. Oh, hey, now that you're back home, are you still looking for college credit?

MAUREEN: Um, yeah.

CECIL: Great. Can you start today?

MAUREEN: Okay. Thanks.

CECIL: Thanks for stopping by, John.

JOHN: Sure thing, Cecil. Beware the unraveling of all things, and support your local farmers.

CECIL: Maureen can you run to the library and do some research on smiling gods?

MAUREEN: Fine.

[*Exit JOHN and MAUREEN*]

CECIL: If John and Maureen are back, that must mean that the doors are working again. This is fantastic news.

I am receiving reports that the rumbling is growing louder. People are saying they can feel it in their feet and teeth. They are becoming forgetful. Objects are becoming transparent. The darkness of Night Vale is washing away. What are we, Night Vale, without darkness, without shadow and secrets?

There's someone knocking on my station door! Carlos! Carlos, is that you? Come in. Welcome home, swee—

[*STEVE enters*]

OH. NO. No!

STEVE: Cecil, I was in the neighborhood and wanted to stop by.

CECIL: No, Steve. You do not stop by the studio. You are not a radio professional.

STEVE: I've been driving in circles around your station all day listening to the show, and it got me thinking. John Peters, you know, the farmer?, was all like "Hey y'all, there's a smilin' god and the world is unraveling because I was in 4-H club." And he's mostly right, but I think that it's not a smiling god but a secret underground missile testing site.

CECIL: The secret underground missile testing site is below the Rec Center, Steve.

STEVE: Well, it's like the Faceless Old Woman said recently while campaigning. She said: "I'm replacing all of your digital photo albums with classified pictures of secret missile testing sites."

I think the Faceless Old Woman understands what's really going on, whereas Hiram is like, "Well, I can't really be bothered with looking into government overspending because I am literally a five-headed dragon." And his blue head is like, "When you consider the mathematics, there's no benefit to us." And gray says, "Thinking about government interference makes me sad." And violet says, "We must be free above all. We must be free and also above all other things." And then his last head just keeps roaring and saying, "YOUR BODY BURNS QUICKLY, SOFT HUMAN PROTESTERS!"

But really, I was thinking about what your boyfriend, Carlos, said.

CECIL: Don't you dare, Steve Carlsberg.

STEVE: He said, "I'm certain I can stop the light from entering Night Vale. I have a simple device that will protect us."

CECIL: That was [*honest assessment of the impression*].

STEVE: But he's, and no offense, Cecil, he's an outsider. He's not from here. How do we know he's not part of the super underground secret military government that is testing missiles?

CECIL: Steve Carlsberg! Did you just accuse my boyfriend of being a secret operative?

STEVE: Well, um, yeah.

CECIL: That'd be pretty cool, actually. But it is not true, Steve! Plus, how many times do I have to tell you there is nothing secret about secret missile testing. It's as American as using drug-laced apple pie to test the effects of hallucinogens on innocent citizens.

KEVIN: I think he brings up a good point, Cecil.

CECIL: You! How did you get in here?

STEVE: Oh, thanks interloper. Whoa, cool eyes.

KEVIN: Oh thank you, I wish I could say the same. Cecil, listen, it's hard to get work done when there is all this fighting. And it's hard to smile when there's no working. And if we aren't smiling, then what value do we have? Watch me smile.

[*Smiles*]

CECIL: You monster.
STEVE: That was really gross! Do it again.
KEVIN: Look at how much better we all feel from that. But right now no one is being productive. There are angels . . .
CECIL AND STEVE: No. Not really. Nope.
KEVIN: . . . and a desert army out there battling for what? For hooded figures? For forbidden Dog Parks? For a glow cloud?
CECIL AND STEVE: All hail.
KEVIN: For the constant terror of a secret police who can invade your home at any time without so much as a letter from Human Resources?
CECIL: They are our hooded figures. It is our Glow Cloud.
CECIL AND STEVE: All hail.
CECIL: This is our town, and it is terrible but it is ours, and we are fighting for it.
KEVIN: I used to feel that way about Desert Bluffs.

So many secrets and conspiracies and darkness in our days. It all felt so important, so permanent. But then we met the smiling god. Oh, it was wonderful. The sun stopped setting. Or maybe there wasn't a sun anymore. Maybe there was just that other, brighter light. Who knows? I do know that we couldn't stop smiling, and our smiles seemed better, fuller, wider.

Soon we had no need for government cover-ups or secrets. Everything was transparent. Literally. You could see through everything and everyone. The bones, the blood, the scurrying insects inside every human body. There was so much work to be done. And such a wonderful company to do it for. Even the ones that resisted the most at first soon found that they loved the smiling god more than anyone. Even the most resistant of radio hosts soon found his way to productive work, happy songs, and a wide, gaping smile.

So let's do this together, Cecil. Believe with me in a smiling god. The greater Night Vale AND Desert Bluffs Metropolitan Area. A town with, not one, but two happy, helpful voices.

CECIL: Listeners, Kevin has just opened up the studio door, only it is not the studio door. It is an oak door, and light, blinding light, is pouring in. Everything is becoming translucent.

KEVIN: Do you see, friends? The beautiful majesty of living as one under the unrelenting love of a smiling god?

STEVE: Wow. It's a very pretty light. You know, that Company Picnic of yours sure wasn't fun. But I got more done in two weeks than in the rest of my life combined.

CECIL: Steve. What are you saying? No.

STEVE: Kevin, before I step into your weird light, let me ask about schools. My stepdaughter, Janice, is ten years old, and the elementary schools are okay, but I don't know if I can afford to send her to private school when she's—

KEVIN: Say no more, Steve Carlsberg, Desert Bluffs schools are top-notch. Young Janice can take college prep courses as early as twelve. Our charter schools even have great medical programs where they can heal her of all her problems.

STEVE: I'm sorry, I don't get it.

CECIL: Yeah, Janice's uncle here. What do you mean, "heal her"?

KEVIN: She can't walk, right?

STEVE AND CECIL: Sure. Right. She can't. Since birth.

KEVIN: Well, rather than build all those crazy ramps and elevators, we just fix people, so that they can become better and more productive.

[*Beat*]

STEVE: YOU ARE AWFUL AND GROSS. AND I WAS ONLY BEING POLITE ABOUT YOUR EYES. THEY ARE WEIRD. NOW YOU LISTEN TO ME.

CECIL: Listeners, Steve Carlsberg just picked up Kevin by his blood-stained lapels.

STEVE: YOU WILL NOT CHANGE MY HOMETOWN. YOU WILL NOT CHANGE MY STEPBROTHER. AND, KEVIN OF DESERT BLUFFS, YOU WILL NOT CHANGE OR FIX OR DO ANYTHING AT ALL TO MY LITTLE GIRL.

CECIL: Steve is carrying him to the open oak door and pushing him through into that blinding, awful light.

KEVIN: [*Screams*]

CECIL: Kevin is gone.

STEVE: I did not like that guy very much.

CECIL: Me neither. Thanks, Steve.

STEVE: Anything for my girl. Try to tell me that there's something about her that needs fixing.

CECIL: You know, Steve. We have our differences. Many differences. More differences than not.

STEVE: Sure.

CECIL: But I'm glad you're there to take care of Janice. She could do a lot worse.

STEVE: Aww, Cecil.

CECIL: Now leave my studio and stop barging in here with your stupid ideas about the world.

STEVE: Yep. See you round, Cecil! [*To DANA who is entering*] Oh, hey there! Steve Carlsberg. Aren't you important-looking?

CECIL: Dana, are you actually back in the studio? Not just an image? Not an apparition?

DANA: I am. I'm home. Our time and space finally, finally meet again.

CECIL: This is a happy day.

DANA: I am glad to see you too, Cecil. But I also came by to talk to the whole city.

People of Night Vale, there is a light drowning out our sun and our minds. But there are angels and an army of masked warriors fighting back this terrible menace. Night Vale, stay safe. Stay home and do not get caught in the dangerous crossfire. The desert army and the angels are here to save us.

TAMIKA: People of Night Vale—

CECIL: Dana, I'm sorry. I think that's Tamika Flynn from her secret broadcast site.

TAMIKA: People of Night Vale, hear me.

DANA: Tamika? THE Tamika Flynn? Hi, I'm Dana. I've heard so much about you. You are an inspiration. You are a hero.

TAMIKA: Thank you, Dana. But I am not a hero. Or we all are. Or the word has no meaning. We must all save our town and ourselves.

People of Night Vale, I am calling you to arms. There are beings claiming to be angels and this foreign army of giants fighting. Why can't we?

CECIL: Good, well . . .

DANA: People of Night Vale, angels are definitely real. I brought them here from the other world. They are powerful and recently very wealthy and they are tough to kill, unlike humans who die easily and unexpectedly all the time from all sorts of little causes. Just wait and let them save us.

CECIL: Ah, so . . .

TAMIKA: People of Night Vale, do not be defined by how you can die, but by how you can live. It is like the great writer and orator Booker T. Washington once said: "In all things social we can be as separate as the fingers, yet one as the hand in all things essential to destroying a smiling god!"

DANA: Stay safe, Night Vale. Stay indoors and we will broadcast to let you know when it is over.

TAMIKA: Get out there, Night Vale, grab anything you can and fight. Grab a slingshot and a book—say an Aimee Bender short story collection or Milorad Pavic's *Dictionary of the Khazar's*, or, if not a book, grab a rock, or the throwing stars that come standard in most issues of *McSweeney's*. Grab anything you can and fight. Do not believe in heroes. Believe in citizens. Be a citizen.

CECIL: Dana, I know you have planned this well. You are incredibly smart. But I think Tamika is right. I think we have to do this together. Let us not repeat our sin of inaction.

DANA: [*Mumbling, overlapping*] All right then, fine, don't listen to me, just brought two different armies here, whatever.

CECIL: It has grown so bright. I cannot see much, and what I can see is nearly transparent. I am forgetting. Everything is coming apart. I can see the great glowing coils of the universe unwinding.

[*Deep rumbling throughout*]

Night Vale our time is now. Let us raise our fists and shout.

I can almost hear it. A crowd shouting "Take down Strex." I can almost hear that crowd but I can't quite hear them. They need to shout louder. They all shout "Take Down Strex." They, every single one of them, shout it louder. "Take Down Strex." Louder than shouting, they scream it. "Take down Strex. Take Down Strex."

But then they stop. Not because they do not care, but because those particular people are far away and not part of this story. They are part of a different story, a different fiction.

Realizing this, they all shrug and sadly murmur to each other: "Take Down Strex." And then they are quiet and hope for that rarest element of all. They hope for the best.

But in this story, in this fiction, I hear the sound of Night Vale fighting back. And as the light of the smiling god grows brighter, and the shouts of a defiant Night Vale grow louder, and as I reach for my copy of Kate Chopin's *The Awakening*, more specifically for the tear gas canisters that came attached to the hardback edition, I take you all now, all of us fighting, all of us together, all of us, all of us—

—to the weather.

[*Exit CECIL*]

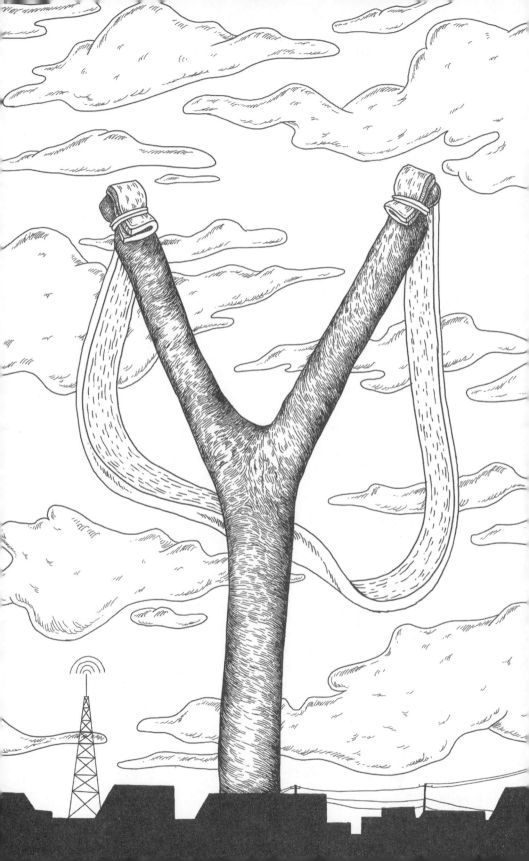

WEATHER: "Call Off Your Ghost" by Dessa

[*CARLOS enters*]

[*Sound cue: Cecil voice mail and beep*]

CECIL: [*Recording*] Hi, you've reached the voice mail of Cecil Palmer. I'm off doing some important journalistic work or maybe just petting Khoshekh, but either way, leave me a message.

[*Beep*]

CARLOS: Cecil, hey. It's Carlos. I hate that I got your voice mail. But listen, I figured it out.

We can't shut the oak doors unless everyone is back where they belong. And every moment those doors are open, more of that light gets through into Night Vale.

I couldn't figure out why we couldn't just keep the doors closed for good.

It was really frustrating to have a problem I couldn't solve. And then I got sad because I couldn't solve it. But then I did solve it and felt happy. Those are some but not all of the emotions I had.

Here is what I found: Night Vale is a place that is difficult to leave and difficult to enter. And connecting a place as weird as that with a place as weird as this was causing a lot of strain on linear time and space.

So those native to Night Vale: Dana, John, the angry woman in the intern shirt, all had to return home, and the masked army all had to come back here. Which they did. Just moments ago the last of them came back through the door.

It's so exciting when you make a scientific discovery like that. I was very happy.

But then, as the last of the masked army members came through the door, it slammed shut and vanished. And I remembered that I am not from Night Vale. I remembered that, as far as the laws of the universe are concerned, it is not where I belong.

Cecil, I don't even remember how I got to Night Vale in the first place. I mean, where is Night Vale even? But I promise, I will find my way back. It'll just take a couple of days. A week, max. I'll be fine. I'm a scientist, Cecil. A scientist is usually fine.

Maybe a few weeks. I don't know.

The upside is Dana was right. I've had 97 percent battery all day and decent reception. So we'll at least get to talk every night. Best of luck at home. I love you.

[CECIL enters]

CECIL: [Normal lighting] Listeners, Night Vale fought together, every citizen.

[Music cue: triumphant music]

High school football coach Nazr al-Mujaheed, in response to the Strex workers' ghastly smiles, showed them that thing he can do with his tongue, which made many of them stop smiling and run screaming away.

A balaclava-clad man wearing a mitre, cloak, and a giant silver star, and speaking through a vocoder—you know, the man we all believe to be the Sheriff of Night Vale?—was dropping heavy bricks down on the invaders from his hover-office in the clouds.

Simone Rigadeau, the transient who lives in the earth sciences building at the community college found some experimental fish in the lab closet there and put them into the fuel tanks of the yellow helicopters, which were already incapacitated by several plastic bags that had blown out of the forbidden Dog Park and wrapped themselves up in the rotors.

Old Woman Josie and her supposed "angel" friends protected the empty lot where she plans to rebuild Night Vale's Old Opera House. The Strex attackers were picked up by her winged friends and flown far into the sky, higher even than the Sheriff's hover-office.

And of course a group of teenagers led by Tamika Flynn chased out everyone at Strexcorp headquarters by slingshotting copies of Steven Covey's bestselling self-help book *7 Habits of Highly Effective People*.

The civilization of tiny people living below lane five of the Desert Flower Bowling Alley and Arcade Fun Complex did something, I'm sure, but they were too tiny to be noticed amid the action.

Which is all to say that Strex has retreated. The blood-covered office workers are gone. The old oak doors are also gone, and with them that penetrating, vicious light. We are safely in darkness again.

A very wealthy-looking and mostly nude being named Erika who introduced itself as "you know, an angel or whatever," then wrote a check to purchase Strexcorp. While it was not technically for sale, there was no one to decline the offer, so according to American business law that's a legal acquisition. It is not yet known what the angels will do with the vast corporation they now own.

I think...at last...we are ourselves. We are Night Vale again.

[*Music starts to warp, go weird, it's...triumphant? Maybe?*]

Even here at the station, the office of Station Management now is just a stone slab covering a dark cave, a pulsing red glow around its edges, filling my mind with sad and monstrous visions, when I walk past that door. So it seems like our old management is back in charge. That's...well, I think that's great news, listeners.

[*Music is really weird, not very triumphant at all*]

It's possible that it is instead terrifying news.
I think, I guess, we...won?

FACELESS OLD WOMAN: Speaking of winning...
CECIL: Oh, right, the election.

It looks like we didn't quite get all the votes in yet. Let's speed things up. Listeners, wherever you are listening to this, just follow along. When I say the name of the candidate you prefer, raise your hand. So I'll say the name, you raise your hand, and the cameras that are everywhere in town watching your every move will count your vote. So:

Raise your hand to vote for Hiram McDaniels.

HIRAM-GRAY: Oh, I thought there would be more. Do they not like me?

HIRAM-GREEN: RAISE YOUR HANDS FOR ME OR I WILL RELIEVE YOU OF THE BURDEN OF HAVING HANDS.

CECIL: Okay, hands down. Now raise your hand for the Faceless Old Woman Who Secretly Lives in Your Home.

FACELESS OLD WOMAN: I am in your home this very moment. I am, in this way, your guest. It would be rude, as a host, if you did not raise your hand for me while I was sitting right there, unseen, next to you. It might make me angry. I've never been angry. I wonder what I'm like when I'm angry. It will be interesting for us to find out together if you do not raise your hand for me.

CECIL: Great, hands down. I'm fairly certain that some of you voted for both, thus negating yourself. You'll know if one of your friends did this because they will soon fade from existence. Anyway, there's all the votes in, but of course, none of the votes matter, because the election is decided by the pulses coming from Hidden Gorge. I am being handed the results now by an election official in full uniform: plague doctor mask, off-brand snuggie, and stilts.

And the next mayor of Night Vale is . . .

HIRAM-GOLD: I thank every person who voted for me. You're all winners in my book.

HIRAM-BLUE: We've recorded all of your names here in this book.

FACELESS OLD WOMAN: I just ate one of your highlighters. I'm sorry. I'm nervous. I'll replace it with a crow's feather just as soon as I am mayor.

CECIL: Oh. Well. It says the next mayor is Dana Cardinal.

[*Beat*]

HIRAM-GOLD: I'm sorry, Cecil. I don't want to get obnoxious about this. But it's pronounced "Hiram." That wasn't even close.

CECIL: I know this must be a disappointment to you both, but I'm just reading what the gorge has decreed.

FACELESS OLD WOMAN: Your former intern Dana? But she wasn't even a candidate. And she's so young and not ancient.

CECIL: Dana, the intern who came home, it is like I told you once. You were always important.

HIRAM-GREEN: THIS IS UNACCEPTABLE. PREPARE TO BURN.

CECIL: You were always somebody. And now age has uncovered the you that always . . .

HIRAM-GREEN: GUAHHHRRHHHRHHRH.

CECIL: Hiram, please. I'm doing something right now. Was. The you that always was.

FACELESS OLD WOMAN: She can't be mayor. She's a murderer. She killed her own double.

HIRAM-GOLD: Well now, I don't know if murder should necessarily disqualify someone from being . . .

HIRAM-BLUE: Irrelevant. There is a 50 percent chance that the victim was Dana original and not Dana double.

HIRAM-GOLD: Oh yeah. Thanks, Blue. Forget that other thing I was saying. She has no proof that she is not a double of herself.

CECIL: Not proof, no . . .

FACELESS OLD WOMAN: Everyone knows that a double is one of the few manifestations of reality that cannot be Night Vale mayor. I do not accept these results. I am continuing my campaign and I will make sure that Dana does not stay "mayor" for long.

HIRAM-GOLD: I find myself agreeing with the Faceless Old Woman. We will not rest until one of us is rightfully mayor.

HIRAM-GREEN: OR UNTIL NIGHT VALE BURNS TO ASH AND FUMES.

HIRAM-GOLD: Yes, Green. Exactly yes.

CECIL: I really must object to all of this.

FACELESS OLD WOMAN: Come Hiram. You and I have planning to do.

CECIL: Well, once again it's just you and me, listeners. The bustle of the day has come and gone, and now there is the quiet night.

The universe is unraveling. It still is.

We won the day. We won the battle. We won whatever unit of measure you care to say we won. We returned to the dangerous equilibrium we had before, which we can only assume, or hope, or wish, is better. But of course we did not stop the unraveling of the universe.

The universe is not a thing that is. It is not a thing at all. It is the very action of its going. It is, in fact, its own dissolve. And our lives, the entire span of human existence going back and back and, if we're lucky, forward and forward, that entire span is spent within the dissolve.

Look at the fleeting stars with fleeting eyes, and feel how the earth beneath you gives. It is all a temporary manifestation of particles. It is all unraveling back to particulate silence. The bustle of the human day will come and go, and then there will be the quiet night.

But how beautiful these moments within the dissolve. What a temporary perfection we can find within this passing world. Everything good ever done, everything good done today, all the good people doing it, and back and back and forward and forward, all of that beauty within a universe unraveling.

Be proud of your place in the cosmos. It is so small. And yet it is. How unlikely! How fantastic and stupid and excellent!

And . . . oh sorry. Hm . . . it looks like I have a voice mail from Carlos. He must have called during the weather. I apologize, listeners. I have to check this.

Stay tuned next for more of us and more of me, until that inevitable, distant point where I, and this, and everything, must end.

Good night, Night Vale. Good night.

PROVERB: "Wonderwall" is the only '90s song visible from space.

DISPARITION MUSIC CORNER

THROUGHOUT THE EARLY YEARS OF DISPARITION I PERFORMED LIVE ON rare occasions, usually for very small audiences at house shows or other small events. One of these was the very first live *Night Vale* event in 2013, which was held in a small bar within New York's Webster Hall as part of a quarterly salon featuring a number of comedians and musicians. The audience was around forty or fifty people, and the setup was very basic, but this first show was similar in format to what we do today: Cecil reading and acting out an episode while I accompany him with a combination of prerecorded loops and improvised live keyboard parts.

Two years or so into *Night Vale*'s existence, the podcast suddenly began to attract a much larger audience, and we decided this was an opportunity to put on our first "big" live show, complete with special guest actors and a full band version of Disparition. We performed it at Roulette in downtown Brooklyn, for an audience of four hundred people or so, which was at the time the largest audience I'd ever performed original music for. I chose several Disparition pieces which had been used frequently in the podcast, and wrote new arrangements of them for guitar, violin, viola, and cello. Joining us as a musical guest at this show was Seattle-based troubadour Jason Webley, whom I had never met, let alone played music with. Nevertheless, we conspired over e-mail to do a cover version of Joseph Fink's song "These and More Than These" at the end of the show as a special surprise for him. We had no time to rehearse it prior to the show, but we managed to pull it off, if in perhaps a somewhat chaotic style. Later, Jason would end up touring with us in the US and UK, and remains a good friend of the show.

Beginning in the spring of 2015, *Night Vale* began to expand its touring operations and I started touring with the show full time, not only providing a live score but also taking on the role of technical director, working with venue sound operators and lighting designers.

As of this writing I have performed in around a hundred live *Night Vale* shows and have several more shows and tours currently scheduled. We tend to tour one particular episode for a year or so, with minor variations in the script according to which guest actors are available on which different legs of a given tour. The core of my live setup is a piece of software called Ableton Live, which is a digital audio workstation known for its versatility in both composition/studio production and live performance. For *Night Vale* shows, I use Ableton to control different sets of simultaneous loops (basic elements of songs divided up according to roles: ambient, melodies, harmonies, drums, and percussion), which I fade in and out as appropriate during the show. On top of these loops I play improvised and composed parts with live instruments. When I first started touring with *Night Vale*, I exclusively used a keyboard, but I have since expanded to include the mandolin, an instrument I chose both for its stylistic adaptability and its portability (it fits in the overheard compartment on even the smallest airliners). I run them both through a number of effects in Ableton—and more recently, I've been experimenting with adding live shortwave radio into this mix.

It has been a joy to spend time working and living closely with the *Welcome to Night Vale* crew and the different guest musicians who have toured with us. It is surprising how easily we all get along, and it's inspiring to travel with a group in which everyone is always working on something interesting and making plans for new creative projects. In fact, I began working with Joseph Fink this year on one such project, a road trip–themed horror podcast called *Alice Isn't Dead*, whose story was heavily inspired by many of the experiences and atmospheres we encountered on the road. Meanwhile, Jeffrey Cranor is writing another new podcast with the music and audio production by Mary Epworth, a British psych rock musician who toured with us in 2015. I look forward to seeing what shape *Welcome to Night Vale* takes in the future, as we continue to develop both the podcast and live show, and to see the creative results that will arise from these other collaborations.

"THE DEBATE"

PERFORMED OCTOBER 10, 2013, AT ROULETTE, BROOKLYN, NEW YORK

CAST:

Cecil Baldwin—CECIL PALMER

Kevin R. Free—KEVIN

Mark Gagliardi—JOHN PETERS, ANNOUNCER/AD

Marc Evan Jackson—MARCUS VANSTON

Hal Lublin—ERIKA 1, STEVE CARLSBERG

Jackson Publick—HIRAM MCDANIELS

Annie Savage—DIANE CRAYTON, ERIKA 2

Mara Wilson—FACELESS OLD WOMAN

IT'S GREAT BEING BOOED.

When I first received the script for "The Debate," I saw that I was playing a couple of characters: Erika the Angel and some guy named Steve Carlsberg. At that point, I had only listened to one or two episodes of the show, and hadn't heard Steve mentioned yet, so I had no idea who he was. All throughout the first show, leading up to my entrance I heard the audience going crazy for Cecil, going crazy for Jackson Publick, going crazy for Mara Wilson, and it made sense—

they were famous people and well known within the world of the show. When I took the stage for my one line, I just wanted to make sure I gave Cecil something fun to play off of, because he had a great rant about me, after which I was supposed to exit.

I opened my mouth, said, "Hi, this is Steve Carlsberg——," and then a wall of sound changed my life forever.

As a cast member of the *Thrilling Adventure Hour*, I've been fortunate to play in front of very generous crowds, but the wall of sound I encountered just by revealing which character I was took me completely by surprise. All of a sudden I felt like a basketball player who hit a last-second, game-winning shot. I'll never forget that.

I thought it would be fun to play the exit like I was the most positive person on earth, almost immune to Cecil's rancor. The audience ate it up. In between shows, Joseph casually said something to the effect of "I'm surprised that they didn't boo you. Steve Carlsberg is generally a disliked character."

The audience for the second performance must have heard him.

When I made my entrance and identified myself, I was met first with a raucous wall of cheers, and then a downpour of boos. It's as if they first had to acknowledge that they were excited to see Steve Carlsberg given a voice, and then play their role of a disapproving mob. I loved every moment of it. Getting to play a character that elicits strong emotions in people is a privilege that not every actor gets. I relished the boos as much as the cheers.

Joseph and Jeffrey got me hooked on being Steve Carlsberg. I've had the privilege.

—Hal Lublin, Voice of Steve Carlsberg

About seven months into *Night Vale*'s run, Ben Acker and Ben Blacker of the *Thrilling Adventure Hour* reached out to us to say (1) hey like your show/good work and (2) we'll be in New York City soon and would love to meet up. They quickly became champions of our little show and mentored us through some early stages of our show and our business.

I assume you know, but just in case you don't, the *Thrilling Adventure Hour* is a live comedy—audio recordings of these shows were made into a podcast—done in the style of the Golden Age of Radio. The acting ensemble—the WorkJuice Players—features some of the funniest people in Los Angeles. They helped us get some of our first live shows on the stage at Largo at the Coronet in West Hollywood, where *TAH* performed and recorded for years.

When we first met the Bens in the spring of 2013, we had not really done a full-fledged live *Night Vale* show. Later that October, around the weekend of New York ComicCon, *TAH* was returning to New York Comic Con for a live show at the Bell House and to attend the convention.

Night Vale was putting on its own live show the night before *Thrilling Adventure Hour*'s. We asked the Bens if any of the WorkJuice folks would be interested in being in a live *Night Vale* show. And five of their cast showed up: Annie Savage, Marc Evan Jackson, Jackson Publick, Mark Gagliardi, and Hal Lublin.

Joseph had written the *Condos* live script, so I led the charge in writing *The Debate*. It was our first show with such a large cast (additionally, Mara Wilson and Kevin R. Free joined us that night). Plus we had no characters for any of the WorkJuice crew, so I set to work figuring out how to take a show that was mostly a Cecil monologue and turn it into a show for eight actors.

Given his incredible voice work on his hilarious Adult Swim show, *The Venture Bros.*, Jackson was obvious to play the five-headed dragon, Hiram McDaniels. And knowing Jackson would be involved help seal the deal that there would be a Hiram vs. Faceless Old Woman (played by Mara) debate that night.

But the rest of the casting was pretty much random. And thankfully it played out the way it did. Mark has remained our John Peters (you know, the farmer?) and Hal Lublin is the only man who could have ever played Steve Carlsberg. Marc was the billionaire turned angel Marcus Vanston and Annie was excellent as Diane Crayton, who later became one of the main characters of the first *Night Vale* novel.

Acker and Blacker helped us out in a lot of meaningful ways our first couple of years, but getting to work with these actors has been the best gift of all.

—Jeffrey Cranor

We found a little piece of heaven here. It is black, smooth, oblong. It hums a soft, but discordant note, and we are afraid to touch it.

WELCOME TO NIGHT VALE.

Listeners, we have a first here in Night Vale: a mayoral debate! Many of you know that Mayor Pamela Winchell will be stepping down soon and that this is entirely her own decision. She issues daily press releases in shaky, uncertain handwriting explaining (emphatically) that she made this choice on her own and that no one is soul-merging with her and forcing her to leave office. Each press release is signed "Yours truly (though not me truly), Pamela . . . PS:", and then there's just a sticky black sludge for a PS.

And we have some new candidates for this coveted office, all of whom I am welcoming in the studio. This is a great day, the first ever mayoral debate the town has seen. Since this is America, and we are a democracy, mayors have always been chosen by counting and interpreting the loud pulses coming out of Hidden Gorge. That's still how it will be done, but we thought we'd offer a chance for citizens to hear from the candidates they'll have no impact on electing.

But first, this breaking news.

The City Council announced the closure of Route 800, for the following reason: deer. The City Council spoke in low singsongy chants, a steady digital bass ululation underneath their unified voice. They stood atop a makeshift pyramid built out of heavily charred copies of the official biography of Sean Penn, heroic mementos of our recent victory over the Night Vale Public Library, and announced that the deer have taught themselves advanced mathematics, telepathy, and short-range time travel.

No official word yet on what these deer have done to cause the only highway in and out of town to be shut down, but the council is asking anyone still out on the roads right now to please return home. If you are not a citizen of Night Vale but cannot currently get out of town to your home because of the road closings, then congratulations. You now live in Night Vale. Please pick up a new citizen welcome packet and mandatory orange poncho at City Hall.

Okay, listeners, it's time to introduce the candidates who will be taking part in our studio debate. First, someone I've known my whole life (and you have too): It's the Faceless Old Woman Who Secretly Lives in Your Home. Welcome.

FACELESS OLD WOMAN: Hello.
CECIL: Where are you? I can hear you, but I can't see you.
FACELESS OLD WOMAN: I'm behind you in a mirror. Just over your shoulder, in the distance. You'll see slight movements in the dark. You'll feel a single fingernail gently run along your cheek.
CECIL: Faceless Old Woman. Can I call you Faceless Old Woman?
FACELESS OLD WOMAN: I have a name, Cecil.
CECIL: You do?
FACELESS OLD WOMAN: Yes.

[*Long pause*]

CECIL: Let's introduce our next candidate, and I'm so glad to finally meet this man, not man, no this person, not person, this entity: Hiram McDaniels. Hello, Hiram.
HIRAM-GOLD: Hello.

CECIL: You know, in the entirety of Night Vale's recorded history, there is no sign of a five-headed dragon ever running for mayor. So it hasn't happened in at least seven years!

HIRAM-GOLD: I am thrilled to be breaking new ground for those of us who do not identify as human.

HIRAM-PURPLE: We are thrilled.

HIRAM-GOLD: Yes, my purple head brings up a good point, I also do not identify as a single being. I have five heads. You will notice that my opponents have one. One head each. Just one.

HIRAM-GREEN: ONLY ONE HEAD. THAT IS IMPOSSIBLE FOR THINKING.

HIRAM-GOLD: Well, Green head, not impossible, but certainly very difficult.

CECIL: And speaking of your opponents, let's meet our last candidate for mayor. It's an honor to introduce our wealthiest citizen and now potential new mayor: billionaire Marcus Vanston. Welcome.

MARCUS: Yep. Hey. I mean, whatever. All this. This is whatever. You know, I used to own a dragon.

HIRAM-GRAY: Excuse me. What an inappropriate thing to say.

FACELESS OLD WOMAN: I agree with Mr. McDaniels's gray head. Ownership of sentient life is cruel and unconscionable.

MARCUS: Yeah, well it was great. It had eight heads though, not just five. I pretty much used it for commuting to work.

HIRAM-GREEN: [*A howl/growl of rage, long and uncomfortable*]

[*Pause*]

CECIL: Great! Let's get the debate started. We'll have opening statements as well as two rounds of questions. So, listeners, if you have a question, call now. Call silently to the sky with pleading eyes. When the birds come, you will feel your question has been received. You will not know for sure, because presumed knowledge is arrogance.

But first, let's pause for a quick word from our sponsors.

ANNOUNCER: It's not easy starting a small business. There are a lot of things to worry about, like building a customer base, developing a strong product, wrestling with self-doubt, crying a lot, bleeding a little, looking up in the small hours at the sagging ceiling over your too-small bed thinking "Why? Why?," being overrun by rats and worms, and discovering that you are just matter, just rotting organic matter, fated to feed the earth and trees. Yes, there are so many concerns facing small businesses, Web design shouldn't be one of them.

Want a simple, low-cost, and beautifully designed Web solution for your small business? Well, do you? It doesn't sound like you do, actually. I'm looking at your Web page right now, and it's lovely. Really smooth, really easy to navigate. It looks like you put a lot of thought into this, and you don't need our help. We won't even tell you who we are because we don't want to pressure you into changing what you've already done with your website. It's perfect.

Wow. Good job. We. Just. Wow. Sorry to have interrupted. I just want to say: You're really good at Web design. Much better than us. Carry on, I guess.

CECIL: Let's get to our opening statements. You have two minutes each. Faceless Old Woman.

FACELESS OLD WOMAN: Night Vale, I want to be your mayor. Who better to serve as leader of a town than the one person who lives secretly in the home of every single resident? I know each and every one of you personally, intimately. Mike Numminen? You need to discipline your children more. Claire Franklin, tell Eva you love her. It's been three years, and you need to take this seriously. Felicia Jackson, there is an enormous spider on the back of your dress right this very moment. You should probably change clothes before you leave the house. Change clothes slowly.

What other candidate can help our community on such a personal level? I have set fire to countless home appliances and stood secretly and stoically over crumbled bodies of sobbing citizens who only thought they were alone. Night Vale, you are not alone. I am there. I am always there, staring at you with curiosity and concern. Look for me out of the corner of your eye just before you fall asleep. I want to brush against your face at the deepest gulf of night. I want to be your mayor.

CECIL: Thank you for that. Let's go next to Hiram McDaniels and his opening statement. Hiram.

HIRAM-GOLD: Ladies, gentlemen, sentient creatures, imagine your perfect Night Vale. Close your eyes and imagine what a perfect town would be like. You can't, can you? That's because you only have one head. I have five. Listen, I don't mean to say I'm better than you. I, after all, have my own faults: caring too much, caring too little, caring just the right amount but at the wrong time, debilitating claustrophobia, an occasional lack of control over my fire-breathing. But one thing I do have is a multitude of heads—heads that can think through problems that the single-head cannot.

Here. Try this. Try solving an easy math problem with me. Quickly, what is fifty-six times ninety-seven?

HIRAM-GREEN: FIVE THOUSAND FOUR HUNDRED AND THIRTY-TWO. THE ANSWER IS FIVE THOUSAND FOUR HUNDRED AND THIRTY-TWO. YOUR MATH SKILLS ARE UNDEVELOPED AND PUNY.

HIRAM-GOLD: See, I have a green head that is excellent at math. I mean, I don't know that mayors have to be that good at math, but the point is . . .

HIRAM-BLUE: Well, mayors have to write budgets and know the population and things like that.

HIRAM-GOLD: Oh! See? Good point from my blue head. You see how we all work together? I can think quickly about a variety of topics, thanks to my many heads and brains and personalities and needs and desires. Some of these desires are nearly unmanageable, and I have a strong desire to be a good mayor. So you know I'll do everything, everything, I will stop at nothing to do that. I will be mayor.

CECIL: Charming! Thank you, Hiram. Marcus Vanston.

MARCUS: Yeah.

[*Pause*]

CECIL: Go ahead with your opening statement.

MARCUS: Let me finish this e-mail to my assistant. [*Mumbling while typing*] "and that is when I first understood what it meant to love myself for who I am. I am a complete person, Jake." Annnnd send. [*Normal*] Okay. So, people of Night Vale, I would like to be your next mayor. I will use all of my resources to do this.

In fact, I have already invested several million dollars into finding and excavating the Hidden Gorge where mayoral races are decided. I plan on developing a single computer voting machine to help streamline elections. So once that is complete, everything should work out fine. We'll all be just fine. Some of us will be more just fine than others, but again, that's also just fine.

CECIL: Thank you, Marcus. Thank you candidates for your desire to serve the Night Vale community with your leadership.

I want to go now to the issues. But first an update on our earlier news story.

Listeners, we've just received word that the newly intelligent deer are stopping on the road and allowing themselves to get hit by moving vehicles. They are then using that physical contact to launch themselves and the drivers and the wrecked vehicles backward in time by several days.

The leader of the deer, a two-headed, spider-eyed mule deer named (as all deer are named) Deer, apologized for the problems they are causing but they just want to experience pain. They have been so numb emotionally, physically, and spiritually, and they want to remember again what it is like to hurt, not just in their bodies but to see others suffer as well. The time travel was a happy accident, Deer admitted, as they had no idea humans experienced such angst, such terror when confronted with multiplicity of self.

The Sheriff's Secret Police remind us that while capable of time travel, the deer don't actually understand the implications of parallel universes versus linear continuity. The deer, while talented, are still very dumb animals. The deer countered that the Sheriff's Secret Police are just being mean now.

The City Council are asking that residents lock their doors and close their windows. The deer are organized and they will stop at nothing to get what they want, Night Vale. Be safe.

And now back to our first ever mayoral debate. Let's reach out to our community and find out what they want from their mayoral candidates. First caller, you're on the air. Who is this?

DIANE: Hi, Cecil, This is Diane Crayton. Candidates, as a member of the Night Vale PTA, one of the most important topics to me is our schools. This past year, we've seen a rise in some concerning trends: declining graduation rates, gun violence, teacher complaints about centipedes crawling out of their eyes at unexpected moments, and clocks that don't work correctly, causing confusion about when the next class is.

What will you do as mayor to improve our schools?

HIRAM-GOLD: The centipede thing is tough, because centipedes are helpful and intelligent beings, so I'm not going to say they have no right to live in and crawl out of teachers' faces. But I think we can find ways to compromise with them about living in different parts of the body so that they do not distract our children from learning.

As for the other issues, we spend an exorbitant amount each year on extracurricular activities, such as sports and art and history. I think we could take some of that money and put it toward after-school programs to help tutor students in important topics like music and brick-laying and how to build great stone shrines to ... well, whoever, I mean, let's say reptiles, just as an example. That's just an example.

FACELESS OLD WOMAN: While I agree with my opponent that we must stop our children from learning too much in schools, I disagree that we need to cut funding from any school programs. Nor should we ask the government for more. We can do this as a community.

I propose selling off unused items from our homes to raise money for our schools. Cecil, you have a whole set of collectible Jade-ite bowls that you never use. I would be happy to sell them on eBay for you. Hiram, you live in a cave that I do not like, but you have a collection of rare jewels and coins in a mahogany chest that you keep locked and buried. Let's put those up for sale. Marcus, you have a coffee table made of human bones.

MARCUS: I need that coffee table.

CECIL: Please let the Faceless Old Woman finish, Mr. Vanston.

MARCUS: I need that coffee table.

CECIL: Okay.

MARCUS: I need it.

FACELESS OLD WOMAN: We all have things we do not use. Books we do not read or care for. Furniture and electronics and dead mice and antiques that could be worth a lot of money to our students. Children are our future. They are a terrible and less enjoyable future than the future we all represented, but they are *a* future nonetheless.

CECIL: Marcus. Do you have a rebuttal?

MARCUS: [*Thinks*] No. It doesn't really affect me at all.

CECIL: Sorry for yet another interruption in our debate, but I've just received an update on the deer situation. The City Council announced that the deer are multiplying. When asked how they are doing this, the City Council rolled their eyes and said the same way deer always replicate, by humming and breathing softly in unison until others that hear them become them. Good thing you're a reporter and not a biologist, the City Council teased, and a sudden, shared laughter broke the tension of the room.

The City Council then announced that they just can't be here anymore and that they wish us all the best in our final moments.

"We're pretty much done for," the City Council reassured reporters. "The deer have taken over the streets, the sidewalks. Many are standing at your window right now waiting for you to see their eyes and hear their hums."

Do not open your windows or doors, listeners. Stay by your radios, stay always by your radios, and we will update you with more information.

Okay, next caller, you're on the air. Who is this?

ERIKA 1: This is Erika.

CECIL: What's your question, Erica?

ERIKA 1: It's spelled Erika. With a *K*.

CECIL: I'm sorry. What's your question, Erika?

ERIKA 1: Well, I'm an angel and I'm concerned. Not concerned, anxious.

CECIL: Let me stop you right there, Erika. Angels aren't real. But go ahead with your question.

ERIKA 1: Of course. Yes. Well, there's a tiny civilization living under lane five of the Desert Flower Bowling Alley and Arcade Fun Complex. Angels have not been able to determine where this nation came from or what it wants. It is rare that angels cannot solve a problem, but when they cannot, they turn to small-town civic leaders for help and guidance. What do you know about this nation of small people in the bowling alley?

FACELESS OLD WOMAN: Erika, let me first say thank you for your hard work. You do not exist, but if you did, we would be extraordinarily proud of the work you do protecting humans. That being said, it is a crime to acknowledge the existence of angels. So I have nothing more to say.

HIRAM-GREEN: BURN IT TO A PIT OF ASH AND DESPAIR.

[*Pause*]

HIRAM-GOLD: We could just burn it down. Or . . . whatever.

MARCUS: [*Off mic*] I'm not crying.

CECIL: What was that?

MARCUS: I'm not crying.

CECIL: Listeners at home, Marcus is hunched over, head turned away from his microphone. He is sobbing.

MARCUS: No I'm not.

CECIL: Perhaps he has been chosen by the angels, who, as a legal reminder, are not real in the slightest. But those who are chosen for special tasks by angels often cannot stop weeping when they talk about angels.

MARCUS: I'm fine. Next question.

CECIL: Caller, you're on the air with the mayoral candidates.

JOHN: Hi, this is John Peters, you know, the farmer? Last year, there was a pretty big glowing cloud that went through town dropping dead animals and things everywhere. And I know that glow cloud is now on the School Board and all, but is there anything one of you could do to keep it from dropping animals everywhere? I nearly lost my organic certification because none of those cows or crows or nurse sharks or spider wolves it dropped had any paperwork. And also all the radiation was probably not healthy.

CECIL: Thank you, John. Candidates, what will you do to protect us from the glow cloud? What will you do to serve the glow cloud? What efforts will you make to hail the all-mighty glow cloud?

ALL ON STAGE: ALL HAIL! ALL HAIL! ALL PRAISE AND REPENT BEFORE THE GLOW CLOUD! GIVE YOUR TEETH. GIVE YOUR EYES. GIVE YOUR ALL TO THE GLOW CLOUD.

CECIL: And to John's point, it's a difficult situation given that the glow cloud is a stand-up member of our community, but the glow cloud is also a—

ALL ON STAGE: TERRIBLE FORCE OF DESTRUCTION. A PUNISHMENT FOR WEAK HUMANS. A CELEBRATION OF UNBRIDLED MADNESS AND PAIN AND FEAR AND PAIN AND PAIN AND PAIN. ALL HAIL THE GLOW CLOUD.

CECIL: Thank you for your call, John.

JOHN: You bet.

CECIL: Next up. Caller?

ERIKA 2: Hi, this is Erika again.

CECIL: Erika, you sound different.

ERIKA 2: I do?

CECIL: Well, yes, I mean, in your earlier call you sounded like a man, and now you sound like a woman.

ERIKA 2: Angels cannot hear gender, Cecil.

CECIL: Well, if angels were real, Erika, what would your question be?

ERIKA 2: Thank you. This question is just for Marcus. Marcus, if called upon by angels to serve a great good, to serve a great calling, to serve a great war, would you serve?

CECIL: Marcus? Are you crying?

MARCUS: [*Off mic*] Hang on. Nope. I'm fine. I'm fine.

ERIKA 2: You are needed, Marcus. You are needed now.

CECIL: Listeners, oh my. Marcus is rising from his chair. His feet are off the floor. He is stretching to inhuman lengths, his eyes are glowing black, and his fingers are spiraling long and diaphanous. Marcus. Oh dear. Listeners, Marcus grew gold feathers from his back as he vanished. He is gone.

ERIKA 2: I am sorry to interrupt your debate, Cecil. Good-bye.

CECIL: Good-bye, Erika.

ERIKA 2: And Cecil . . .

CECIL: Yes?

ERIKA 2: I am afraid. . . .

CECIL: Yes? Go on.

ERIKA 2: No. That's it. Just: I am afraid. Good-bye, okay?

CECIL: Okay. This debate has certainly taken an odd turn listeners, but also none of this happened and we will comment no further.

One last caller. You're on the air.

STEVE: Hi, this is Steve Carlsberg. I have a question for Hiram. Hiram—

CECIL: NO STEVE. NO. STEVE CARLSBERG, WE ARE OUT OF TIME FOR QUESTIONS. GOOD-BYE.

Candidates, let's get to closing statements. Faceless Old Woman.

FACELESS OLD WOMAN: My fellow Night Valeans, my opponent talks about human children, but he has never been a human child. I have. It has been centuries, but I have. He claims he wants to improve fitness and health in our schools, but he cannot even regulate his own body temperature. I can. I can also regulate yours. He says he cares about you, but I am the only candidate who is actually in your home at this very moment, writing down the grim specifics of your eventual death on the backside of one section of drywall. You'll see it someday when getting some pipes or wiring fixed, and you'll be impressed. Not impressed. Terrified. This is a promise I make to you. My other opponent is now an angel, and cannot legally be thought about. So vote for me, the Faceless Old Woman Who Secretly Lives in Your Home. I'm touching your neck right now. You smell nice.

CECIL: Thank you. Hiram?

HIRAM-GOLD: Night Vale . . . sure, there is a faceless old woman secretly living in your home, and I respect that. She is vaguely familiar and unsettlingly comfortable, and I admire that. But isn't it time we stopped this politics as usual? Isn't it time we got the government out of our homes? There once was a day when we all needed government agents snooping around in our books and dishes. That was a different time. Should the government really be able to touch our necks and be aware that we smell nice? I say no. I'm literally a five-headed dragon. I don't know anything about being a human. I do things like breathe fire, fly, regenerate limbs, and molt. I don't care anything about your personal lives. They're your choice. I wouldn't even know how to interfere.

HIRAM-GREEN: YOU ARE INFERIOR AND EMOTIONALLY CONFUSING ANIMALS.

HIRAM-GOLD: So vote for me, Hiram McDaniels. I'm literally a five-headed dragon with no regard for human life . . . choices. Human life choices.

CECIL: Thank you both. I'm sorry for the technical difficulties. I don't know if you can hear that, but there is a very soft humming sound coming from the mics or the soundboard or something.

FACELESS OLD WOMAN: I don't hear it, Cecil.

HIRAM-GOLD: I don't hear a thing.

CECIL: I remember this sound from before. We'll have an engineer come take a look at it. In the meantime, ladies and gentleman and all in between, the deer have gotten quite out of hand. One of the Sales staff, thank you, Roberta, just handed me a note that says there are dozens of deer surrounding this station and trying to peer into the windows.

HIRAM-GOLD: That's your humming sound right there then. I could go outside and set fire to them. That would be a very mayoral solution.

FACELESS OLD WOMAN: That's a fool's errand, Hiram. Did you never play Deer-Duck-Dragon? Dragon beats duck, but deer beats dragon.

HIRAM-GOLD: So we need a duck?

FACELESS OLD WOMAN: No! Deer beats duck too. Deer beats everything. It's a terrible game.

CECIL: She's right, Hiram, but it's not the deer. The humming is something worse. Listeners, I fear something much worse is lurking. So as we all hide from the deer, hide from the hum, and hide from it all, I take you now . . . to the weather.

WEATHER: "Promise to the Moon" by Jason Webley

CECIL: Listeners, the quiet humming is not the deer, but a swirling, black vortex just outside our studio door. In fact the deer have backed away from the station. I have seen this vortex before, listeners, and I am afraid to approach it, but Hiram went to look inside.

HIRAM-GOLD: Hey, I found this guy in the vortex.

KEVIN: Hello.

CECIL: Who is this man? Not man. Who is this . . . creature? Why is he covered in blood? Where are his eyes?

KEVIN: Hi, I'm Kevin.

CECIL: You stay away!

FACELESS OLD WOMAN: Hello, Kevin. That's Cecil. Wow, you guys look almost just alike.

KEVIN: Oh, hello, Cecil. Nice to meet you. And yes, I completely see the resemblance. It's mostly in the eyes, I think. I met Hiram and now Cecil. Who are you?

FACELESS OLD WOMAN: I am the Faceless Old Woman Who Secretly Lives in Your Home. Well, most homes. Not yours. I've never seen you before.

KEVIN: Faceless? You're not faceless. You have a beautiful face. A memorable face. I don't know if I've ever seen such deep hazel eyes or proud lips or archaic jaw.

FACELESS OLD WOMAN: I do not have a face, Kevin. I have never had a face.

KEVIN: You do have a face, and it's unlike any other face in history.

CECIL: Why are you here? Explain to me what you are doing here.

KEVIN: Oh, sure! Well, I was sitting in my own radio studio in my own town and I heard that humming again. I saw a spiraling white vortex, and rushed into it. It has been months since I have seen it, and I once met a man there who looked like me, with my eyes and my smile. I think he was you, Cecil. I know that I am Kevin. I know I have been in this strange studio before, with its old-timey microphones and acoustic gray-foam walls. A place like this is usually covered in clumps of hair and reddish-brown handprints streaking down the only remaining un-shattered window. But they do things differently here in . . . Where is this?

HIRAM-GOLD: Night Vale.

KEVIN: Oh my! So this is Night Vale. How delightful. Hello out there, Night Vale listeners. This is Kevin from Desert Bluffs. You know, I was just telling my intern, Vanessa. I was telling Vanessa just today how much I have wanted to come here. I'm always telling her that, as a matter of fact. I just never get around to actually visiting. Work and family, and you get so busy, it's hard to find the time. And so here I am. I wish

Vanessa were here. She would love Night Vale. You guys have such . . . you know? We always talk about coming here, and here I am without her. Oh, I wish you could have met Vanessa. Always a joke to start the day. She had one about limestone this morning. I don't remember it but it was a hit. Always a laugh. Always a smile. A big smile where she'd show me all these perfect teeth and I would just imagine the rest of her perfect skull. Funny how the skull is so visible in your mouth. Weird. Who thinks about that stuff? I don't know. Weird, right?

FACELESS OLD WOMAN: Maybe next time you come you could bring her.

KEVIN: Oh gosh, I wish, but no.

FACELESS OLD WOMAN: No?

KEVIN: Oh, dear, I'm sorry, no. Vanessa died many years ago. We're all still very upset about it. Very upset about what we saw. Some of us never came back to work again. Some of us never left our houses again. Most of us never woke up again. I don't like to talk about it much.

FACELESS OLD WOMAN: I'm sorry.

KEVIN: Night Vale, I don't know why I was brought here, but I am starting to see we are connected, and by more than just a two-lane highway. We are connected much more deeply, Night Vale. And if this is true, I imagine your town too has been seeing a rise in the deer population this evening. It is a blessed event, of course, as these deer have been so very helpful to all of us in Desert Bluffs. Doing all our math problems . . . Gaining us extra work hours by time traveling us back and forth . . . So productive and adorable, those deer! But of course there is sometimes too much of a good thing.

Strexcorp, our parent company—and I believe yours too now, Cecil—is issuing a recall on all these time traveling deer. They tried to implement the project slowly, but it got a little carried away. If you have lost loved ones or are no longer in your original timeline or universe, then we apologize. Please contact Strexcorp attorney Luisa Reyes, as she is preparing a class action lawsuit against Strexcorp. We've already budgeted for the remuneration for community harm, so don't you worry about us. We're fine.

We've sent helicopters to dispatch the deer. If you have earplugs, you may want to put them in now, or simply turn up some loud music to drown out the machines and screams for the next hour or so.

I can hear the fading hum of the vortex that fortuitously connects our two radio studios, Night Vale. Cecil, I will see you again, I am certain. I can't wait to tell Vanessa what a great town this was. I must go.

It was nice to meet you two.

[*Exits*]

FACELESS OLD WOMAN: He saw that I had a face. I have never seen my face. What do I look like Hiram? Am I beautiful?

HIRAM-GOLD: You are beautiful when you do beautiful things. Do you do beautiful things?

FACELESS OLD WOMAN: I think that I do.

HIRAM-GREEN: THEN YOU ARE BEAUTIFUL. IT IS A SIMPLE CALCULATION, YOU SMALL, DEFENSELESS SACK OF BONES AND MEAT.

FACELESS OLD WOMAN: Thank you, Hiram. You are beautiful too. Cecil, you are . . . distracted.

HIRAM-GOLD: Cecil? You all right?

CECIL: I . . .

FACELESS OLD WOMAN: Cecil? It's going to be okay. Actually, that's a lie. In general, it's not going to be okay.

HIRAM-GOLD: That man with missing eyes, bloodstained skin, and teeth like an abandoned cemetery was certainly terrifying, but he's gone now.

CECIL: He was . . .

FACELESS OLD WOMAN: Cecil. We all get frightened and freeze in the face of unbearable terror. I mean, only if we can see that face. Some faces are apparently there, but unseeable.

CECIL: I . . . You are right. Thank you both.

Candidates, thank you also for coming on the show tonight. I think you both would make an excellent mayor. I look forward to casting a meaningless vote for one of you soon.

Listeners, thank you for listening to the show tonight. Remember that you may hear terrible machines and screams as corporate agents terminate the false deer. Their attempt to destroy our way of life by bringing us together as one has failed. We are free to remain ourselves and find our own connections—beautiful or grotesque. Either way, a beauty or grotesquery of our own choosing.

So relax tonight Night Vale. You are yourself. You are safe. Tonight is a good night. Tomorrow is unconfirmed. We will all find out together.

Thank you again, candidates, and listeners do not forget to cast your vote on election day. We do not know where votes will be cast, what day election day is, or if votes are even read. But it is your democratic duty.

Stay tuned next for a chasm of subjectivity and bravado between yourself and every other human being.

Good night, Night Vale. Good night.

PROVERB: Don't judge a book by its cover, by its leather cover, by its human skin—looking cover. Don't ever judge that book.

ABOUT THE AUTHORS

Joseph Fink created the *Welcome to Night Vale* and *Alice Isn't Dead* podcasts. He lives with his wife in New York.

Jeffrey Cranor cowrites the *Welcome to Night Vale* podcast. He also co-creates theater and dance pieces with choreographer wife, Jillian Sweeney. They live in New York.

ABOUT THE CONTRIBUTORS

Cecil Baldwin is the narrator of the hit podcast *Welcome to Night Vale*. He is an alumnus of the New York Neo-Futurists, performing in their late-night show *Too Much Light Makes the Baby Go Blind*, as well as Drama Desk–nominated *The Complete and Condensed Stage Directions of Eugene O'Neill Vol. 2*. Cecil has performed at the Shakespeare Theatre Company, DC, Studio Theatre (including the world premiere production of Neil LaBute's *Autobahn*), the Kennedy Center, the National Players, LaMaMa E.T.C., Emerging Artists Theatre, and at the Upright Citizens Brigade Theatre. Film/TV credits include Braden in *The Outs* (Vimeo), the voice of Tad Strange in *Gravity Falls* (Disney XD), the Fool in *Lear* (with Paul Sorvino), and *Billie Joe Bob*. Cecil has been featured on podcasts such as *Ask Me Another* (NPR), *Selected Shorts* (PRI), *Shipwreck*, *Big Data*, and *Our Fair City*.

Disparition is a project created by Jon Bernstein, a composer and producer based in Brooklyn, New York. More at Disparition.info.

Kevin R. Free is a writer/performer whose work has been showcased on PRX's *The Moth Radio Hour* and NPR's *News & Notes*. His most recent work, created with Eevin Hartsough, is the Web series *Gemma & the Bear!* (www.mycarl.org), which is the recipient of several awards, including an Award of Excellence from the Best Shorts Competition. His full-length plays include *(Not) Just a Day Like Any*

Other, written and performed with Christopher Borg, Jeffrey Cranor, and Eevin Hartsough; *A Raisin in the Salad: Black Plays for White People; The Crisis of the Negro Intellectual, or TRIPLE CONSCIOUSNESS; Night of the Living N-Word;* and *AM I DEAD?: The Untrue Narrative of Anatomical Lewis, The Slave* (commissioned by Flux Theatre Ensemble through the FluxForward program, 2015). He is an alumnus of the New York Neo-Futurists, with whom he wrote and performed regularly in *Too Much Light Makes the Baby Go Blind (30 Plays in 60 Minutes)* between 2007 and 2011. More at www.kevinrfree.com and on Twitter ©kevinrfree.

Glen David Gold is the author of the novels *Carter Beats the Devil* and *Sunnyside.*

Jessica Hayworth is an illustrator and fine artist. She has produced a variety of illustrated works for the *Welcome to Night Vale* podcast since 2013, including all posters for the touring live show. Her other works include the graphic novels *Monster* and *I Will Kill You with My Bare Hands*, as well as various solo and group exhibitions. She received her MFA from Cranbrook Academy of Art, and lives and works in Detroit.

Maureen Johnson is the *New York Times* and *USA Today* best-selling author of several YA novels, including *13 Little Blue Envelopes, Suite Scarlett,* and *The Name of the Star.* She has also done collaborative works, such as *Let It Snow* (with John Green and Lauren Myracle) and *The Bane Chronicles* (with Cassandra Clare and Sarah Rees Brennan). Maureen has an MFA in writing from Columbia University. She has been nominated for an Edgar Award and the Andre Norton Award, and her books appear frequently on YALSA and state award lists. *Time* magazine has named her one of the top 140 people to follow on Twitter (©maureenjohnson). Maureen lives in New York, and online on Twitter (or at www.maureenjohnsonbooks.com).

Ashley Lierman is a professional university librarian and an occasional writer. Apart from contributing guest episodes to *Welcome to Night Vale*, she writes the monthly column "Queer Quest" for the news blog of the American Library Association's GLBT Round Table, in which she discusses LGBTQ+ representation in video games, comics, speculative fiction, and other forms of niche media. She has also contributed to two short story anthologies by the independent genre fiction press the Sockdolager (www.sockdolager.net), and has appeared as a guest on the podcast *I Haven't Seen That* (www.ihaventseenthat.com).

One of the creators and cohosts of *We Got This with Mark and Hal* on the Maximum Fun Network, **Hal Lublin** is an accomplished actor and improviser. Best known for his work as one of the core WorkJuice players in *The Thrilling Adventure Hour* and Steve Carlsberg on *Welcome to Night Vale*, Hal plays Wide Wale and Manolo on *The Venture Bros.* and will recur on Cartoon Network's upcoming series *Mighty Magiswords*. His work runs the gamut from animated films and television programs to radio shows and video games for CBS, Happy Madison, Disney, SyFy, JibJab, Wired, and more.

Originally from Birmingham, Alabama, **Jasika Nicole** studied theatre, voice, and dance at Catawba College in North Carolina before moving to New York City to pursue a career in the arts. She got her start in musical theatre but is best known for her role as Agent Astrid Farnsworth on Fox's sci-fi series *Fringe*. In addition to performing, Nicole has a degree in studio art and is an accomplished illustrator as well as a published author. An avid DIYer, Nicole knits, sews, bakes, makes shoes, and builds furniture in her spare time. Miss Nicole resides in Los Angeles with her lovely wife, Claire.

Zack Parsons is a Chicago-based humorist and author of nonfiction (*My Tank Is Fight!*) and fiction (*Liminal States*). In addition to

Welcome to Night Vale, he has worked with Joseph Fink on the website Something Awful and can also be found writing for his own site, the Bad Guys Win (www.thebadguyswin.com). You can call him a weird idiot on twitter at ©sexyfacts4u.

Lauren Sharpe lives in Brooklyn with her husband and twin daughters. She listens to trees and believes in magic. More at www .LaurenSharpe.com.

Mara Wilson is a writer, storyteller, and voice actress. Her voice can be heard on *BoJack Horseman,* and her writing can be read on the Toast, McSweeney's, Jezebel, Reductress, Cracked, and her own web-site, www.MaraWilsonWritesStuff.com. She is the author of the book *Where Am I Now?* available from Penguin books.

ACKNOWLEDGMENTS

Thanks to the cast and crew of *Welcome to Night Vale:* Meg Bashwiner, Jon Bernstein, Marisa Blankier, Desiree Burch, Nathalie Candel, Emma Frankland, Kevin R. Free, Mark Gagliardi, Angelique Grandone, Marc Evan Jackson, Maureen Johnson, Kate Jones, Erica Livingston, Christopher Loar, Hal Lublin, Dylan Marron, Jasika Nicole, Lauren O'Niell, Flor De Liz Perez, Teresa Piscioneri, Jackson Publick, Molly Quinn, Retta, Symphony Sanders, Annie Savage, Lauren Sharpe, James Urbaniak, Bettina Warshaw, Wil Wheaton, Mara Wilson, and, of course, the voice of Night Vale himself, Cecil Baldwin.

Also and always: Jillian Sweeney; Kathy & Ron Fink; Ellen Flood; Leann Sweeney; Jack and Lydia Bashwiner; Anna, Sam, Levi, and Caleb Pow; Rob Wilson; Kate Leth; Jessica Hayworth; Holly and Jeffrey Rowland; Zack Parsons; Ashley Lierman; Russel Swensen; Glen David Gold; Marta Rainer; Andrew Morgan; Eleanor McGuinness; Paul Sloan; John Green; Hank Green; Patrick Rothfuss; Cory Doctorow; Andrew WK; John Darnielle; Dessa Darling; Aby Wolf; Jason Webley; Danny Schmidt; Carrie Elkin; Eliza Rickman; Mary Epworth; Will Twynham; Erin McKeown; Sxip Shirey; Gabriel Royal; The New York Neo-Futurists; Freesound.org; Mike Mushkin; Ben Acker and Ben Blacker of *The Thrilling Adventure Hour;* the Booksmith in San Francisco; Mark Flanagan and Largo at the Coronet; and, of course, the delightful Night Vale fans.

Our agent Jodi Reamer, our editor Amy Baker, and all the good people at HarperPerennial.

FOR MORE OF NIGHT VALE, CHECK OUT
WELCOME TO NIGHT VALE
── A NOVEL ──
BY JOSEPH FINK AND JEFFREY CRANOR

The *New York Times* bestselling novel from the creators of the *Welcome to Night Vale* podcast is now available in hardcover, CD, digital audio, and ebook.

"This is a splendid, weird, moving novel . . . It manages beautifully that trick of embracing the surreal in order to underscore and emphasize the real—not as allegory, but as affirmation of emotional truths that don't conform to the neat and tidy boxes in which we're encouraged to house them."

—NPR.org